MURDER WITH LEMON TEA CAKES

Aunt Iris pulled her camel-colored coat from the coat rack, then went to the counter for the bag of lemon tea cakes she'd set there. "Don't work too hard," Aunt Iris told Daisy as she gave her a hug. "Oh, and can you pick me up in the morning and bring me to work? I'll leave my car here because we'll probably take Harvey's. He'll just drop me off at home."

"That's fine," Daisy said. "Why don't you have a cup of tea with me until he gets here?"

"He's usually prompt, or even early. I'll just go out to the garden and wait for him."

"Don't sit out there alone if Harvey's late."

"I won't," her aunt assured her, gave her hand a squeeze, and then left through the side garden door, carrying her purse and the bag of tea cakes.

Daisy had picked up her two-cup vintage teapot with its hand-painted lilac pattern when she heard a blood curdling scream.

"Aunt Iris," she called as she set down the teapot, exited the side door and ran through the garden.

She froze when she spotted Harvey's body crumpled in the herb garden . . .

Books by Karen Rose Smith

Caprice DeLuca Mysteries
STAGED TO DEATH
DEADLY DÉCOR
GILT BY ASSOCIATION
DRAPE EXPECTATIONS
SILENCE OF THE LAMPS
SHADES OF WRATH
SLAY BELLS RING

Daisy's Tea Garden Mysteries
MURDER WITH LEMON TEA CAKES

Published by Kensington Publishing Corporation

Murder with Lemon Tea Cakes

Karen Rose Smith

KENSINGTON PUBLISHING CORP.

http://www.kensingtonbooks.com

KENSINGTON BOOKS are published by

Kensington Publishing Corp.
119 West 40th Street
New York, NY 10018

All Kensington Titles, Imprints, and Distributed Lines are available at special quantity discounts for bulk purchases for sales promotions, premiums, fund-raising, and educational or institutional use. Special book excerpts or customized printings can also be created to fit specific needs. For details, write or phone the office of the Kensington special sales manager: Kensington Publishing Corp., 119 West 40th Street, New York, NY 10018, attn: Special Sales Department, Phone: 1-800-221-2647.

Kensington and the K logo Reg. U.S. Pat & TM Off.

ISBN-13: 978-1-61773-960-6
ISBN-10: 1-61773-960-X
First Kensington Mass Market Edition: January 2018

eISBN-13: 978-1-61773-961-3
eISBN-10: 1-61773-961-8
First Kensington Electronic Edition: January 2018

10 9 8 7 6 5 4 3 2 1

Printed in the United States of America

Chapter One

"Harvey, that's so kind of you to say." An almost giggle escaped from Daisy Swanson's Aunt Iris.

Daisy watched her aunt as she set a hand-painted porcelain teapot that was steeping blackberry black tea before a man Iris had dated merely a month. Yes, her aunt was acting like a teenager, and Daisy definitely knew teenagers. Her own daughters giggled like that around guys they deemed crush-worthy. Her aunt practically twittered like an adolescent when she was around Harvey Fitz, owner of Men's Trends in the small town of Willow Creek, Pennsylvania.

Business at Daisy's Tea Garden was slowing down for the day. Willow Creek was a semi-busy tourist town set in the midst of Amish country near Lancaster. It was a town where neighbors knew neighbors, talked about neighbors, and proved there might be less than six degrees of separation between everyone.

Her aunt's ash-blond, short curls bounced as she slid a bone china sugar bowl painted with a rose design near Harvey's cup.

"Half a teaspoon should be just right," he said,

looking at the blushing older woman as if she was more important than any tea brew.

Harvey was tall and thin, with a shock of silver hair still thick and long enough to give him a distinguished look. It even turned up at his neck in the back.

Daisy had to wonder if he'd had hair plugs transplanted on the top of his head. That hair looked too good for a man of his age. He had to be seventy, about ten years older than her aunt.

She wanted to break into their conversation to find out how far into dating they'd gotten. She didn't want her aunt to get hurt. They hadn't known Harvey very long, and they didn't know him nearly well enough. As far as Daisy was concerned, Iris should stay far away from him because he was still married.

Separated, but married.

That was trouble, no matter how you looked at it.

Keeping her ear tilted toward the couple's conversation, Daisy glanced around the business she and Iris had grown from scratch. Well, not exactly from scratch. There had been a bakery on the first floor of an old Victorian before they'd bought it. Now they rented the upstairs to a high school friend of Daisy's, Tessa Miller, chef and kitchen manager of the tea garden. They'd developed the downstairs into a tea, baked goods, and soup business.

The interior wasn't froufrou like many tea rooms, though it did have a subtle flower theme. They'd considered the fact that they'd wanted men to feel comfortable here as well as women. Besides merely drawing from Willow Creek's tourist trade—Lancaster County Amish country was a popular get-away destination—they wanted to draw from the professional offices in Willow Creek and Lancaster too.

In keeping with that plan, they'd decorated the

walk-in "be served or buy-it-and-go" room with oak, glass-topped tables and mismatched antique oak, hand-carved chairs. A yellow bud vase adorned each table. The walls had been painted the palest green in the walk-in tea-serving area because Daisy believed the color green promoted calming qualities, just as tea did.

In contrast, the more private room was a spillover area. On specified days, it was also the room where they scheduled reservations for afternoon tea which included multiple courses. The space reflected the best qualities of a Victorian with a bay window, window seats, crown molding, and diamond-cut glass. In that room, the walls were the palest yellow. The tables were white and the chairs wore seat cushions in blue, green, and yellow pinstripes.

Tessa emerged from the kitchen with a bright smile and a serving dish in her hand.

Tessa was Daisy's age—thirty-seven—with rich caramel-colored hair that she wore in a braid. She always dressed like the artiste she was with colorful and flowy tops and skirts. She wore smocks to work in lieu of the usual chef's coat. Today, in tribute to the fall weather, her smock was adorned with bright swirls of orange and rust. She set a cut-glass plate filled with cookies in front of Harvey. On the top of the plate perched a lemon tea cake fresh from the oven.

"My favorite," Harvey announced, picking it up and taking a large bite. "I don't know how you do it, but every one of your cookies is delicious, not to mention your scones. You *are* going to have the lemon tea cakes at my celebration this weekend, aren't you?"

One of the reasons Harvey had stopped in today was to consult with her and Iris about his store's twenty-fifth anniversary celebration. That would be a big to-do, with engraved invitations that the manager of Men's Trends had sent out. It was a large party for Daisy and her staff to cater. Besides the main event here at the tea garden on Sunday, tomorrow—on the store's actual anniversary date—Men's Trends would be serving tea and accompanying snacks to any of their customers who wandered in during the afternoon.

"We'll have lemon tea cakes at your store tomorrow too," Daisy assured him.

Harvey finished his cookie, wiped his fingers on his napkin, then gazed once more at Iris. "Will you be at Men's Trends tomorrow, or do you have to stay here to hold down the fort for Daisy?"

"I'll be holding down the fort here," Iris responded.

"But you will be here to celebrate with me on Sunday, won't you?" Harvey asked. "A celebration is only a celebration if you have the people around you who matter."

Iris's cheeks reddened. She said in a low voice, "I'll be here. You matter to me too."

Warning bells went off in Daisy's head. Harvey had not signed his final divorce papers. Trying to be realistic, she knew her Aunt Iris didn't run in Harvey's social set by any means. *His* friends played golf at Willow Creek Country Club. The women in his soon-to-be ex-wife's circle shopped in New York, Baltimore, and D.C. They might live in Willow Creek, but they were world travelers, food connoisseurs, and wine aficionados.

Her aunt was a tea aficionado.

Yet when Harvey and Iris gazed at each other, Daisy saw something genuine there. Maybe when one reached a certain age, all the rest didn't matter.

Maybe when one reached a certain age, one could learn to live with loss and move on.

Daisy knew she hadn't moved on from her husband's death three years ago. Thank goodness, she had her girls and Aunt Iris, her mom and dad, and her sister. Thank goodness, she'd moved back to Willow Creek and started this new venture with her aunt. Come to think of it, in some ways she *had* moved on. In others—

One step at a time.

"I'll go over the list with Harvey for tomorrow and the weekend if you want to work in the kitchen with Tessa and Eva," Iris said to Daisy.

Eva Conner, who was nearing her forty-fifth birthday, was their dishwasher and girl Friday.

Studying her aunt, Daisy suspected Iris might be trying to get rid of her. Did this meeting of hers with Harvey really include business?

"Have a wonderful celebration tomorrow," Tessa said as she excused herself and crossed to the doorway that led to the kitchen. Daisy was about to do the same when the front door of the tea garden opened and her daughter Jazzi blew in with the end of September breeze. A few dried leaves did too.

Unlike herself and Daisy's oldest daughter, Violet, who both had honey-blond hair, Jazzi's hair was black, thick, glossy, and straight. Jazzi glanced at Harvey and her aunt and the few other customers in the tea room. Then she shifted her backpack from her shoulders and swung it into one hand. She was frowning, and that wasn't unusual these days. Daisy wasn't exactly sure what was going on with her fifteen-year-old.

There was a tradition in Daisy's family that all the women were given flower names. Her mother's name was Rose, her aunt's name was Iris, and Daisy's sister's name was Camellia. Daisy had named her daughters Violet and Jasmine. But Jazzi never used her full name. She preferred her nickname.

Now Daisy went toward her to greet her with a hug. Her daughter slipped out of her hold.

Daisy studied the sullen expression on her daughter's face and said, "Just in time to help Tessa with a batch of scones to refrigerate for tomorrow."

"Maybe I don't feel like making scones," Jazzi returned as she ducked her pretty face and didn't look at her mother.

"Do you have lots of homework?"

"The usual."

Daisy wrapped her arm around her daughter and guided her over to a quiet corner of the tea room. Jazzi had been unreliable and rebellious lately. There could be any number of reasons for that, but Daisy suspected the main one. Violet had gone off to college at the end of August, and Jazzi didn't seem to know how to deal with her sister's absence.

"I know you miss Vi."

Jazzi shrugged. "I don't. She's not around lording it over me."

"She's not around for you to talk to or borrow clothes from or ask for advice on makeup. When your Aunt Camellia moved to New York, I felt lost without her. Our lifestyles became very different, and I didn't know if we'd ever have common interests again. Your relationship with Vi will change, but you can still be close."

"Easy for you to say," Jazzi muttered.

Daisy gave her a long look. "If you don't want to help Tessa with the dough for scones, you can work on the cookbook."

Daisy's office was located beside the kitchen, and

Jazzi was familiar with her computer. This was a family business, and Jazzi was supposed to be taking over collating recipes for this year's Daisy's Tea Garden cookbook. But she hadn't gotten very far.

"That's like doing schoolwork. I'll help Tessa with the scones."

With that announcement, Jazzi spun on her espadrilles and headed for the kitchen. With her slim-legged jeans, her long, tunic-style sweater, and her black hair flowing down her back, Jazzi looked older than fifteen. Daisy wished she could keep her from growing up altogether, but she couldn't. Just as she couldn't keep Violet tied to Willow Creek after college.

Daisy was about to ask Harvey if he'd like her to pour him a second type of tea. Okay, she was nosy and wanted to know what his conversation with Iris was about. But the glass door to the tea garden was suddenly pulled open. As the bell rang, Cade Bankert strode in.

Daisy stopped in mid-step to gaze at him a couple of seconds longer than she should. He too had been a high school classmate. When she'd moved back to Willow Creek and she and her aunt had decided to look for a place to buy for the tea garden, as well as a second property for her and her girls, she'd consulted Cade, who was a real estate agent. She'd always liked him. He'd taken her to their high school prom. But then she'd left for college, and they'd gone their separate ways. Whenever she saw him, sparks of male and female interest seemed to cross over between them. But neither of them had let a spark ignite, maybe because Cade had realized she hadn't been ready for that.

When Cade saw her, he smiled and headed for a table for two. She smiled back and approached him, noticing how well his charcoal suit fit his broad shoulders. His long legs stretched out under the table as if he could finally relax after a long day.

He often stopped in for a snack and a respite before going back to his agency's office for the night. She knew he worked long hours. What self-employed person didn't?

She could let Cora Sue Bauer, the middle-aged bottle redhead with a bubbly personality, serve him. However, she signaled to Cora Sue that she'd take care of their latest tea connoisseur. As she neared his table, his gaze swept over her royal blue sweater and slacks, and the yellow apron with the daisy emblem for Daisy's Tea Garden stamped on the front. Cade ran his hand through his dark brown hair, putting it in some order after the wind had disturbed it.

He glanced around, noticing tables with other customers sampling Daisy's baked goods. "You're busy. A cup of hot tea hits the spot at the end of a day."

"If I remember correctly," she teased, "when we first opened the tea garden, you didn't know black tea from white tea, or what a tisane was."

"And you've educated me," he responded. "I've become a tea lover. How about orange pekoe today."

"Coming right up. We have fresh baked lemon tea cakes too."

"Three of those," he said with a smile. "On second thought, make that six to go. For a change, I'm headed home at a reasonable hour."

"Satisfying day?"

"Yes, it was. House sales have picked up. I have two new listings and closed on another. How about you? Satisfying day?"

"Steadily busy with lots of tourists out on a drive

enjoying the fall weather and the countryside. We do have beautiful scenery in Pennsylvania."

"Yes, we do. Did you miss it when you left?"

"I did. I didn't realize until I moved back here that Florida never really felt like home, not in the way Willow Creek does. Maybe it was the lizards and alligators. I prefer squirrels and fox and deer."

He laughed. "Or two feet of snow in the winter."

"Only some winters," she joked.

She heard her aunt laugh again. Harvey did that for Iris, and maybe Daisy was being too protective of her aunt. The same way she was protective of Violet and Jazzi?

As she thought of her older daughter, her heart hurt a little. Vi was making her way through the maze of classes and friendships at Lehigh University. Daisy missed her. And Jazzi—she was growing up too. It was hard to believe three years had passed since Ryan had died. Maybe there was a more substantial way for Daisy to move on besides checking her daily balance sheets at the tea garden.

She could fetch Cade that pot of orange pekoe tea and his lemon tea cakes or . . .

"If you have the evening free," she began and then stopped. Her mouth suddenly went dry. Still she plunged ahead. "I started stew in the slow cooker this morning before I left. How would you like to come home with Jazzi and me and have a home-cooked meal?"

Cade's brown eyes didn't waver from her blue ones. "You've just made my day."

His expression told her there could be more than friendship on his mind. Had she just made a mistake?

* * *

Daisy's house was different than most. It once had been a barn!

She parked on the gravel in front of the building that had once been an equipment shed. Now it served as a detached two-car garage. Cade pulled up beside her. They'd agreed to meet here at seven-fifteen, and he was right on time.

"How come you asked him to dinner?" Jazzi asked from the passenger seat, curiosity in her voice.

Daisy switched off the ignition of her purple PT Cruiser and gave her daughter her full attention. "I've known Cade for years. He went out of his way to negotiate the best deal for the barn and for the tea garden property. Asking him tonight was just an impulsive decision. Do you mind?"

Jazzi gave her a one-shouldered teenage shrug. "I guess not. I have friends over. You can have friends over. I just wondered if you're . . . forgetting about Dad."

Daisy reached out and put her hand on Jazzi's arm. "I will *never* forget about your dad. I promise." This particular subject had never come up between her and her daughters. She was glad Jazzi felt so deeply about her father. Where Violet had been born from Daisy's womb, Jazzi had been adopted. She and Ryan had worked hard to make sure Jazzi knew she was a child of their hearts as much as Violet was.

Jazzi pulled away, unfastened her seat belt and opened her car door. "I'm not going to hang with you guys anyway. I have a paper due in a few days."

She was out of the car before Daisy could take another breath. Just what was going on with her? Fifteen-year-old angst? Or something else?

As Cade joined Daisy and walked with her up the path leading to the house, he glanced up at the multi-paned window that had once been a hay hatch where hay bales had been hauled into the barn and out. A smaller window above that one let light into the attic space. A floodlight at the peak of the roof had gone on with dusk, and Daisy could catch a glimpse of the blue plaid curtain that draped the window in Jazzi's room. The second floor had been divided into two bedrooms with a bath and had suited her daughters perfectly. Jazzi had chosen white-washed furniture as well as a spread that was blue trimmed in white. Violet's room, however, was less country and more contemporary, with sleek-lined walnut furniture. The drapes and spread were hues of green.

"You know," Cade said, "I couldn't envision this the way you did. I can't wait to see the inside."

Cade had witnessed the outside makeover with its barn-red siding and repointed and cleaned stone base. White trimmed the windows as well as the dormers. But he hadn't seen the structural changes inside. Ryan's insurance money had made this new life in Willow Creek possible. She'd always be grateful for that.

"You can have the five-cent tour. Anyone who comes to dinner gets it."

Jazzi had her own key. She'd already unlocked the wide white front door and punched in the code to switch off the security alarm.

As soon as Cade stepped inside the barn house, he whistled. "Wow! You should do this for a living."

"Decorate barns?" she asked with some amusement.

"No, buy them and redesign them."

He was staring at the open stairway to the rear of the living room. A huge wagon wheel chandelier lit up the area which was open to a dining area and kitchen. A floor-to-ceiling stone fireplace was a focal point on the east wall.

"Come on," Daisy said. Leading Cade into the

kitchen area, she motioned down a short hall. "My room's down here."

Cade went down the hall, and Daisy knew he could see the sleigh bed.

"A Sunshine and Shadow quilt," he said when he returned to the kitchen.

"It's my mom's favorite design. When I saw it in a shop in Bird in Hand, I couldn't resist it. I put one of those bowl sinks in the powder room and my bathroom to add a country touch."

"The antique pine furniture does that too." Cade admiringly shook his head again. "You did this all yourself?"

"I did it with the help of Mom and Iris and the girls. It was a joint project. I especially wanted Vi and Jazzi involved so it would feel like home to them."

In the living room once more, Daisy tried to see the entire space through Cade's eyes. The furniture was all upholstered in blue, green, and cream. The braided blue and rust rugs had been woven by a local Amish woman.

Jazzi had run upstairs to her bedroom to drop her backpack. Daisy smiled when she noticed her two cats, who had started down the stairs. Was Cade an animal person?

"Are you going to introduce me to the rest of the family?" he asked Daisy, pointing to the stairway.

The cats apparently sensed another friendly human because they descended the rest of the stairs. Daisy motioned to Marjoram, who was a tortoiseshell with unmistakably unique markings. One side of her face was mottled like a tortoiseshell in tan, brown, and black. The other side was completely dark brown. Various colors including orange to cream spotted her back and flanks, while her chest was a creamy tan and rust.

"This is Marjoram," Daisy said as she scooped up the cat and cuddled her against her body. The other feline, black with white fluffy spots on her chest, crossed to Cade, sat on his shoe, looked up at him, and gave a small meow.

"That's Pepper," Daisy added with a smile.

"How old are they?" Cade asked.

"Probably about eighteen months. We found them last fall in the garden, hence their names Marjoram and Pepper." After another cuddle—the tortie couldn't abide cuddling for long—Daisy let Marjoram down to the floor. "Another cup of tea before I put supper on the table?" she asked.

Pepper moved from Cade's shoe, walked a circle around his legs, then crossed to a deacon's bench under a window and settled on an afghan there.

"What kind do you have?" Cade asked.

"I have an Assam that I like. It's a black tea from India."

"If *you* brew the tea, you have to give me something to do."

"Guests don't have chores in the kitchen," she told him as Marjoram joined her sister on the bench.

"Consider it a contribution," he said. "What can I do? Really."

"You can toss the salad. I'll warm up the bread."

They worked companionably together as Daisy brewed tea, popped the bread in the oven, and watched Cade slice the carrots at the island. She pulled a basket from one of the knotty pine cupboards and lined it with a napkin, preparing it for the warmed bread. It had been over three years since she'd worked beside a man in the kitchen. Ryan's cancer had taken him so fast, they'd hardly had time to say good-bye. Not nearly enough time. But she shouldn't be thinking about loss now, not if she wanted to move on.

"I really appreciate this. Home-cooked meals are hard to come by," Cade said as he set the salad bowl on the table.

The round pedestal table was oak with a distressed wood finish. The chairs were antiques that she'd found at the flea market and refinished herself. All of it had been part of rehabilitation, grieving, and starting over. For the most part, it had worked.

"Are you saying you live on my scones?" she joked. A former dietician, she was aware of eating habits, both good and bad. When Cade did stop in at the tea garden, he usually bought a dozen scones. He'd told her that he often froze them and pulled them out when he needed them.

"Of course, I don't just live on your scones," he answered, faking injured pride. "I can fry burgers and cook an omelet."

When Daisy looked at Cade, she saw the man he'd become, but she also remembered the boy he'd been. "Why haven't you ever married?"

He shrugged. "Maybe after our prom date, no other woman could compare to you."

His explanation stunned her for a moment, and before she could decide whether he was serious or not, her cell phone rang. It wasn't exactly a ring. It was a sound like a tuba bellowing.

Cade's eyebrows arched.

"It's the only ringtone I can hear when I'm in the tea garden with customers." She saw her Aunt Iris was calling. "It's Aunt Iris. Excuse me for a minute?"

He nodded. "I'll take the bread from the oven."

Daisy moved into the living room and answered the call. "Hi, what's up?" Maybe Harvey wanted to change their plans for tomorrow afternoon in his store. Maybe he wanted her to bring a particular tea.

"Harvey just left."

"You're still at the tea garden?"

"We were talking," her aunt said defensively, and Daisy knew she'd better back off with any disapproval she might be feeling.

"Were you talking about tea at his shop tomorrow or the party on Sunday?"

"Both. He finalized everything he wants served for afternoon tea service on Sunday. But that isn't why I'm calling."

Daisy waited.

"Harvey left because he received a phone call from his lawyer. It's about the divorce settlement."

"I thought all that was finalized."

"He did too. But apparently Monica made new demands, or else changed her mind about something they'd already agreed on. He didn't go into detail. He said he had to leave and take care of it. He didn't want anything to hold it up. I think he was going to see his lawyer . . . or maybe even Monica. He didn't say exactly."

Daisy could hear the worry in her aunt's voice and the fear that maybe the dreams she was beginning to weave weren't going to come true.

"Aunt Iris, what would you say if I told you I was dating a man who wasn't divorced yet?"

Iris was silent for a few moments, but then she said, "I'd tell you to be very careful. I'd tell you to keep your eyes wide open and listen to your sixth sense."

"Is that what you're doing?"

"I am. Harvey Fitz is one of the special ones. He's worth waiting for."

Daisy wasn't sure of that. She wasn't sure of that at all.

Chapter Two

The following afternoon, Daisy noted the latest styles in men's clothing for fall as she put the finishing touches on the dessert and tea display at Men's Trends. Shawl-collared sweaters were back, as well as waffle-knit pullovers. Color-blocked hoodies hung on the racks with raglan crewneck sweaters.

Ryan had preferred classic cable-knitted sweaters, but then he'd been a traditional, or maybe you could say an old-fashioned, kind of guy. He never would have worn the leather jacket trimmed with fur, or the black and orange anorak. He might possibly have tried on the double-breasted peacoat, simply because it was retro and might have appealed to his traditional sense. As far as sport coats . . . he also might have succumbed to buying the houndstooth blazer, but not with its notched lapels. The black sharkskin would have been out. Definitely forget the plaid. He would have asserted that the floral blazer didn't belong in the store.

But Men's Trends was all about trends, from Hugo Boss to Kenneth Cole to Saint Laurent and Brioni. Harvey Fitz also took measurements for custom-made suits. He had an impeccable reputation as a men's clothier, and Men's Trends was the reason why.

Daisy added a sprinkle of powdered sugar to the double chocolate chip cookies. She knew the cookies would melt in anyone's mouth.

Turning her attention to the sandwich tray, she was pleased Tessa had created the triangles with avocado pepperoni spread and others with smoked turkey and farmer's cheese. For now, they had steeped Earl Grey tea and a peach-infused green tea. Harvey's manager, Bennett Topper, had helped her move in three tall tables this morning where customers could stand, sip tea, and eat dessert. That had seemed the prudent thing to do.

As customers stopped by to sample the cookies and sandwiches she displayed, she could hear snippets of conversations that told her these men and women came from a pay echelon she'd never reach. They spoke of trips to Europe and BMWs, cruises in the Mediterranean and excursions to Thailand.

Just how rich was Harvey Fitz?

As so often happened, the people flowing around the dessert and tea table paid her no mind. It was as if she were just part of the furnishings. She didn't feel that way when she was serving at Daisy's. There, conversation was everything. It was critical to the success of her endeavor. Customers came to talk and relax. Businessmen wanted efficient service. The word was spreading that she provided conversation, relaxation, and darn good food.

Daisy was keeping the water heater for the tea in the break room next to Harvey's office. Now Tessa came down the short hall carrying two teapots covered with embroidered cozies. She set them into place on the display between twinkle lights, flower arrangements, and the array of desserts. She added Asian pear white tea and pomegranate tea to the other selections. The pomegranate was one of Daisy's favorites. It was a blend of Ceylon black tea from Sri Lanka with a sweetly tart pomegranate flavor.

"Quite a crowd," Tessa said as she readied cups and saucers.

"Do you think they're here for the tea or the fashion?" Daisy joked.

"More likely for the free desserts," Tessa returned with a wry smile.

Abruptly, Daisy's concentration was distracted from tea and dessert and shifted to a woman rushing after Harvey Fitz in between the tie racks.

"Harvey. Don't walk away from me like that," the woman protested. "I know your divorce is going to be final, and I think we should talk."

Bennett Topper, the store's manager, smoothly stepped between the woman and Harvey.

"Miss Darren," Bennett Topper said, "Mr. Fitz is handling his twenty-fifth anniversary open house. Now isn't quite the time for conversation. Maybe you could make an appointment with him for next week."

Harvey swiftly escaped into his office and shut the door.

Daisy couldn't help but wonder what his connection was to this Miss Darren. She really didn't have the right to know. On the other hand, if her Aunt Iris was involved with Harvey, maybe she did.

A couple who had been hovering near the shirt display suddenly moved closer to the desserts. They each nodded to Daisy. The man picked up a chocolate chip cookie, the woman one of the lemon tea cakes. They seemed to dismiss Daisy as they turned away.

With shoulder-length, wavy blond hair and blue

eyes, Daisy was usually underestimated. Because of the blond hair? Not exactly. But teachers, and in her adult life businesspeople, seemed to think she was window dressing and not particularly serious-minded. That was before they got to know her. After they did, they realized she could be as serious as a category-four hurricane when she was determined to do something . . . or when anyone she loved was threatened.

For now, however, as she assembled teacups and saucers, she listened to the couple's conversation. The man said, "That Darren woman has been after him for years. Now that Harvey's finally getting a divorce, she probably wants to hook up."

"Maybe she didn't hear about his latest will change," the woman responded. "First of all, he could lose half of his assets in his divorce. But Agnes told me that he was changing his will to reflect his divorce proceedings. He's giving everything to charity."

"Even though he has a son and daughter who expect to inherit?" the man asked.

"Agnes said he's disinheriting them because they feel entitled to everything he has. His boy, Daniel, isn't satisfied no matter where he takes a job."

"I heard that when Daniel worked here, he tried on clothes more than he sold them."

"And Harvey's daughter is just like her mother. She spends every penny she makes. Neither of them deserves his fortune."

"They're his kids," the man reminded her.

"Exactly," the woman agreed. "They're his children. But do they even visit him, have dinner with him, spend any time with him? They've taken their mother's side in the divorce, so why should he leave them anything?"

All of this was news to Daisy, and she wondered if it would be news to her aunt too. After all, if Aunt Iris was serious about Harvey, she'd have to deal with his children and possibly his ex-wife.

Aunt Iris was soft-hearted, and Daisy couldn't imagine her in a world where she had to deal with the likes of Miss Darren . . . and maybe even Harvey's wife.

Two hours later, Daisy reduced her speed as she approached the slanted parking spaces with hitching posts for the tea garden's Amish customers who drove horse and buggies. She turned her van left onto the lane that led to the rear of the property and a few private parking spaces. Handicapped customers could use this parking area. She always parked here when she was serving tea off the grounds and had to load up the van or empty it after an off-site party.

Afternoon tea inside should be over by now. Iris, Karina Post, a temporary employee who helped mainly with the afternoon teas, and Cora Sue Bauer would be clearing tables and serving any of the after-work crowd who joined them on a Friday afternoon. Eva would be tending to the kitchen.

Before Daisy and Tessa exited the van to go inside, Tessa asked her, "Are we really ready for Sunday and Harvey's official anniversary party?"

"We'd better be ready. He's renting out Daisy's for the day and paying us big bucks."

"We need to do it more often. It would help the bottom line."

Daisy knew that, but she also hated to close the tea room to her regular customers. "I'll be coming in around six AM Sunday morning to make sure the lemon tea cakes are freshly baked. The other cookie and scone dough will be ready to be scooped and baked too. But we'll mix up those batches tomorrow," she reminded Tessa. "All the ingredients for the salads will be prepped and ready, along with the dressings. The mini cheesecakes just need to be thawed, and I'll start the soup before I begin anything else."

"That new recipe for leek and potato soup?"

"I think that will be a good one."

"Will Karina be helping us serve?"

"Jazzi, Karina, and Cora Sue will be doing most of the serving. Iris will watch over the tea brewing, while you and Eva handle the kitchen. I think we've got it all covered. How about if we go in and have a cup of tea ourselves before we start to unload?"

"Sounds good."

To make a business succeed, everyone involved needed to work together easily. Daisy's rapport with Iris was perfect for a work environment. After all, she'd learned a lot of her cooking and baking skills from her aunt as well as her mother. So being in the kitchen together was a natural thing. Working with Tessa was companionable. They'd known each other for so long they didn't have to watch their words or worry about what they were going to say next. Tessa was a good friend, and Daisy was grateful she'd joined her in this venture.

A stiff wind blew fallen leaves here and there as she and Tessa rounded the back corner of the tea garden. They could have used the kitchen door, but Daisy enjoyed checking the herbs and flowers in the garden off of the patio. A profusion of mums in purple, yellow, burnt orange, and cranberry colors formed a border. No one sat at the tables outside. When Daisy brushed against a pot of rosemary, the scent drifted into the air.

Herbs were interspersed with flowers for their decorative value and their scent. The ornamental oregano had been a particularly unusual eye catcher this year. In between the large pots on the patio floor sat whimsical statues—a foot-high unicorn and a bronze cat seated on a stone reading a book, glasses perched on its nose. A flameless candle on a timer in a tall lantern glowed near the side door since the late-afternoon light was already becoming dim.

Tessa entered first, and Daisy let the door shut behind them. Inside the general serving area, she could see a table of six happily chatting. Daisy never knew if a Friday afternoon would be slow because residents were rushing home to get ready for the weekend, or busy because groups of employees from a business had decided a cup of tea and a scone at the end of the day was just what they needed before they started their weekend. Today she was happy to see three of the other tables occupied too. A full house for afternoon tea and a steady business was all she could ask for.

"How did it go?" Iris asked Daisy and Tessa.

"We didn't have much left over," Daisy assured her. "And all of the teas went over well. Harvey's crowd knows tea."

Iris laughed. "He said as much. I think he has several English friends who started the trend."

The party of six in the main tea room started to stand. One of them waved to Iris and called, "That apple bread is particularly good. I might have to order a loaf the next time it's your goodie of the day."

"I'm glad you liked it," Iris called back.

As the group left the restaurant and the atmosphere grew quieter, Daisy followed Tessa to the kitchen.

Tessa asked Daisy, "How about a pot of green tea with rose hips?"

"That sounds calming. Just what I need."

As Tessa released water from a temperature-controlled urn, she said, "We hardly had any time to talk this afternoon. I have some news."

"What kind of news?"

"I'm taking several of my paintings to Revelations. Reese Masemer has agreed to give my work a showing. Apparently, he had scheduled an artist who wasn't really ready, and Reese is giving me that slot."

"That's wonderful!" Daisy gave her friend a hug. Although Tessa had joined Daisy working at the tea garden, her true love was her art. Every spare moment, she painted upstairs. She'd turned the Victorian's attic into a studio, and it was perfect for her.

"Maybe you'll sell everything."

"That's a dream I've almost been afraid to dream."

"If you can see it, it can happen," Daisy assured her. She told her daughters that all the time.

"Speaking of seeing and dreaming," Tessa said slyly, "how did dinner go with Cade?" She had known Cade back in high school too, though not as well as Daisy had.

"It went just fine," Daisy said, though she wasn't sure it had. After Cade's surprising remark about the prom, he'd acted like a longtime friend, not a man with a romantic interest in her.

"Did he ask you for a date?"

"Nope," Daisy said with a shrug.

"Did he try to kiss you?"

"Nope," Daisy said again, as if it didn't matter at all. She didn't even know if it did. "It's possible he didn't like me making the first move—you know, asking him to dinner."

"Don't be silly. Men these days consider that a turn-on."

Cade hadn't seemed romantically turned on, even though she was attracted to him. Maybe she was deluding herself, thinking something romantic could develop between them.

Before their conversation could go any further, Daisy's cell phone vibrated in her pocket. She'd put it on vibrate while they were serving and mingling with Harvey's customers.

Slipping it from her pocket, she saw Violet's number. She said to Tessa, "It's Vi. I'm going to take it." She always took her kids' calls. They always came first.

"What's up, honey?" Daisy asked Vi as she headed to her office.

Violet just started right in. "You know I said I might come home next weekend?"

"Yes." Jazzi was so looking forward to seeing her sister, and Daisy missed her oldest more than she could ever say.

"I don't think I will be. It's so crazy here—crazy busy in a good way, and I just love it. In fact, I might not be home until Thanksgiving."

Relief rushed through Daisy because she was pleased that Violet was adjusting to college so well. Yet dismay weighed her down. She definitely felt the effects of a half-empty nest, especially when Jazzi seemed to be pulling away from her.

"Not until Thanksgiving?" she repeated, trying to keep her voice even so Vi didn't hear how very disappointed she was.

But her daughter must have heard a little of that disappointment. "It's really not that far off, Mom. As busy as you are, and as busy as I am, it will be Thanksgiving before we know it."

"I suppose you're right. If I book many parties like

the one I have on Sunday, I won't have time to think about anything else." Though, of course, that wasn't true. Her daughters were on her mind every waking moment and many sleeping ones.

"You'll kill them dead on Sunday, Mom. Make it a splash Willow Creek will remember."

Daisy didn't know about making a splash. She just hoped her servers wouldn't spill tea on anyone.

On Sunday, Aunt Iris patted Daisy's shoulder. "We've outdone ourselves."

As Daisy glanced around Harvey Fitz's twenty-fifth anniversary celebration, she had to agree with her aunt. White tablecloths gave an immaculate appearance. Vintage china with its roses and tulips and gold trim welcomed everyone who sat down at one of the place settings. Lace doilies on multi-tiered serving dishes spoke of refinement. The guests could choose from pots of green, black, and oolong tea, including Daisy's Blend, a decaffeinated green tea infused with raspberry and vanilla.

"Tessa's sandwiches with the smoked salmon on cream cheese and rye are being gobbled up first," Daisy commented. They never knew what their guests would like best.

"The lemon tea cakes are a hit, and so are the strawberry layered-cake pastries."

"Harvey seems happy with it all."

At the moment, he was dipping his spoon into the leek and potato soup Daisy had created. The expression on his face said he liked it.

Tessa passed by Iris and Daisy after she checked on the status of service. "I think it's time for a tea toast. Maybe that will break up the argument between Harvey Fitz's daughter and son."

As Daisy looked their way, the two siblings seemed to be squabbling over something. Daniel was a good-looking young man in his mid-twenties. His light brown hair was stylishly gelled, and his patrician nose replicated his father's. However, the expression on his face was dark, and his scowl gave him the appearance of a much less handsome young man. Harvey's daughter, Marlene, was shaking one long, graceful finger at her brother. Her blond hair was upswept in a messy topknot, and Daisy noted that her roots showed. She was obviously a brunette at heart. Giving her the benefit of the doubt, Daisy wondered if that was special effects highlighting. Who knew these days?

"A toast would be good right now," she agreed.

She poured herself a cup of tea and went to stand at Harvey's table. She'd done this before for birthday parties, anniversaries, and bon voyage celebrations. The tea garden was becoming popular for all of those. But she'd never before rented out her business space for the whole day to someone as well connected and rich as Harvey Fitz. When she stood between his son and daughter across from him, they stopped arguing, realizing something more public was about to occur.

Daisy rang a crystal bell that tinkled prettily. She'd hidden it in her apron pocket. It was perfect for occasions like this.

Everyone in the room looked her way, and she smiled. "Daisy's Tea Garden is so pleased to welcome Harvey and his family and friends here today. Harvey Fitz's business acumen has made Men's Trends a roaring success for all these years. Harvey, we just want you to know we recognize your achievements, and we applaud them. We hope you enjoy your celebration here at Daisy's as much as we enjoy having you."

She lifted her teacup in a toast. "To Harvey Fitz. To success, health, happiness, and at least twenty-five more years to come."

The whole room stood to applaud after their sips of tea, though Harvey's children were two of the last to stand. They looked as if they knew they had to give their father his due.

Daisy glanced at her aunt and saw the adoring expression on her face as she watched Harvey. Did Aunt Iris know what she was getting into with this family? Did she think Harvey's children would go their separate ways and not concern themselves with their father or her?

Love really was blind sometimes, Daisy thought.

The front door of the tea garden suddenly flew open. Although Daisy had put the CLOSED sign in place, she, of course, hadn't locked the door. Harvey's guests needed to feel free to come and go. But now she wished she had locked the door because the woman who blew in looked altogether entitled and enraged.

Everyone on Harvey's guest list had appeared and been checked off. Daisy didn't know who this woman was, but she had the feeling she was about to find out. The glaringly fake redhead, with her long wavy hair, red manicured nails, and Prada purse quickly canvassed the room and made a beeline toward Harvey.

In her designer orange and brown color-blocked suit, she shook her fist at him. "You can't hide your assets and get away with it."

To Harvey's credit, he didn't respond in kind. Rather, as everyone else sat down, obviously cowed by what was happening, Harvey regally stood.

"I assure you, Monica, that nothing is hidden."

"I don't believe it for an instant," she snapped back. "You won't return my calls. You won't answer your door if I visit. You *are* hiding something."

So this was Harvey's wife. Daisy considered Monica and then her aunt and just shook her head.

Harvey responded, "My financial statements are an open book. I think you should leave before Daisy has to call the police."

Monica's cutting sideways glance at Daisy told her the wife didn't think she was a threat.

A woman at a nearby table—Daisy remembered her name as Colleen Messinger—stood and went to Monica's side. She whispered something in Monica's ear.

Harvey's wife's face seemed to deflate. She studied the gathering, and Daisy thought she glimpsed tears in the woman's eyes.

However, Monica's shoulders remained rigid. "Your lawyer better set up a meeting with my lawyer. Don't think you can avoid me forever."

Then, with Mrs. Messinger taking her by the elbow and walking her to the door, after a last look at her soon-to-be ex-husband, Monica Fitz left.

There almost seemed to be a unanimous sigh of relief in the room. Harvey's children had their heads together now instead of squabbling, but they made no move to leave. In fact, Harvey's daughter reached out a hand to him.

Were Harvey's children now leaning toward their father's side because they were hoping they could still inherit his fortune?

Daisy had stepped away from Harvey's table, giving the guest of honor time to recover. At a nearby table she spotted empty teacups. Taking her hostess duties seriously, she picked up the pot sitting between guests and refilled their cups. They paid her no mind because they were involved in conversation. In fact, as she poured the second cup, she heard one man say, "To keep the coin collection Harvey inherited, he gave up the house and forked it over to Monica. I don't know what else she wants. This divorce is costing him big. It will take a long time to recoup what he settled on her."

If Monica was receiving a more than generous settlement, then what was her problem? Maybe this divorce was something Harvey wanted and she didn't.

Could the couple still reconcile?

Aunt Iris was studying Harvey again as if he was the secret to happiness for the rest of her life.

Daisy would stand by her aunt, especially if she was headed for a fall. She just wished she could keep her from falling.

Chapter Three

After Monica Fitz left, everyone tried to fake a cheery atmosphere again. Daisy and Iris both went from table to table, making sure teacups were filled and the guests felt welcome in spite of what had happened. Tessa kept the sandwiches and desserts coming, as Karina and Cora Sue carried in more tiered dishes when the first ones emptied.

Daisy caught sight of Jazzi, who was supposed to be helping to bus the tables. She was standing near the kitchen, her back half turned to Daisy, and in her hand—

Daisy caught sight of her daughter's smartphone. Maybe it had been a mistake to get her one of those. But Jazzi had missed Vi so much, and this was a way for them to text and send photos and video conference.

Daisy had upgraded hers so it was compatible with Jazzi's. She still wasn't familiar with it.

Harvey Fitz was an important client. He and his guests deserved their full attention during the course of the celebration, including Jazzi's.

Although Daisy didn't want to ruffle Jazzi's feathers

any more than they seemed to be, she crossed to her daughter and in a low voice said, "Can you put the phone away until after the tea party?"

She waited to see if Jazzi would explain what was so important, but Jazzi didn't. Daisy wasn't into snooping, but she did want to snatch Jazzi's phone sometime when she wasn't looking and check text messages and calls. Nevertheless, as Jazzi solemnly slipped the phone into the back pocket of her khakis, Daisy knew they were going to have to have a serious talk soon. Something was up with her younger daughter, and she wanted to know what it was.

Jazzi said, "I suppose you're going to want me to help wash up the teapots too. If you weren't so concerned with the vintage look, you could buy new ones that you could load into the dishwasher."

Daisy took a deep breath. She was better with praising than with counting to ten. "Look around here, Jazzi. This tea garden is what supports us, and it supports us because Iris and I make it unique. If we used dishes and teapots we could throw in the dishwasher, this place wouldn't have the same atmosphere. If you're worried about dishpan hands, there are three different kinds of lotions in the ladies' room. The apricot is especially nice."

Jazzi gave her mother a look as if she lived on another planet. "Dishpan hands have nothing to do with it. Time does. I want to get out of here and get back home."

"Do you plan to go to college someday?"

"You know I do."

"Then get used to working, and not always working where you want to work. Life gets bumpy sometimes, Jazzi. It's what we make it."

But Jazzi wasn't taking any advice, not today anyway. She just said, "I'll make sure everyone who's finished has their place cleared."

Daisy wanted to advise her to do it with a smile, but she wasn't going to push her luck with her daughter. Not today. Maybe tonight.

Suddenly a deep voice behind her asked, "Teenage rebellion?"

She turned to face Jonas Groft. She'd noticed he was one of Harvey's guests, but hadn't thought much about it. Jonas, a former Philadelphia detective, owned the furniture store down the street. Woods had been opened about a year. No one really knew his story or why'd he settled in Willow Creek, but he came in for tea many afternoons, and they chatted about their businesses, Willow Creek, and the customers who came and went.

She wasn't sure she'd ever stood this close to him before. Someone had mentioned he was thirty-nine. He had thick black hair with a few strands of silver at his temples and green eyes that seemed mysteriously intense. Tall and exceedingly fit, he had shoulders that were broad and long legs. He moved as if he'd once been an athlete, though sometimes he seemed to work his shoulder as if it had been injured. She hadn't asked him any personal questions over the months he'd been coming in to sample their teas because he'd seemed to keep his guard up. He hadn't delved into her personal life or she into his. That had been okay with her. Now, however, he was asking something personal. What did *he* know about teenage rebellion?

"Are you aware that teenagers are a species unto their own?" she asked him.

He laughed, and she enjoyed the sound of that laugh because he seemed to be somber much of the time.

His green eyes studied her as he explained, "I dealt with juveniles back in Philly who could have been considered to have come from an alien race."

She had a feeling he'd dealt with more than juveniles. "Jazzi wants to earn money, but not by working here. She's supposed to be helping me with the tea garden's yearly cookbook but isn't accomplishing much in that direction either. And why don't I feel guilty listing her faults to you?" she asked with a wry smile.

"Because I imagine you need someone to unload on once in a while."

"I have Aunt Iris."

"But you don't want to worry her," he guessed.

"You're an astute man."

"I've been working on it for years."

Daisy had to laugh at that.

"I'm so astute," he went on, "that I've noticed what a fine celebration you've given Harvey. He looks pleased in spite of the unpleasant interruption."

"Something like that can ruin a business's reputation if everyone doesn't have a good time."

"Look around," he said, motioning to the room and all the guests in it. "They're smiling, drinking, eating, talking. That's just what you want here, isn't it?"

"It is. I couldn't have done it without my staff's help."

His half smile told her he appreciated her outlook. That appreciation felt good.

He put some of that appreciation into words. "I admire the way you're making Daisy's Tea Garden a Willow Creek success. Many places like this fail. But you have loads of regulars and tourists who like to stop here."

"Woods will be a success too. The furniture in your store is beautiful. It takes time to build a brand. I hear you're making some of the furniture yourself now."

"That's true. I am. Woodworking has always been a hobby."

Ah, something else she hadn't known about him.

"Do you hear much from your older daughter now that she's in college?" he asked, switching the attention from himself to her again. He obviously paid attention to detail. She often mentioned Vi and her college aspirations in conversations with regular customers.

"She calls once a week, but in her last call she said she's busy and might not be home until Thanksgiving."

"That upsets you?" He was looking at her as if he were a detective again trying to ferret out the truth.

No reason not to be honest. "It upsets me because I'm her mom and I want to see her. I miss her as much as Jazzi does. But on the other hand, I know she has to make the most of her college experience. She'll form friendships that could last a lifetime and learn social skills she needs. But I worry about her weekends there—everything you hear about college, including frat parties. I don't want her getting into trouble. Since I'm at a distance, I have very little say about whether she does or not. She's only two hours away, but it seems a world away."

"Being a parent isn't for the fainthearted."

"No, and thank goodness I have my parents, my sister, and Aunt Iris. Raising kids really does take a village."

He looked thoughtful for a moment, then said, "When kids go wrong, most of the time they don't have the village behind them. They don't even have that one person that matters behind them. I can't tell you that you're worrying for nothing, but it seems to me Jazzi and Vi have a lot behind them—everything they need."

Daisy studied Jonas's face, the scar on his cheekbone, the slight wave in his black hair, the intelligence and maybe even curiosity in his eyes. They hadn't spoken like this in all the afternoons he'd come in to enjoy a mug of tea. He liked his tea in a mug, unlike most of her clientele.

She heard her name called. Checking over her shoulder, she found Tessa waving to her. Her kitchen manager was standing at the table with some of Harvey's guests, and two of them were leaving.

"I have to see what Tessa wants."

"Go," he said easily. "I'm leaving too. I'll see you around."

"See you around," she repeated as Jonas walked toward the door.

Daisy gave Jonas's back one last look, then crossed the room to Tessa. One of the women who'd stood to leave said to Daisy, "I just wanted to tell you I enjoyed that strawberry layered-cake pastry that I tried. Is that always on your menu?"

Daisy hadn't seen this woman come into the tea garden before. "We have different offerings every day, but you can always order one you especially like."

The woman seemed pleased with that notion. "I'd like to take home a dozen of the lemon tea cakes, but your waitress says you're not prepared to do that after a celebration like this. Does that mean I have to come into the tea garden tomorrow to buy them?"

What to do? Of course, she wanted this woman to come to the tea garden tomorrow when their cases were full of goodies and she'd probably buy more than the lemon tea cakes. However, pleasing the customer was all part of the marketing package.

"I have extra lemon tea cakes stowed away that I was going to take home tonight. You're welcome to those. I'll get them for you."

As Daisy hurried to the kitchen to gather up the tea cakes, she wasn't thinking about the woman who had asked for them. She was thinking about Jonas Groft and their conversation. In her experience, men especially underestimated her. But that didn't seem to be the case with Jonas. He appeared to see clearly what she could do. She liked the feeling that gave her.

Over the next half hour, the celebration wound down, as Harvey's guests slowly took their leave, continuing their conversations on the front porch of the pale green Victorian with white and yellow trim. As the guest of honor, he went from table to table, talking to them all. He was a congenial man. After all, his store couldn't have been so successful if he didn't have good public relations skills. A hands-on owner, he made sure of details, checked displays, and went over orders himself, according to her aunt. Daisy respected his dedication to Men's Trends.

Tessa crossed to Daisy and took a look around. "Jazzi did a good job bussing the tables after you talked to her."

"I shouldn't have had to talk to her."

"She's in the back on her phone. Is there anything you'd like her to do?"

After Daisy thought about it, she shook her head. "No. I have to pick my battles or I'll never win the war, though I'm not even sure what the war's about."

"It could be a new guy she likes."

"She's too young."

Tessa gave Daisy a "you're kidding me" look.

"All right, so I want to *think* she's too young," Daisy countered. "I really don't want to get into the subject of a steady boyfriend with her. It's group dates or nothing at her age."

"She's going to tell you that you're living in the Dark Ages."

"Maybe I am," Daisy said with a sigh. "It's not like I even know how to date. It's been a long time since I gave off signals to men that I was available."

"You didn't seem to have any trouble talking to Jonas."

Tessa was a good friend, and someone who could maybe understand where she was in life. "That conversation was a little different from the surface ones we usually have."

"Maybe he's making his move."

Daisy laughed outright. "I don't think so."

"Maybe *you* should make one."

Daisy thought about Cade and how she'd asked him to dinner, and how that hadn't turned up anything romantic. "I tried that, and it didn't work."

Just then the last table of Harvey's guests bade him good-bye and left, chatting among themselves.

Daisy was about to cross to Harvey herself when she suddenly changed her mind. Harvey was pulling her Aunt Iris over to a corner table that was a little more secluded than the others. He held up his hand as if telling her to stay there, went to his chair, and produced something from his trench coat pocket. When he sat down across from her aunt at the table for two, Daisy could see that he was presenting Aunt Iris with a tea tin. It was painted with sunflowers and wrapped with a yellow ribbon tied into a bow. Her aunt beamed at him and nodded. Then Harvey stood, went to Iris, pulled her to her feet, and gave her a giant hug.

By that time, Daisy felt she should duck back into the kitchen, but it was too late for that.

Spotting her, Harvey came over to her and gave her a wide smile. "I just want to tell you how much I enjoyed the celebration today and your lovely service." He produced an envelope from his pocket and handed it to her.

"You've already paid me in full," she reminded him.

"This is something extra that you deserve. Everyone had a wonderful time in spite of my wife's attempts to spoil it. But she didn't, and you and your staff picked up admirably after she left."

Daisy tucked the envelope into her apron pocket. "Thank you."

He gave Daisy a nod, said, "See you sometime soon," waved to Iris, and left.

Fingering the envelope in her pocket, deciding to split the money with her staff, Daisy walked over to the table where Iris was still sitting. She pointed to the tea tin. "That's a beautiful tin. It looks as if it's hand painted."

"It might be. It's filled with one of those very expensive silver needle white teas from China. But it's not for my everyday enjoyment. Not yet. When Harvey's divorce is final, we're going to celebrate by brewing a pot and talking seriously about our relationship. He's been separated from Monica for over two years. I think he's going to ask me to marry him."

"And that's what you want?"

"We're both too old not to enjoy the time we have with each other. Don't you think?"

What Daisy thought was simple. Harvey's divorce had to be more than final before he became involved seriously with her Aunt Iris. Was it so much easier for men to put the past behind them?

She'd find out when and if Harvey asked Aunt Iris to be his wife.

On Tuesday evening, Daisy was grateful that the tea garden had been busy all day. Usually, she took one day a week off, and that was Sunday, unless they had a special party like the one they'd thrown for Harvey Fitz. In that case, she took Monday off. So yesterday had been crammed with errands, making a few meals for the rest of the week, and tidying up the house. When she'd returned to the tea garden today, she'd been pleased to see that Harvey's celebration had brought in more customers.

As Tessa bumped Daisy's shoulder, she was already wearing her poncho and was ready to leave for the day. "We almost ran out of lemon tea cakes again. Some of Harvey's guests came in today and bought dozens of them. They're a hit. Iris had to grab a half dozen for Harvey before I sold the last ones. Are you going to put anything new on the menu this week?"

"How about chicken soup? With colder weather, I think there will be a call for it. Mrs. Grant makes her own fine noodles, and I placed an order for them."

"Do you have a recipe for the soup?"

"I finally jotted one down that I've been making for years. It should work well."

"I'm all for cooking chicken soup. Soothes the soul as well as the stomach. Maybe we should send some to Harvey's wife."

"Tessa," Daisy chided.

"Some of the guests who stopped in mentioned

how awkward that whole thing was. Imagine Harvey having to deal with her."

Daisy didn't like to engage in gossip, and they certainly heard plenty of it at the tea garden. She and Iris and Tessa had found out early on that they were sort of like bartenders. When customers came in for a soothing cup of tea or soup or dessert, they liked to talk too. Mostly Daisy and her staff just listened. A nod and then "I see" was often what someone needed to feel better. Understanding went a long way.

"Are you going to be here much longer?" Tessa asked.

"I'm going to check tomorrow's menu and make sure everything's ready. Aunt Iris has a date with Harvey. What about you? Not painting tonight?" Daisy asked.

Tessa didn't usually wear a poncho to go back up to her apartment.

"I'm going to stop at Revelations. Maybe I can convince Reese to go to dinner and talk art."

"Good luck."

Tessa left by the side garden door.

Iris was pushing a broom one last time over the tile floor.

"I'll do that if you want to get going," Daisy offered.

"Just because I'm going to dinner and a play doesn't mean I'm going to have you do my work. I still have a half hour before I meet Harvey in the garden. That will give me time to cover some of these lines on my face, add a little mascara, and freshen up my lipstick. Where's Jazzi tonight?"

"She's working on a social studies project with a friend. I'm supposed to pick her up around nine."

"Are you going to stay here until then?"

"I have receipts to enter on the computer, and I can work on the cookbook."

Aunt Iris took the broom to the closet in Daisy's office and stuffed it inside. When she returned to the green room, she said, "I brought a pantsuit along and dressier shoes to change into." She untied her apron.

"Now I see why you need a half hour," Daisy joked. "This isn't just a dab of lipstick date."

"Not *too* dressy. After I meet Harvey in the garden, we're going for an autumn walk along the creek to admire the leaves. We're both looking forward to the play at Willow Creek Little Theater tonight. Then afterward, we're going to Harvey's condo. He's having a personal chef prepare our meal. Though he did ask me to bring along lemon tea cakes to hold us over until dinner."

"You could get used to that—a personal chef, a BMW, cruises, and trips to Europe."

Her Aunt Iris frowned. "When you put it like that, it does sound like a whole different life, doesn't it? I can get used to that as long as I have ordinary pleasures too. And I certainly wouldn't want to give up working here with you."

Daisy wasn't sure cruises and trips to Europe left much time for her aunt to be working at the tea garden if she and Harvey got married. But that was a discussion for another day.

Daisy had decided to brew herself a cup of a pomegranate green tea when her aunt returned to the kitchen, looking like a woman who couldn't wait to go on a date. She was indeed wearing makeup, which had been rare before Harvey Fitz. Her taupe pantsuit, a string of pearls, and her brown flats were perfect for an autumn walk and a play. Dinner at Harvey's condo? Daisy didn't know what would be perfect for that. Had Harvey and her aunt progressed beyond kissing?

Not going there.

Aunt Iris pulled her camel-colored coat from the coatrack in the office, then went to the counter for the bag of lemon tea cakes she'd set there. "Don't work too hard," Iris told her as she gave her a hug. "Oh, and can you pick me up in the morning and bring me to work? I'll leave my car here because we'll probably take Harvey's. He'll just drop me off at home."

"That's fine. Why don't you have a cup of tea with me until he gets here?"

"He's usually prompt, or even early. I'll just go out to the garden and wait for him. I really should check the thyme and oregano. If they're not producing as much as we need, you might have to order from the supplier."

"Don't sit out there alone if Harvey's late."

"I won't," her aunt assured her, gave her hand a squeeze, and then left through the side-garden door, carrying her purse and the bag of tea cakes.

Daisy had picked up her two-cup vintage teapot with its hand-painted lilac pattern when she heard a bloodcurdling scream.

That was her aunt!

"Aunt Iris," she called as she set down the teapot, exited the side door, and ran through the garden.

She froze when she spotted Harvey's body crumpled in the herb garden.

Her Aunt Iris had spilled the bag of lemon tea cakes and was on her knees next to him. "Harvey! Harvey!" she called.

However, Daisy saw where Harvey's skull had been bashed in. She saw the blood. She rushed forward to take Harvey's pulse and to look for any sign of life.

But there was none.

Harvey Fitz was dead.

Chapter Four

An hour later, Daisy's Tea Garden was buzzing with activity. Daisy felt shaky but so vigilant that her skin crawled every time she heard a noise. Her aunt, who had been separated from her and led to the office by a patrol officer, didn't look much better. Even through the glass partition, Daisy could see that her aunt was pale, pale enough to faint. Daisy's thoughts sped through her mind much too fast to catch. Willow Creek's chief of police, Eli Schultz, stood in the office with Iris who sat in the desk chair. Eli was gruff, no nonsense, and abrupt. Daisy wished she could be beside Iris, giving her support. Eli Schultz had better not browbeat her.

In Willow Creek, the chief was mostly a paper pusher. His force took care of petty crimes, domestic disturbances, and traffic violations. But he did have one detective under his command, and that was the man who came in the door to the tea garden now. The detective didn't come for tea, although he'd been in a time or two for scones. Willow Creek was small enough that the locals knew each other. Detective Rappaport, whose keen eyes fell on Daisy now, had spoken to the high school kids about drinking and drugs.

When Chief of Police Schultz spotted him, he emerged from the office and consulted with the detective out of earshot.

Aunt Iris gave Daisy a little wave to let her know she was okay. But neither of them was really okay. How could they be? Harvey Fitz was dead, and he'd been murdered in their garden.

Detective Rappaport came toward her first. He looked to be in his late fifties. He had thick, blond-gray hair, grooves along his mouth, and plenty of lines on his face. As he approached her, he took a notebook and pen from his trench coat pocket.

"I'm Detective Rappaport," he said. "And you're Daisy Swanson, co-owner of the tea garden?"

"That's right."

"How about you tell me what happened here."

"I already told the chief of police."

The detective gave her a steady look, then warned her, "You're probably going to be telling this several more times—down at the station tomorrow, for instance, where you'll give your signed statement. But for now, I need to take a few notes and make sure exactly what happened. So go over it for me, all right?"

She quickly did, all the while glancing through the glass partition to where her aunt was. She was worried about her.

After she told Rappaport what had happened, he asked, "Why do you keep trying to make eye contact with your aunt?"

Daisy was tired, queasy, and not in the mood for suspicion. "Because I'm worried about her. She thought she was going to marry Harvey, and now the man is dead. Wouldn't you be worried about somebody you cared about?"

Rappaport studied her up and down, from her blond hair, down her apron with its huge daisy, to her flat shoes. "I'll be talking to your aunt in a few minutes. No one mentioned she was dating Harvey Fitz."

"It wasn't a secret. They'd been going out for a month or so."

"I see," the detective said.

Daisy didn't like his tone. "What do you see?"

"I'm asking the questions, Miss Swanson."

"It's Mrs. I'm a widow, but still Mrs."

"Mrs. Swanson," he acknowledged. Then he took a look around the kitchen and the interior of the tea garden again. "You were finished for the day?"

"We were closed, if that's what you mean. I was going to stay and work on the computer."

"What kind of work?"

If he was trying to catch her in a lie, he wouldn't. "I had receipts to enter and orders to study. We're also preparing a cookbook for the tea garden, and I was going to work on that."

"How long were you considering staying?"

"Until around nine. I was going to pick up my daughter at a friend's."

"How old is your daughter?"

"She's fifteen. I don't see what that has to do with any of this."

"My job is to ask the questions, and yours is to answer them. If you'd like to leave now, you can."

"I'm not going anywhere without Aunt Iris."

"Do you live together?"

"No, but she's shaken up. It might be a good idea for her to come home with me tonight."

He studied her again and then nodded. "You'll

have to wait out here," he ordered her. "I need to speak with your aunt alone."

Although Daisy wasn't happy about that, she did understand. The detective was interested in seeing whether their stories matched up. She'd watched enough cop shows to know that.

As gossip came and went, she'd heard tidbits about the detective. It was rumored he'd once worked with the Pittsburgh PD, but he'd taken this job in Willow Creek for a slower-paced position. There were also rumors that he'd left Pittsburgh after an internal affairs investigation. But just like with Jonas Groft, no one knew the real story.

Daisy wasn't sure she cared to know it. The less she had to do with the police chief and Detective Rappaport, the better.

However, five minutes later, Daisy peered through the glass partition and decided Detective Rappaport could put his rules and regulations back in his source book. Her aunt looked pasty and white.

Suddenly, Iris put her head down between her knees.

Daisy had run from the kitchen and opened the office door before anyone told her she couldn't go in. She went to her aunt and put her arm around her.

"What happened?" She stared at the detective accusingly. "What did you say to her?"

The detective didn't answer her but crouched down in front of her aunt, took an ampoule from his pocket, and pressed his finger into it.

He waved it under her aunt's nose. "Take a whiff of this. You'll feel better."

When Iris did take a whiff of it, she sat up and waved his hand away.

The ampoule contained smelling salts, and Daisy wondered if the detective had found himself in situations like this before with fainting witnesses all around him.

Daisy took her aunt's hand. "Aunt Iris?"

Her aunt shook her head as if trying to clear it. "I just got a bit fuzzy, lots of black dots, ears ringing."

The detective looked up at Daisy and then rose to his feet. "I just asked for her name and address, nothing tough yet. Mrs. Albright, would you rather go home now? You can come into the station tomorrow to answer my questions."

"It's Ms. Albright," her Aunt Iris told him. "I've never been married."

The detective shook his head. "I'll get this right eventually. Are you sure you're feeling well enough to continue?"

Iris looked at Daisy. "Could you make me a cup of black tea? That should help."

"I don't want to leave you."

"Mrs. Swanson, I assure you that your aunt will be safe with me," the detective told her gruffly. "I'm not going to badger her. I just need the facts. By the time you steep the tea, we'll probably be finished."

"You know about steeping?"

With obvious patience, he explained, "My mother was a tea drinker."

"Could I get you a cup of tea, Detective?" Daisy asked politely.

He shook his head vigorously. "I'm a straight java man all the way. Though I'm not opposed to all of the food that goes with the serving of tea. Your desserts are excellent, and so are your soups."

"You've had them?"

"I've had your scones and sampled the rest. Some of the officers stop in here, and they bring a selection back to the station. Word does get around about practically everything."

Daisy was sure that was true. With another look at her aunt, and her aunt's affirming nod, Daisy left to steep the tea.

While Daisy was in the kitchen, she heard the footsteps and clatter of a team arriving through the Victorian's front door. She peeked into the green room and spotted a man carrying a camera. He was followed by another gentleman who carried what looked like a toolbox. A patrol officer motioned them toward the garden entrance.

By the time Daisy had steeped the tea, sliced lemons, and assembled sugar cubes with the teacup and saucer on a tray, Detective Rappaport seemed to be winding down.

As Daisy set the tray on the desk in her office, the detective asked her aunt, "When were you and Mr. Fitz planning to be married?"

Now it seemed her aunt was flustered, her cheeks going rosy. "I don't know. He hadn't signed his divorce papers yet. After he did, we were going to discuss our next step."

"Are you sure there was going to *be* a next step?"

Daisy almost protested, but the detective's sharp look cut her off.

Her aunt was precise when she said, "All I know, Detective, is what Harvey said and what he did. He was acting like a man who was in love with me. He said he would talk about our future as soon as his divorce was final. I believed him."

Rappaport suddenly closed his book and pocketed

his pen. "That's it for now. I'll need to see you both at the station tomorrow, say around ten AM?"

"But the tea garden—" Iris began.

"I'm afraid you'll have to close it at least for tomorrow," he explained. "The techs will finish with the crime scene as soon as they can. Someone will contact you when you can get back in."

"This could be mightily bad for business," Daisy said. "It's a horrible thing to have happened. Customers coming in might not want to even think about it."

"On the other hand," Rappaport said, "you could have a lot more customers who are interested in gawking. You know—see the place where the man was murdered."

Her aunt was thoroughly outraged. "Detective Rappaport! We would never, ever encourage anything like that."

The detective looked from Iris to Daisy. "Maybe. Maybe not. And something else. Where are your vehicles?"

Daisy answered, "My van is in the back lot. Aunt Iris's car is there too."

"I'll be issuing search warrants for them and impounding them. Let me walk the two of you out."

When Daisy emerged with her aunt from the front door of the tea garden, all she wanted to do was find a quiet spot to call her dad so he could come and get them. Thank goodness, she'd driven the van today and her car was still at home. Daisy's father could still be at Gallagher's Garden Corner—the nursery her parents owned—with end of the day customers.

In the midst of the noise and commotion, a woman shouted to them from beyond the perimeter tape.

"What happened in there?" she yelled. "I'm with Channel 18 news. The public deserves to know."

There were others with cameras beyond the tape, many just curious citizens. But Daisy saw one familiar face, and he was motioning to her.

Jonas Groft looked tall and sturdy and like a port in the storm. He was gesturing to her and Iris, and pointing toward a black SUV. His vehicle?

Daisy clung close to Iris. "Come on. Let's hurry over there to Jonas Groft." She took her aunt's arm to guide her.

Jonas came to meet them at the tape, and he formed a bodyguard stance as he led them to the vehicle. He'd already opened two doors. Daisy quickly hopped in the front, and her aunt hiked herself up into the back. They slammed the doors shut, and soon Jonas was in the driver's seat.

"We can sit here, but they might surround us, or I can take you home. Your call."

"It would be great if you could take us to my place. Oh, but I have to pick up Jazzi." She looked at the time on her phone.

"My clerk's locking up the store," Jonas said. "We can pick her up along the way."

"Are you sure you don't mind?"

"I don't know what happened back there, but I do know what a commotion it is. I don't have any other demands on my time, so it's no problem."

"Thank you," Daisy said gratefully and gave him the address of Jazzi's friend.

Daisy called Jazzi, and she answered after one ring. "I know I'm late," she told Jazzi. "But I'm on my way to pick you up." She glanced at Jonas. "Or rather I'm with a friend and Aunt Iris, and we'll pick you up. Watch for a black SUV."

"Did something happen with your van?"

"No. But something happened at the tea garden. I'll explain when I see you."

"Mom . . . ," Jazzi started, and Daisy knew her daughter was ready to ask questions.

"We'll be there in ten minutes. I love you, honey."

Something in Daisy's voice must have warned Jazzi to be patient. She responded, "I'll see you then."

Jonas just drove, without asking questions, until Daisy couldn't keep it in any longer. "Harvey Fitz was murdered in our garden."

With that burst of news, Jonas cut her a quick sideways glance. "I thought you might have had a break-in."

"I wish it were that simple. Someone bashed in Harvey's head with something, and he was lying in the herbs."

Jonas glanced in the rearview mirror. "Ms. Albright, are you all right?"

"I'm not going to pass out, but I'm anything but all right. I just can't believe . . ." Her voice broke.

"Murder is unbelievable," Jonas said, as if he knew, and he probably did. After a silent moment, he asked Daisy, "Who took your statements?"

"Chief of Police Schultz and then Detective Rappaport."

"What kind of things did they ask you?"

"Just what happened, what I saw and heard, that kind of thing."

"Nothing about how you and your aunt knew Harvey?"

"Yes. I told him Aunt Iris and Harvey were dating."

Jonas gave a small grunt.

"What?" she asked, puzzled.

"You shouldn't tell Schultz or Rappaport anything you don't have to tell them."

"I don't understand. We want to help."

"In a murder investigation, whoever finds the body is always suspect."

"You're not serious!"

"I'm very serious. Do you have to go down to the station tomorrow to give statements?"

"Yes, around ten."

"When you do, just tell them exactly what happened tonight and nothing else, not until you know where this investigation is headed."

"But how am I going to know that?"

"There will be scuttlebutt. I'm friendly with some of the patrol officers, and I might be able to get details. But protect yourself."

"You sound more like a lawyer than a cop."

The silence in the SUV was weighty until Jonas said, "I've seen a detective go after the right suspect with a vengeance. I've also seen suspects railroaded because there was no one else to find."

"Do you know anything about Detective Rappaport? Is he fair?" Daisy asked.

"Whether he's fair or not, he's going to look hard at your aunt because she and Harvey were dating. But there will be other suspects too. After the scene at Harvey's twenty-fifth celebration, his wife will definitely be a suspect. I'd be looking at her and maybe his kids. But a man like Harvey could have lots of enemies. You can't be as successful as he was, and as rich as he was, without ruffling feathers or being a bit ruthless."

All of a sudden Daisy realized Jonas Groft's outlook on life could be altogether different from hers. As a former detective in a big city, he'd probably seen the unthinkable. He'd probably seen way too much. There was a reason he owned a furniture store in Willow Creek and had left the law enforcement profession behind. She'd been a bit intrigued by him before. Now she was even more interested.

However, her mind was on her aunt, and how she was going to tell Jazzi and her parents about this whole thing. "My parents are going to be worried sick if they see anything about this on the news."

"And they will. You can bet some of those lookie-loos with cell phones were uploading their video to the news channels. You'd better give your parents a call to prepare them."

Prepare them. How could anyone ever be prepared for murder?

Daisy drove her purple PT Cruiser into the parking lot of the Willow Creek Police Department the following morning. The police department building was almost as old as the town, settled back in the late eighteen hundreds. The building had been revamped and refurbished, but its brick exterior needed sand-blasting. It was located smack-dab in the middle of the downtown. The town council had allotted funds a few years back for automated front doors and refurbishment of its only jail cell. At least that's what the *Willow Creek Messenger* had reported. Daisy had never been inside the building and really didn't care to go in there now.

But she and her aunt had no choice.

"I shouldn't have had that coffee this morning," Aunt Iris said from the passenger seat. "I feel like I'm buzzing like a radio with static. I should have stuck to our herbal tea."

"I think you'd be wired no matter what you had to drink. Jazzi said you didn't sleep at all last night. She heard you tossing and turning."

"I just kept seeing . . ." Her aunt's voice broke.

Daisy took her hand. "I know, and we're probably going to have post-traumatic stress syndrome symptoms for a while. You can talk to me about it any time."

"What do you think the police are going to ask me?" Aunt Iris inquired, worried.

"I don't know. But it's two minutes before ten, so let's go find out."

Other than those electronic front doors, the inside of the police station took Daisy back to earlier decades. A dispatcher sat near the front door at a desk that had seen years of wear and tear. The woman sitting there looked to be in her forties. She had short brown hair and was wearing headphones and typing on the computer. A wooden fence of sorts cut off the reception area from the space farther back in the room. A swinging door in the middle reminded Daisy of a gate one might see in a nineteen-forties film. Inside that gate sat six desks with computers. Officers occupied two of the desks.

Daisy and Iris stood at the gate, not knowing whether they should push it open or not. One of the officers saw them, and he approached them with raised brows.

"We're here to see Detective Rappaport," Daisy said.

The officer glanced over his shoulder to another cop. "Rappaport's in, isn't he?"

"Yes sirree," the other officer answered. "He's taking statements this morning."

The first officer, who wore a nametag bearing the

name Bart Cosner, motioned them inside the gate. "Follow me."

Daisy and her aunt did just that. After they went inside the officers' area, they followed the man to the right and down a short hall. Detective Rappaport emerged from an office.

"Mrs. Swanson," he said. "Ms. Albright. Right on time. Mrs. Swanson, Officer Cosner will take you into Interrogation Room One. He'll take your statement. Ms. Albright, how about if you come into this room?"

"I thought we were going to do this together," Daisy protested.

"No, ma'am. You're not. I'm mostly finished with you, but I need to ask your aunt more questions before I tape her official version of what happened. She'll meet you out in the reception area when she's finished."

Daisy didn't like this wrinkle at all, but there wasn't much she could do about it. She could call Jonas, she supposed, and ask his advice. But ever since Ryan had died, she was used to standing on her own. She'd retell her experience from last night, then she'd wait for her aunt, hoping Detective Rappaport didn't shake her up too much. Daisy wanted to be there to hold her aunt's hand, to support her, to back her up. But she'd have to do all that after the detective had finished with her aunt.

An hour later, Daisy sat on a ladder-back chair near the dispatcher, waiting. She'd checked her phone for messages about a dozen times. Last night, when she'd reached Tessa, who'd been having dinner with Reese, she'd related everything that had happened. Her friend had been shocked, then appalled at the events and had decided to spend the night with a friend in town since she probably couldn't get into her apartment. She'd also been interested in how Jonas Groft had become involved, how he'd dropped off Daisy, Iris, and Jazzi at her home, but yet he hadn't come in.

Tessa had said, "You invited him in, didn't you?"

"Of course, I did. He'd gone out of his way to help us."

"So why didn't he come in?"

"I don't know. Maybe he thought Iris and Jazzi and I needed the time alone, and he was probably right. Jazzi was upset. Iris was upset. I was just trying to keep us all calm."

"Have you told your parents?"

"Before I called you. Mom wants Aunt Iris to stay with them for a few days."

"Do you think she might?"

"She's not sure what she's going to do, but I don't think she should be alone."

Yet Daisy knew her aunt probably felt very alone right now.

When Iris emerged from the hall that led back to the interrogation rooms, she looked terrible. She even looked as if she might have been crying.

Daisy stood and crossed to meet her at the gate. "Are you free to leave?"

"For now," Aunt Iris said, her lower lip trembling.

Daisy saw the officers watching them, the dispatcher not that far away. She took her aunt's arm. "Come on, let's go. We can talk outside."

Once they'd exited the building and headed toward Daisy's car, Iris stopped her a few feet from the door.

"He wanted to know everything about my relationship with Harvey," Iris said, sounding dejected.

"What do you mean *everything*?"

Her aunt blushed. "He wanted to know if we were intimate."

"I hope that wasn't his first question," Daisy muttered, feeling outraged for her aunt.

"No, not his first. He asked when we started dating. Then he wanted to know if I'd ever gone to Harvey's condo."

"You told him you had."

"Yes, of course. I'm not going to hide anything. He asked if I knew Harvey's wife . . . if I had spent any time with his children. Finally, he wanted to know if I was aware of how rich Harvey was and if I had access to his bank accounts."

"Seriously?"

"Seriously. I'm worried, Daisy. I think I'm their number one suspect, and I don't know what I'm going to do about it."

Chapter Five

After Jazzi climbed on the school bus the next morning, Daisy felt at loose ends. She hadn't received a call from the police yet to say she could reopen the tea garden. After giving their statements yesterday, she'd made sure Aunt Iris was tucked in with Daisy's parents. It would be good for Iris to have her sister to talk to about everything, Daisy hoped.

When Daisy felt unsettled like this, as if she had to organize her mind and her heart, she cooked or baked. It was just her go-to activity to settle herself down. This morning she decided to make chicken soup and take some to Jonas. After all, he'd been a big help, and she wanted to thank him.

Daisy was just about to add vegetables to the simmering chicken when her landline rang. She dumped the carrots and corn into the pot, repositioned the lid, and then picked up the cordless phone. After her "hello," a male voice asked, "Is this Daisy Swanson?"

She didn't recognize the voice and was wary. "Yes, it is."

"I'm Trevor Lundquist from the *Willow Creek Messenger*."

Ever since the murder, she hadn't picked up the phone and had just let her voice mail handle calls. Most of the calls had been from the press and interested residents of the town who wanted the scoop on what had happened. She didn't want to *give* the scoop.

However, Trevor Lundquist wasn't a stranger. Willow Creek was small enough that she'd met Trevor when the tea garden had set up a stand during the May Fling at the carnival grounds this past spring. She, of course, suspected what the reporter wanted, but she'd be polite and listen. Being friends with the local press was important to business.

"I'd like an interview with you," he continued. "After all, the hometown paper deserves to know what happened first."

"I don't know any more than the report the police gave on the news," she hedged.

"I'm sure that's not true. This happened at your tea garden. You and your aunt were there."

Gossip flew fast and furious in a town this size. Still, she told him the truth. "I'd rather not talk about what happened."

"An interview could be good for me and good for you. Did you ever think about the lift it would give your business?"

"I don't want to capitalize on a tragedy."

"Mrs. Swanson, it's my job to report the news. If you benefit from that, so much the better."

"I also don't know any more than anyone else," she repeated.

"Nonsense. You could give me the whole background story. People saw your aunt and Harvey Fitz together.

They were dating. I want to know all about that and what led up to the murder."

"That topic isn't for discussion," Daisy said firmly.

"Maybe not by you, but what about your aunt? If you won't give me what I need, I'll get in touch with her. She's the source. Maybe I could draw the true story from her."

"I don't want my aunt badgered."

"Then give me *something*."

Daisy considered what she could and couldn't do, what she would and wouldn't do. She'd seen Trevor Lundquist's byline many times, and he seemed to write an honest perspective on whatever the subject was. This murder, she imagined, was his chance to write about something meaty. If she didn't help with it, he'd find a way to do it. She didn't want him bothering any of her family.

"How about this, Mr. Lundquist. For now, stick to the reports the police give you. I'm sure you're experienced enough to have a contact there."

After a beat of silence, he admitted, "I am and I do."

"When the murder is solved, I'll give you an exclusive."

"What if one of those network shows come calling?"

"If I tell you I'm going to give you an exclusive, then that's what I'm going to do. Believe me, my aunt won't want this story blared nationwide."

"I've checked around about you," he said. "You seem to be an astute businesswoman."

"Thank you, I think."

"I've also heard that if a customer has a problem with service or any of your products, you make it right."

"I won't stay in business very long if I don't please my customers."

There was a moment of hesitation. "All right," he said. "I won't badger anybody right now. But I'll tell you this. If the investigation goes on too long, I might need a tidbit or two to keep the public interested and to fill in my weekly byline."

"That's not our deal."

"You're tough."

"When it comes to protecting my family, I am," she assured him.

He grumbled, "It's a deal. But if some L.A. movie producer comes calling—"

"I'll tell him to go back to L.A. I don't want the notoriety, and neither does my aunt. We just want the killer to be brought to justice." She added silently—*and for Aunt Iris to be cleared of any suspicion.*

After Daisy hung up, she pulled a spoon from the drawer, dipped it into the chicken broth, and tasted it. She added more pepper, then pulled a bag of frozen peas from the freezer. Should she add rice or noodles?

For Jonas, she'd add noodles.

Daisy drove by the tea garden and the crime scene tape and pulled into a parking space in front of Jonas's store. She'd dipped the soup into a mason jar, wrapped it in a navy tea towel, and stowed it in a small wicker basket. She'd also slipped a half dozen chocolate chip cookies into a Ziploc bag and added that to the basket. Now as she exited her car and took a whiff of the crisp autumn air, catching just a hint of wood smoke, she wondered if this was a good idea. It was a simple thank-you, right?

Maybe not so simple, considering their visit to the police station yesterday. Maybe, just maybe, she wanted Jonas's advice.

Woods had a distinctive flair, if not a usual furniture store arrangement. Giant cubicle shelves lined one side of the store. In each square stood a ladder-back chair in a different color and finish—one in a pretty lemon color, another in a robin's-egg blue, and a third in distressed green. But there were wood finishes too—cherry, dark walnut, and a chair that was unfinished. A variety of styles of tables, from pedestal to traditional to library to octagonal occasional tables, stood along the other side of the room, their finishes gleaming in the sunlight that shone through the windows. Throughout the store stood armoires, chests, and highboys, the most beautiful Daisy had ever seen. All of the furniture here was handcrafted by local craftsmen, including Jonas himself.

Jonas sat at a counter at the rear of the store, studying something on the computer monitor. He looked up, however, when the bell over the door rang and Daisy walked in. She had to admit that when she'd picked out her wardrobe today, she'd taken a little extra time. Jazzi and Vi kept her up to date on trends. Today she'd worn cranberry-colored skinny-leg jeans and a sweater with geometric shapes in cranberry and black. Although Vi insisted she should have highlights added to her hair, she preferred keeping it natural, letting the sun do its thing in the summer. This morning she'd simply brushed it, letting it wave where it wanted to, rather than confining it in a ponytail. At the last minute, she'd inserted a wooden barrette over her right temple. Her bangs were getting a little long, but Jazzi insisted that was the style. When she took her daughter's advice, that pleased Jazzi, so she did it whenever she could.

Jonas's gaze seemed to study her a moment longer than usual, but that simply could have been her imagination.

She set the basket on the counter. "Just a thank-you for helping me the other night. I'm grateful you saved us from that mob."

"I don't need a thank-you. That kind of thing is second nature to me."

"You had to lead witnesses to safety?"

"Some of the time."

He was always so enigmatic about his past and his work. She was sure there were reasons, so she didn't like to pry. Whether he considered it second nature or not, she was still grateful for what he'd done.

"Chicken soup and cookies. The soup's still warm."

"I have a small refrigerator and microwave in the back. You've saved me from a burger and fries."

She wrinkled her nose. "Don't tell me that's your mainstay."

He laughed. "Along with doughnuts. Old habits die hard."

"We have good restaurants along with fast food joints in Willow Creek."

"Yes, I've seen that," he said. "But it's really no fun eating at a restaurant alone, and gourmet food in takeout containers just isn't the same."

She knew what he meant. She wondered if he'd ever had someone special to have those meals with, because he sounded as if he missed it, just as she did.

"I had another reason for stopping by, other than the chicken soup." She wanted to be honest with him.

"You need to buy a table, chair, or armoire?"

She smiled. "Not right now." After a moment's hesitation, she explained, "Iris and I went to the police station yesterday to give our statements. They wouldn't let me stay with her. They separated us and recorded everything."

"That's standard."

"From what Iris told me, she was interrogated more than interviewed. They wanted to know every detail about her relationship with Harvey—how well she knew his wife, if she associated with his children, how intimate she and Harvey had been."

Jonas's eyebrows arched at that one, and she felt herself blush. That was not something she wanted to talk about with a stranger, but she wanted Jonas to know exactly how the police were looking at Iris.

"Iris should have had a lawyer with her. She needs to consult one immediately."

"She just wants to tell the detective what she knows. She's vulnerable right now and completely open."

"Open isn't good, not in this situation. You and Iris are honest people, not used to dealing with something like this. Rappaport and the chief of police are. No, we don't have many murders in Willow Creek, but that's even more reason why they're going to go after this with a pick and shovel."

Jonas took a notepad from alongside his computer, picked up a pen, and wrote something on the top sheet. "Marshall Thompson is a friend. He's also a criminal defense attorney who's worth every penny of what he charges."

"Iris doesn't have unlimited funds."

"Marsh also works on a sliding scale. She needs to talk to him, Daisy, whether she hires him or not. He'll do a free consultation if you tell him I recommended him." He tore off the sheet of paper from the tablet and held it out to her.

When Daisy took it, her fingers brushed his. Her heart sped up, and she felt something electric when she looked into Jonas's green eyes. That scared her.

When she was scared, she retreated in order to figure out what to do next. After slipping the piece of paper into her purse, she waved at the soup and cookies. "Enjoy. Maybe for just this one lunch you'll forget about burgers and fries."

"Maybe," he agreed enigmatically.

With the scent of wood and glossy finishes still in her senses, she left Jonas's store, not exactly sure what had just happened between them, yet certain something had.

Daisy couldn't get her stop at Jonas's shop out of her head the rest of the afternoon. Maybe it was because she was distracted by the fact that she couldn't go to her place of work, the murder that had taken place there, and her worry about her Aunt Iris. Thinking about Jonas was more . . . pleasurable. Of course, when she thought about his advice, she started worrying all over again. It didn't help that when Jazzi came home from school, she went straight to her room. Daisy had called up to her twice now, and she hadn't answered or come down.

Her daughter hadn't heard her? Or she was ignoring her?

It had to be one or the other. So Daisy climbed the stairs. Even though the door to Jazzi's room was partially open, she knocked. She respected her daughter's privacy.

Nevertheless, when Jazzi didn't call "Come in," she

went in anyway. Privacy was one thing, rudeness was another.

Jazzi's room was about the millennial teenager, not frills and polka dots as her own room might have been at her daughter's age. Well, maybe she would have had a poster or two of her favorite idol on the wall. But Jazzi's room was about empowering a girl or a woman. There was a poster of Malala Yousafzai. She'd framed photographs she'd taken of some of her favorite places—her grandmother's house, a nearby covered bridge, an Amish horse and buggy. Jazzi might have her fingernails painted in the latest designs, but she was the type of girl who created those designs.

Now as Daisy entered her younger daughter's room, she saw that Jazzi was so engrossed in what she was doing, she hadn't heard or noticed her.

"Jazzi?"

Her daughter gave a startled jump and then quickly closed her laptop where she sat using it at the corner desk.

That was a red flag if ever Daisy had seen one. Being secretive as well as being sullen were causes for concern.

"I didn't mean to startle you. I called up to you twice. What are you working on?" She tried to monitor Jazzi's computer use. She had monitored Violet's too before her daughter had gone to college.

But Jazzi wasn't giving Daisy any explanations. She wasn't opening the laptop. She was looking . . . scared. What was her daughter into? Pornographic photos? Singles chat sites? E-mailing with a boy she didn't want Daisy to know about? All of those things created chaos in Daisy, so much chaos that her daughter's privacy was put on the back burner. She opened Jazzi's laptop.

The screen had gone dark with Jazzi closing it, but now Daisy hit a key.

"Don't!" Jazzi said. "I don't want you—"

But Daisy had already seen the website. At first, she didn't understand what she was looking at. But then the title began to make sense. The name of the website was Bonds Forever. After a quick look, Daisy could see it was one of those websites where children who were adopted could register to find their birth parents.

Jazzi must have seen the stunned look on her mother's face. "This has nothing to do with you," she told Daisy quickly. "I mean, nothing to do about you being my mom. I want to find my birth parents."

Over the years, they'd had plenty of discussions about being adopted—how Jazzi had been a gift to her and Ryan, how she'd been a child of their hearts. But since Ryan had died, they hadn't had any of those discussions. In fact, since Ryan had died, they hadn't talked as much as they should have. Violet had expressed her grief and sadness over her dad's loss much more openly than Jazzi, and Daisy had given her younger daughter the opportunity and the time to grieve in her own way. But maybe that hadn't been the right thing to do. After all, their life had been in Florida. With Ryan gone, Daisy had moved them back here, changing everything.

At this moment, she knew she had to accept whatever Jazzi was feeling or she could lose her. "Have you been registered on this site for very long?" Her voice quavered a little, and she didn't want that. She didn't want Jazzi to know she was as scared as she was.

"I've been registered on the site for about a month. I thought about registering a few months before that."

"You could have come to me about this." She tried

to keep her tone even, not letting any hurt show. But Jazzi must have seen some of the hurt.

"Really, Mom? You would have tried to talk me out of it."

After Daisy took a moment to consider Jazzi's conclusion, she shook her head. "You're wrong about that. I wouldn't have tried to talk you out of it, not if it's what you really want. If you need to find your birth parents, I'll do whatever I can to help you."

Now Jazzi was the one who looked surprised. "You really will?"

Daisy lowered herself onto Jazzi's bed, needing to sit before she sank like a puddle to the floor. "I really will."

"Then tell me what you know so I can plug in the information. All I know is my birth date."

"Your dad and I didn't tell you anything about the adoption because we didn't know much. Your adoption was a private one, through a lawyer. Your dad and I didn't want to wait for an agency to find us a baby, so we pursued all of our options. He spent hours on the Internet and found this lawyer's website. We filled out the forms, and Glenn contacted us that he'd found an unwed mother in Pennsylvania who wanted to give up her baby. He'd taken into account that I was from here and still had family here. We came to Pennsylvania to adopt you because you were born here. I know your mom's first name is Portia, but that's all I know because it was a closed adoption. But I'll see if I can find out anything else if that's what you want."

"Since Dad died—" Jazzi stopped and swallowed hard. "I've just felt this big hole. It was there a little bit before he died, I guess because I didn't know exactly where I came from. But after he died, it's gotten really big. I thought finding my birth parents might help fill it. I want to do it, Mom. I keep checking back on the website to see if anybody's tried to connect with me, but nobody has. It's like waiting for an e-mail that never comes. Do you know what I mean?"

"I know exactly what you mean. Let me see if I can find out anything else."

Jazzi hopped up from her chair and threw her arms around her mother's neck. "Thank you."

In a way, Daisy felt as if she had her daughter back. In another way, she was worried she might lose her.

In the end, after a long discussion with her aunt the following day, Daisy made the call to Marshall Thompson and scheduled an appointment for late that morning. His office was located a few streets north of downtown, on Cherry Tree Road. It was an older section of town with row houses, cherry and blue spruce trees, and ivy crawling up the front of brick homes. His establishment was gray brick on the first floor with white siding on the second. Dark gray shutters accentuated the double-hung windows. The front stoop had two steps and no porch, though there was a sign that proclaimed the handicapped entrance was in the back.

When Daisy rang the front doorbell, a young woman answered. She looked to be in her mid-twenties, with a fresh face without much makeup, just a dab of lipstick, a flowered blouse in orange and green, and slacks in the same green color.

She smiled. "You must be Daisy Swanson and Iris Albright. Appointment at eleven?"

"That's right," Daisy said with a nod since her aunt still seemed incapable of speech. Iris hadn't wanted to come and didn't want to be here.

"Come on in," the young woman said. "I'm Olivia. Uncle Marsh will be right with you."

The reception area was wallpapered in a thin cranberry and navy pinstripe. The receptionist's oak desk was L-shaped. Daisy could see that the monitor sitting there was state of the art. She recognized good quality when she saw it because she had done a thorough perusal of computers to buy one for the tea garden. A set of headphones lay beside the keyboard, and Daisy guessed that Marshall Thompson's niece transcribed for him.

Daisy could see steps leading to the second floor. To the left of them was a short hall. Now a door along that hall opened and a man walked toward them. He was tall, at least six feet two. His hair was thick, though snow white, and his dark brown suit was impeccably cut. He wore a white shirt with a tan pinstripe and no tie. He extended his hand to Iris. "I'm Marshall Thompson. And you're Iris Albright?"

"That's right," Iris said in a clipped voice that said she was nervous.

After he shook Daisy's hand, he said to Olivia, "I'll take care of them now. You can go back to what you were doing."

Olivia gave her uncle a smile, nodded, and went back to her desk. Marshall Thompson led them down the hall into his office.

This room was very different from the reception area. It was large, with wood paneling, a sofa, coffee table, and chairs. A long credenza lined one wall. They faced a huge mahogany desk with a matching side table that housed a computer. From the high-end coffee pot on the credenza to the oil paintings of Lancaster County farms hanging on the walls, the room shouted quality, just as Marshall Thompson did.

Instead of going behind his desk as most lawyers would, he motioned to the sofa and chairs.

"Let's have a seat. Coffee?"

Iris shook her head, and so did Daisy. They both just wanted to get into this and find out what they were facing.

Marshall nodded as if he understood. He lowered himself to the sofa next to Daisy and across from Iris. "When you phoned, Olivia told me you said Jonas Groft recommended me?"

Daisy nodded. "His store is down the street from my tea garden. He was a big help the night—"

She stopped and hesitated. "The night the murder happened."

The lawyer nodded, but he didn't say how he knew Jonas or anything else about their relationship.

Aunt Iris, who had laid her purse on the sofa next to her, was now twisting her hands in her lap. "I need to know how much this is going to cost. I don't know if I can afford you."

"Is it Miss or Mrs. Albright?" he asked.

"Miss. I've never been married. I thought I was going to be—" Her voice broke.

Marshall Thompson asked, "Instead of coffee, how about a cup of tea? I always have water heating. I don't have loose tea like you probably use in your tea garden, but I have a selection of tea bags."

"You enjoy tea?" Iris asked.

"I do. Unfortunately, I've never stopped in at your tea garden. I begin my work days early, and I end them late." He picked up a hand-carved wooden box sitting on the credenza. He opened it for Iris and said, "Pick one."

Daisy saw her aunt pick chamomile for calming. No decision to make there.

"Miss Swanson?" he asked.

"For me, it is Mrs. I'm a widow."

He opened the box in front of her.

She chose a green tea. She needed the antioxidant these days. If she had a cup of tea with them, maybe her aunt would relax a bit.

After he'd poured the tea and offered them cream or a slice of lemon from his small refrigerator, they both prepared their tea, and Daisy felt more comfortable. She hoped her aunt did too.

"Now fill me in," the lawyer directed.

"We haven't discussed your fee," Iris reminded him.

"Let me hear your story first."

Daisy let Iris do the telling. Her aunt needed to talk about what had happened, to empty her head of the images, to try to diminish their impact. Maybe if she said the words and described it often enough, that would happen. It could make it worse too, Daisy supposed, but she hoped it was more like a desensitization exercise.

After Iris was finished, the attorney looked thoughtful. Then he leaned forward. "I'd like to tell you that you have nothing to worry about. However, it was your tea garden, Miss Albright, and *you* found the body."

"But I didn't touch him. I could see he was . . . dead."

"Lots of things come into consideration here, some of them accidents, some of them not."

"What do you mean by accidents?" Daisy asked.

The lawyer looked at Iris. "You said you were dating this man?"

She nodded.

"For instance, the suit he was wearing. Had he worn that same suit when he'd been with you before?"

Iris thought about it. "He wore that blue pinstripe suit often. He might have. Why?"

"Because your hair could be on that suit. Your DNA could be on that suit, even if you had merely touched his arm. That wouldn't mean you touched him that night, but it would be evidence."

"Oh, my," Iris murmured.

Daisy patted her hand.

"Could you tell what might have been the murder weapon?" he asked Daisy.

Daisy didn't want to remember that scene either, but she called it up again. Thinking about it made her want to gag. "The way Harvey's head was bashed in, it could have been a rock or a bat," she offered.

"There's a difference," Marshall said. "A rock would mean an impulse murder, while a bat could mean it was premeditated."

"But Iris was with me in the tea garden until she left to meet Harvey."

"The police will work a story around that if they think they have the evidence to prove she's the one who did it. So listen carefully, Miss Albright. This is what I want you to do. Do *not* talk to the police again."

Iris appeared shocked. "But what if they call me for another interview?" she asked.

"Then you call me. I do not want you speaking to them, and I definitely don't want you speaking to them without counsel. Understood?"

Her aunt nodded. "Will you need a retainer? I do watch crime shows. I know about these things."

Marshall Thompson smiled. "I think Jonas probably told you my first consultation would be free. It is. So no worries about a retainer today. If you need my services, then we'll discuss it."

"I know lawyers like you have to be expensive," Iris murmured.

"Lawyers like me?" he asked with a quirk of his lips.

Iris motioned to the room, to the bookshelves with law volumes, to Marshall himself. "You're obviously successful."

"My practice has never been just about money," he responded.

Daisy wondered just what it *had* been about, but he didn't elaborate, and she didn't ask.

The criminal defense attorney stood, indicating that their meeting was over. Iris and Daisy picked up their purses and stood too.

"Put my number on your speed dial," he directed them. "The police can sometimes take you by surprise. If I don't pick up, leave a message. I *will* call you back."

It was funny, Daisy thought. She got the same feeling around Marshall Thompson that she did around Jonas Groft. Call it woman's intuition or whatever, but they gave off an aura of deep-seated integrity.

That was exactly what she and her aunt needed right now.

Chapter Six

Daisy and her aunt had just left the lawyer's office when Daisy received a phone call from a police officer telling her she could reopen Daisy's Tea Garden. When she told Iris, she realized from the expression on her aunt's face that she was a little scared to do it. What were she and her aunt going to find? What was she going to relive? What was Aunt Iris going to relive?

Whatever the repercussions, Daisy drove them to the tea garden and parked in the back lot. The crime scene tape was no longer strung across the edge of the yard or around the front.

Daisy knew this would be difficult for Aunt Iris. They had chosen to go in the side entrance for many reasons, mainly because this was where it had happened. This was where the police had been. This is where they had to start, not only to heal, but to forget what they had seen here.

It was easy to notice that the garden area, with its outside tables, needed not only straightening but a professional cleaning. The flagstone where Harvey had lain was blood-covered. Fingerprint dust was here, there, and everywhere.

Aunt Iris mumbled, "I can't bear to be out here," and she hurried inside.

Daisy looked around the area and knew what she had to do. Last evening, she'd searched online and found a service in Lancaster that specialized in this type of cleanup. She took her phone from her purse and called the number she'd added to her contact list. Someone answered on the first ring.

"Kline's Cleaning Service. This is Maria. How can I help you?"

Daisy didn't quite know what to say but finally plunged in. "My business, Daisy's Tea Garden, had a murder take place here. My aunt and I need cleanup before we can open again."

"Fingerprint dust and blood?" Maria asked as if she were used to dealing with Daisy's request.

"Yes," Daisy responded.

"Fingerprint dust is the worst. It's best you don't try to remove it yourself. We start with a dry sweep-up, then use a special cleaner that breaks down the elements so it can be wiped away. If you try soap and water, you'll leave a muddy mess."

"Can you give me a price estimate? Could you do it soon?"

Maria explained, "My guys have to examine the scene to give you an accurate estimate. But I can have a team there in about an hour, if that suits. They're just finishing a job in Lancaster."

"An hour would be wonderful. I'll be here." They couldn't open the tea garden again until it was put right, no matter what the cost.

After Daisy ended the call, she looked around. The police and techs had retrieved evidence. If that had meant stepping in the bushes, that's what they'd done.

If it had meant smashing the herbs, there went the herbs. If it had meant tracking mud on the flagstone, so be it. She understood all that. She just wished a terrible situation hadn't been made worse by the whole investigation process. But she supposed that's the way it had to be.

Daisy couldn't help studying the area, deciding what herbs she might have to replace, thinking about whether they still had time to grow more before winter set in or whether seasonal plants in colorful ceramic pots with decorative plant stakes, like she had on the front porch, would be a better solution.

She walked all around, estimating in her mind what they'd need. Leaving the immediate area, she moved past the tables and the flagstone patio to the path down the yard. Along that path she and Aunt Iris had planted pineapple sage that grew into more like a shrub than an herb plant and chocolate mint that took off and spread if she didn't carefully watch and prune it. And then there was the lemongrass. At this time of year, it rose about three feet tall and accented either side of the handcrafted cedar bench. Patrons often sat there at the rear of the property and listened to the creek and contemplated the blue sky.

As Daisy walked back to the patio with its pots of herbs and flowers, she suddenly noticed something was missing—the foot-high sculpture of a unicorn.

Had the police taken it, thinking it was evidence? If they hadn't taken it, had that been the murder weapon? If so, did the killer just dump it, or take it with him or her? The statue was white alabaster, and blood would stain it. It was quite possible the killer could have dumped it in the creek or somewhere around town and the police had found it . . . or would find it.

She didn't know if her Aunt Iris would want to be involved in a discussion about it. So Daisy made a unilateral decision, looked up Detective Rappaport's number in her contact list, and called him. It was his direct line—at least that's what he'd told her—so she assumed she wouldn't have to go through a dispatcher. But when he said in a gruff voice, "Detective Rappaport here, how can I help you?" she wondered if she was being silly . . . if this information mattered at all.

"This is Daisy Swanson."

"Hello, Mrs. Swanson. Did you have a question about what we did at your place?"

"Not exactly a question."

"I can't talk about what we did or didn't find, if that's what this call's about."

"Not exactly."

"Mrs. Swanson, I'm a busy man."

"Don't you think I know you're busy? Don't you think *I'm* busy? I have a tea garden to set up and get running again after losing three days of revenue. So I'm not calling simply to chat."

"Tell me why you called," he said in an impatient voice.

"After studying the garden, I realized something was missing. It's a foot-high statue of a unicorn. It's only missing if your men didn't take it. Did they?"

"Hold on a minute," he said, and he was gone less than that. "No unicorn was brought in as evidence. Are you sure it's missing and it didn't just fall someplace? Maybe a customer took it before the murder."

"I examine everything around the tea garden each

evening before we close. Either I or Iris would have noticed it was missing."

"There wouldn't have been one night you simply didn't notice?" he asked skeptically, obviously not convinced.

"Every aspect of the tea garden is important to us. A white unicorn that's a foot high isn't going to go unnoticed."

She heard him sigh. "Is this another strategy to cover up for your aunt?"

"I don't know what you mean."

"You said your aunt was with you until she went outside to meet Harvey Fitz. You said only moments passed. I suspect your aunt got into a heated fight with her lover and conked him on the head with a rock."

Daisy was absolutely flabbergasted. "You're wrong!"

"No surprise you'd say that. But enough time could have passed that she'd even dumped that rock in the creek. It's a deep creek with lots of rocks."

"You're fabricating a scenario that isn't true," she protested.

"So you insist. But I'll get to the truth."

Daisy met his statement with, "Will you?"

A combative silence ensued until Detective Rappaport asked, "Do you have a photo of this unicorn?"

"I do. I can text or e-mail you one."

"Text it. But don't expect anything to come of it. Thanks for calling, Mrs. Swanson. Have a good day."

After Rappaport ended the call, Daisy just studied the phone. She was dismayed by his attitude. It was probably his job to question everything about everything. But how far would he get doing that? Maybe she should fish around herself just to make sure Aunt Iris would be in the clear.

* * *

Daisy and her aunt decided to keep the tea garden closed on Saturday. After the cleaning service had finished yesterday afternoon, they'd both felt too emotionally spent to do the prep work for opening. With Jazzi going to a friend's to work on a science fair project, Daisy had called Tessa and Cora Sue and asked them to come in this morning to help ready the tea garden to open again on Sunday. This evening, she, Iris, and Jazzi would be having dinner with her parents. With that, hopefully life would regain a more "normal" tone.

After Tessa arrived, Daisy started soups while Tessa created a new salad with carrots, grapes, raisins, and pecans with a sour cream, mayo, lime, and honey dressing. Iris didn't talk as she mixed up batter for chocolate raspberry scones.

It was almost noon when Daisy took a call from Jazzi. She said, "Mom, Nicole and I are in the middle of making our display for the science fair. Can you just pick me up on your way to Gram's tonight?"

Actually, that sounded like a good idea to Daisy. She didn't want Jazzi to be alone at the house in case news vans or reporters came calling. Up to now, freezing them out with "No comment" had worked. Although Harvey's murder wasn't to be taken lightly, the news people from other areas who'd hoped to pick up juicy tidbits would move on to the next crisis or crime.

"You can stay at Nicole's. I'll pick you up around five, okay?"

"Sounds good," Jazzi answered, then added, "I love you, Mom."

"I love you too, honey."

With everything that had happened, Daisy hadn't yet tried to find the lawyer who'd handled Jazzi's adoption. Or was that just an excuse because she was stalling? Maybe she merely didn't want to contemplate what would happen if Jazzi found her birth parents. She'd promised her daughter she would help, so she had to put it on the top of her priority list.

But first, she wanted to make sure her aunt wasn't in deep water with the police by beginning an investigation of her own. She had texted the detective the photo of the unicorn yesterday but had heard nothing in return.

Cora Sue was making certain the serving rooms were spic and span. Daisy gave her a nod of approval and went to the kitchen. "Do either of you mind if I scoot out for about an hour?" Daisy asked her aunt and Tessa.

Iris waved at the dough she'd already mixed up. "I have this ready to refrigerate. I'll start on another batch. Tessa's watching the soup. Go ahead and run your errand. Where are you going?"

"My dad's birthday's coming up, and I need a new tie for him, an expensive one."

Iris narrowed her eyes. "You're going to Men's Trends, aren't you?"

"Yes, I am. Employees talk. They often hear things they shouldn't. I think we need background on Harvey that you don't know. Knowledge is power, right? And it's better than just standing around doing nothing while the police could be building a case against you. We need to be prepared, and a few answers could prepare us."

Aunt Iris looked worried. "I don't know if that's a good idea. But if you feel you have to . . ."

"I do." She gave her aunt a hug. "It will be fine. I'm

just going to talk to Harvey's manager and some of the employees while I buy a tie."

Before Iris could convince her not to go, she took off her apron, grabbed her purse from her office, and left.

Men's Trends was a three-block walk from Daisy's Tea Garden. Daisy walked when she could because she didn't have much time for other exercise. Today the air was musky with fall, downed leaves, and the coming of the next season. She was looking forward to Thanksgiving, when Violet would be home. She knew it really wasn't that far away; it just seemed to be so. Harvey's murder and Iris's sadness had seemed to make her miss her daughter even more. And then there was Jazzi and what she wanted to do. What if she found her birth parents?

Walking was good for thinking too. She wasn't exactly sure how to help Jazzi, and she was thinking through options as she passed a candle shop, an insurance office, a store that sold hand-made purses and travel bags and Woods. But she wasn't ready to share those options with Jazzi yet.

After another two blocks she arrived at Men's Trends. The clothing store might have been established a few decades ago, but there was nothing out of date about it. From setting up the tea and dessert display there, Daisy knew the security system was top-notch, unlike at her tea shop. When the door opened at Men's Trends, no buzzer or bell sounded, not in the store area. But a red light went on when the security monitors detected motion, and a buzzer sounded in the back room.

A clerk approached her right away. She looked to be near Daisy's age, was dressed in a two-piece dress in a rust color, and wore a name tag that read CAROLINE.

Her dark brown hair was expertly cut in a pageboy, and she looked professional.

She smiled broadly. "You're Daisy Swanson, right?"

"I am."

"I was really impressed with the tea and dessert celebration you brought to the store, as well as the one at the tea garden. Many of us employees suggested to Mr. Fitz that we put in a permanent tea bar for our customers. They often stand around waiting for measurements and alterations while a mate or boyfriend makes a selection. Mr. Fitz was thinking about it." Caroline looked sad at the thought.

Daisy said, "I'm so sorry for your loss."

Caroline's eyes glistened a bit. "We're all still in shock."

"I imagine you are. Is Bennett running the store now?"

Caroline pointed to the east end of the store, where the men's off-the-rack suits were located. Bennett Topper stood there talking with a customer. Bennett reminded Daisy in a lot of ways of a tall, slender, pointed-nose English butler.

"Yes, Bennett has stepped in. I think he's overwhelmed with it all. Not so much the store, but Mr. Fitz's murder."

"How long has Bennett been with Mr. Fitz?" Daisy inquired.

"He's been here over fifteen years," Caroline said. "At least that's what I've heard."

Daisy would like to talk to Bennett, but he was obviously tied up at the moment.

Caroline lowered her voice. "Bennett received a call from Mr. Fitz's lawyer. He's going to run the store until decisions are made about it."

Since Caroline was chatty, Daisy took advantage

of that. "Tell me something, Caroline. Did Mr. Fitz's employees like him?"

"Well enough," she admitted. "He was tough but fair. He just fired a saleswoman last week, and she made a scene before she left."

"If he was fair, he must have had good reason," Daisy concluded. "Do you know what that was?"

Moving a little closer to Daisy, Caroline lowered her voice even further. "Mallory Yoder liked to flirt, especially with the rich men. One of the customers' wives had complained, and Mr. Fitz didn't hesitate to give Mallory her walking papers. I heard that she said she was going to bad-mouth the store all over town."

Someone else who held a grudge. The list was growing.

"Do you think you could give me Mallory's contact information?"

At that point, Caroline looked puzzled. "Why would you want that?"

"I'll be honest with you," Daisy said. "The police consider my aunt a suspect."

"Iris Albright? You're kidding, right? She was so in love with Mr. Fitz. Anybody could see it when they saw them together. Why would she ever want to hurt him?"

"Exactly. My aunt is loyal and honest to a fault."

"How does Mallory play into it?" Caroline asked.

"Well, if the police are focusing only on Aunt Iris, they're not looking at other suspects. I want to find another viable suspect so they'll take their focus off of my aunt."

"Just like on those TV shows."

"Exactly."

"I really shouldn't hand out an employee's information," Caroline debated. "But the murder of a man I respected is involved."

Caroline went to one of the cashiers' desks, took a coupon card from beside the register, and turned it around to the back. "You can use the coupon on the front, but the info is on the back." She wrote it out and then handed it to Daisy.

"Don't expect her to welcome you with open arms. She's mad, and I'm not sure what she's mad about—losing her job or losing her connection with the customer she hooked up with."

"Maybe they were in love."

Caroline huffed. "In love? He's older and married, whether he wears a wedding ring or not. He has money. She has none. She scrapes by and borrows money from friends. So if anything, this thing with the customer is pure lust. He *is* hot . . . for an older guy."

"Does the store have a policy about employees fraternizing with customers?"

"It does. No hanky-panky between employees and customers, or between employee and employee. It just muddles up store workings. If the sparks are two-way, the fireworks are awkward for everyone else working in the store. And if one person is enamored with the other and the other isn't interested, it's basically a fatal attraction, and that can lead to some pretty nasty scenes. So no collusion here, no canoodling, no anything."

"I think talking to Mallory could help me understand the dynamics here."

"You mean between all the people who work here?"

"And their attitudes toward Mr. Fitz."

"You could possibly be right."

"Thank you for her contact info," Daisy said in a low voice.

"If you need anything else to help your aunt," Caroline said, "just let me know."

In the next few moments, as Caroline helped Daisy choose a blue tie for her dad, Daisy realized she'd made an ally. She needed more of those to learn answers to her questions. Maybe Mallory Yoder could be an ally too . . . or a murder suspect. If Daisy called her, the sales clerk could hang up. But if Daisy paid her a visit . . .

Daisy drove down the Pike following her GPS's directions. The Old Philadelphia Pike, now Route 340, once called the King's Highway, had been the first "planned" road between Lancaster and Philadelphia. That's when inns were built every few miles as safe rest stops for people who were traveling. Signs in front of each inn identified them with painted pictures. The signs could be read by all—English-, German-, or Dutch-speaking. The other reason? Many of the travelers were poorly educated and could not read. Anyone could recognize the paintings on a sideboard and know where they were going.

Signs that hung along the Old Philadelphia Pike took many forms—a ship, a wagon, a plow, a buck, a white horse, a black horse, a hat. Although a lot had changed since Conestoga wagon times, much remained the same. Anyone coming to the town could expect friendly shopkeepers, homegrown Lancaster County foods, and restful lodging. All of that was what was important.

Sometimes Daisy's GPS took her in roundabout ways. Today it seemed to be on a straight course until the female voice directed her to make a right turn. For almost a quarter of a mile, Daisy's car rumbled down a road that led to a farm. The house was rustic as farmhouses went, with a big porch accented with white supports and tan siding.

Daisy parked on a gravel patch near the house, then took the paver path to the front door. As she climbed the six steps, she noticed the door opening.

"May I help you?" The girl was younger than Caroline, possibly her early twenties. She had the bluest eyes, a piquant face with a delicate chin, long eyelashes that would bat very well, and luxurious chestnut-brown hair.

"Are you Mallory Yoder?" Daisy asked.

"Yes, I am. Why do you want to know?"

"I'm Daisy Swanson."

"From the tea garden," Mallory remembered.

"Yes. I'd like to ask you a few questions about Harvey Fitz."

Fear stole into Mallory's eyes. "The police already talked to me about Harvey. They talked to all the employees."

"But you weren't an employee when he died, were you?"

"Who told you that?"

"Does it matter?"

Mallory pulled on a wave of hair along her face. "No, I suppose it doesn't. I lost my job there. Now I have to muck out stalls here and clean the house to get me through. I have to do something to pay my way until I find another job."

"You live here?"

"I rent a room from the family. It's not like it's a B&B or anything; it's just me. We connected on one of those Internet sites. They needed the money from renting the room, and I needed a place to stay that was cheap."

"Is Willow Creek your home?"

"It's my home, but no family live here anymore. I wanted to come back here because I was happy here when I was a kid. I thought I still had friends here. Most of them have moved on too, so I'm kind of stuck. I needed that job at Men's Trends."

"Then you should have followed the rules." Daisy couldn't help when her motherly advice fell out.

Looking defensive, Mallory said, "One of his customers flirted with me. I liked him. We went out for drinks one night. But Mr. Fitz just thought I was playing around and wanted to catch a rich husband."

"Could that be part of it?"

"Maybe. Robert was fifteen years older than me, but I liked him. I'm looking for love, just like anybody else. Mr. Fitz was paranoid about that kind of thing because his wife married him for money."

Was that true? Daisy wondered. "What are you going to do now?"

"I don't know. Flirting with Robert was exciting. I miss that."

Daisy wanted to roll her eyes and say a prayer. Heaven forbid her daughters should think like that.

"But what happens after the excitement's gone, Mallory, especially if the man's married. You've broken up a marriage, and you walk away broken-hearted."

"He could have ended up with me."

Daisy had to give her cold, hard facts. "That rarely happens, and if it happens, he won't stay. Once a cheater, always a cheater."

"You act as if you know."

"No, I don't know, but I have friends who know."

"I have to look for another job," Mallory said, biting a nail.

"Then look for one where you can do something you're good at. Look for one where you can get ahead.

Then when you meet a guy, you'll have something to give him besides a good time, and he'll respect you for it."

"You're telling me respect is better than money?" Mallory asked with a little laugh.

"Believe me, respect is way better than money. The money comes and goes, but the respect will stay. So will love and trust, if you're lucky enough to find them."

"Do *you* have that?"

"I had that once. I'm a widow now. My husband and I had rough times, but we got through them together. Don't you think your own parents would tell you that?"

"They're divorced."

Unfortunately, that was modern life.

Daisy didn't believe Mallory was a murderess. She doubted she had it in her. Although she might have been angry at Harvey for firing her, she seemed to know deep down that he'd done the right thing.

"Do you know anybody who would have wanted to hurt Mr. Fitz?"

Mallory thought about it. "No, not really. But if I think of anybody, I'll let you know. I can always find you at the tea garden, right?"

"Right. And I'd better get back. Take care of yourself, Mallory."

When Mallory waved good-bye, Daisy wondered if any of her advice would sink in.

Chapter Seven

Later that afternoon, Daisy was at the counter in the tea garden planning the arrangement of the baked goods for the following day when she heard a rap, rap, rap on the front door. She spotted Cade smiling at her through the glass. She crossed to the door and unlocked it.

He said, "I know you're not open for business, but I wanted to see how you are. The police have left you in peace?"

"They've let us back in, but it might be a while until we feel peaceful again." She nodded toward the kitchen. "Especially Aunt Iris."

Coming into the main serving room with her, Cade flipped out a chair with his foot and pointed to a seat across the table. That meant he wanted to talk.

She called in to her aunt, "I'll just be a few minutes."

"Take your time, honey. I'll get started on the chocolate chip cookie dough."

Seating herself across from Cade, Daisy took a deep breath. It was good to chill for a minute or two.

His dark brown eyes gentled as he seemed to see

that. He said, "I saw the truck for the cleaning service was here yesterday. How did that go?"

"It went all right. Thank goodness there's a service like that. Fingerprint powder is terrible to clean up. They have special materials to do it, and they left some of the cleaner in case we need it. Some things couldn't be cleaned—like the flagstone blocks that were stained. The landscaping service is coming Monday morning to replace those."

Cade reached out his hand and covered hers with his. "So how are you holding up?"

She liked the warmth of his hand on hers. She'd missed that kind of touching. "I'm okay. I'm keeping busy. Once we open tomorrow, I won't have time to think about much else. But earlier, I did walk down to Men's Trends. Bennett Topper is managing it, and he's taking over until the estate decides what to do with it."

"Why did you go down there?"

"Because Aunt Iris is a prime suspect, and I don't want her to remain one."

Cade scowled. "It's not a good idea for you to get involved in it or ask too many questions. Leave the investigation to the police."

Cade's words reminded Daisy of past experiences. Her mother always said she had a china doll face . . . meaning she could use her prettiness to get what she wanted. She'd never done that. She had brains behind that face, and she wanted to be respected for them. She could feel her temper flare. She pulled her hand away from his.

"If I want to ask questions, I will. If I want to find another suspect for the police other than my Aunt Iris, I'll do that too. We've engaged a lawyer for her, but that might not be enough, not if the police target her. I'm not going to let that happen."

Cade frowned. "Look, Daisy, the killer is still around. If you ask questions of the wrong person, you could be in danger."

"I can take care of myself," she said indignantly. "I've taken those women-be-safe courses. I know about poking a guy in the eye with your key, kneeing him where it hurts, slashing at knees for self-defense. I haven't been a hothouse flower."

"Do you have a gun?" Cade asked, maybe intending to shock sense into her.

"Of course not! I'd be more likely to hurt myself or someone else if I did, even if I knew how to use it."

"Do you have a can of pepper spray?"

Daisy shook her head. "No, I didn't think I needed one in Willow Creek."

"You should think again, especially if you're going to be in the middle of this."

"I didn't say I was," she insisted stubbornly.

Blowing out a frustrated breath, Cade pushed his chair from the table and stood. "I can see you're not in the mood to talk about this rationally. Maybe after a few days, you'll see the wisdom behind my advice. I don't want anything to happen to you, Daisy."

She saw his concern, but she also saw the fact that he didn't think she could make a difference in an investigation like this. He was dismissing her because she was a woman, or because she steeped tea and baked for a living . . . or just because.

At her silent defiance, Cade said, "I suppose Iris needs you in the kitchen. I won't hold you up. Take care of yourself, Daisy."

She'd hardly gotten "You too" out of her mouth when he turned and left. She might have just damaged a longtime friendship. Then again, what kind of friendship was it if Cade didn't have faith in her?

Usually Daisy enjoyed dinner at her mom and dad's. However, when she and Jazzi had arrived this evening—

She learned her sister had dropped in for a surprise visit!

As Daisy and Jazzi entered the kitchen, Camellia saw her, broke into a wide smile, and came over to hug them both. But Aunt Iris, who was standing at the counter mixing dressing for the chopped cabbage in a bowl beside her, wore a deep frown.

Over the years, Daisy had felt the rivalry between her mother and her aunt. It had probably stemmed from childhood. Daisy wasn't sure because the two of them never talked about it. Yet Daisy could always feel the push-pull tension between them.

She could especially feel and understand the tension because of her relationship with her own sister. As Daisy had grown up, she'd done it in the shadow of Camellia. She had loved her sister dearly, but Camellia was everything she wasn't. Daisy had been somewhat of a tomboy, not caring much about her appearance. On the other hand, Camellia had cared about hair and makeup and the latest styles. She wore her brunette bob in a chic cut. She'd always been chic. She'd always been outgoing and more popular than Daisy. In college, well, Camellia had majored in marketing. What more was there to say? She had PR skills up the kazoo. She'd never been married and seemed to flit from one relationship to the next without much concern.

But Daisy did love her, even if they were as different as night and day. The problem, if there was one, was that she'd always felt her mother favored Camellia. She was sure it wasn't intentional. Camellia was the first-born and had gotten lots of attention because she was so cute . . . and so accomplished. That's probably why Daisy and her Aunt Iris had gravitated toward each other.

When all of them got together, there were vibes in the air that even Jazzi and Vi could feel. Her daughters had often asked her about it. She'd tried to explain, but that wasn't easy. How did you admit you'd always felt *lesser than* with your mom? How could she con-fess that, yes, she'd always been slightly envious of Camellia? All she could do was keep reassuring her own daughters that she loved each of them equally, that they were both beautiful and accomplished, that one didn't deserve more attention than the other. That's what she and Ryan had always tried to do. Had they succeeded? She wasn't sure about that. Would Jazzi be searching for her birth parents if they had?

That was a bomb she'd been intending to drop today at dinner. Now she wasn't so sure.

After she hugged Camellia, she asked, "What are you doing here?"

"I drove down for a pop-in visit. I have a ton of comp time because of working overtime. I do miss you all. Phone calls aren't the same. Mom, you really have to learn to Skype like Daisy and I do."

She and Camellia tried to video conference at least every few weeks. New York and Willow Creek weren't that far apart. Yet sometimes New York seemed a world away.

Her mother waved Camellia's Skype suggestion away. "I don't need to know all that tech stuff. I do just fine on the phone."

Her mother usually used a landline because she

was always afraid the conversation would be cut off on a cell phone. And it was true that some areas of Willow Creek had spotty reception, even with the best carrier. On the other hand, when her mother held a preconceived idea, there wasn't much anyone could do about it.

"Dinner's ready," Rose said now as she pointed to the platter of ham. "Jazzi, will you go call your grandfather, please?"

Daisy knew her dad was probably settled in front of the TV, already engrossed in a football game. He enjoyed those in the fall whenever the nursery was closed. After Thanksgiving, Gallagher's Garden Corner would be open later on Saturdays as well as offer Sunday hours. His free time would be cut considerably. Her father was usually the buffer against the women's tensions. She hoped that would be true tonight too, because already she felt something brewing between her aunt and her mother. It was in a look, in an expression, in a nod. You didn't live around this all your life and not be able to tell.

Jazzi brought her grandfather from the living room, and he smiled at them. "You all look so pretty today. Must be the fall air."

Jazzi just shook her head. "Granddad, that's lame."

"Maybe it's lame but it's true."

Daisy noticed her dad's sandy-brown hair was mostly gray now. His part had inched back over the past five to ten years. He had a long face, high cheekbones, and blue eyes. He kept himself in shape with his work at the nursery—lugging tree balls, carrying shrubs, and working outside a good part of the year.

He took his seat at the rectangular maple table and motioned for them all to do the same. "Look at this spread your mom and your aunt put on. We have much to be thankful for. I just wish Vi were here to share it too."

As they all held hands and her father offered the blessing, Daisy stole a look at Iris. She was concerned about her. The past few days, the lines around her aunt's eyes and her mouth seemed to cut even deeper than they usually did.

After they began passing the food, Camellia took a slice of ham and said, "Mom's been catching me up. There's quite a lot going on in Willow Creek, and you all seem to be in the middle of it."

That wasn't the conversation opener Daisy had hoped for. Before she could turn the topic to something else, her mother said, "Yes. All of it's a shame and so unnecessary. If Iris hadn't gotten involved with a married man—"

"Mom!" Daisy exclaimed.

Even Jazzi looked a bit shocked that her grandmother had brought it up.

Daisy's father said in a warning tone, "Now, Rose . . ."

"It's true," Rose continued. "No good can come from something like that."

Her mother was a by-the-rules kind of person and most of the time was rigid in her thinking. She kept her ash-blond hair permed but in a short, manageable cut. She precisely applied lotion to her face every night and makeup with sunscreen every morning. For her, right was right and wrong was wrong. Usually the whole family accepted her mother's precise attitudes, but Daisy saw that the expression on Aunt Iris's face said she wasn't going to let Rose Gallagher's opinion stand this time.

Daisy tried to intervene. "Mom, Harvey's divorce was in the works. Soon, those final papers were going to be signed. He and his wife hadn't been together for a long time."

"A long time? Do you mean years or months? Because months could mean they were involved in a rift that could be mended again. Isn't that true, Sean? Anything between two people can be solved if both partners work at it. Iris got involved and maybe interfered."

Suddenly, Iris stood and threw her napkin onto the table. "I didn't interfere. Harvey and his wife were finished, and the fact that you brought this up again makes me wonder if you weren't a tad jealous that a man was interested in me—a rich, suave, sophisticated man." At that, her aunt left the table and went into the living room.

Beseechingly, Jazzi gave Daisy a "What are you going to do about it?" look.

Daisy marshaled assertive forces she'd developed over the years. "Mom, that was uncalled for, and I think you should apologize."

"My daughter telling me what to do?" Rose asked with raised brows. "I won't apologize for the truth."

With a shake of her head, Daisy pushed her chair back and crossed to the living room, where her aunt stood at the bay window, staring outside.

She wrapped her arm around her. "Aunt Iris, I'm so sorry for all that. You know it's not true."

"But what if it is?" Iris responded weakly. "What if *I* was the reason for Harvey and his wife not getting back together again?"

"From what I've heard and what I've seen, they had more problems than could ever be solved. The important thing you have to know is that you're not at fault here. You weren't the cause of Harvey's murder. You didn't do anything to hurt him."

"But as your mother keeps reminding me, I dragged you into this by being involved with him."

"I don't feel dragged. Things happen in our lives that make them complicated."

Camellia had come into the room now too. She crossed over to Iris and gave her a hug. "I'm sorry I brought the whole thing up, Aunt Iris. I had no idea Mom would act like that. I think maybe she's just worried about all of you, and that's why she reacted the way she did."

"She's not going to apologize, you know," Iris said. "She believes what she believes."

Daisy took her aunt's hand. "Come on. We have a delicious meal to eat, and we're going to enjoy it," she said with more determination than belief.

Once they were in the kitchen and seated around the table again, Rose didn't meet Iris's eyes. Daisy addressed her mother. "Mom, Iris and I have had enough questions and enough badgering about everything that's happened."

"I didn't badger," her mother insisted.

"Maybe not. But we just don't want to talk about it. There's no merit in it. So can we just enjoy dinner and listen to Camellia's stories about her escapades at the winery? I'm sure she has adventures to tell us about." Camellia's work often took her into New York City.

Now her father gave Daisy a knowing look. That look said that he understood both of his daughters. He understood that Daisy thought she lived a boring life and Camellia an exciting one. It said he understood the differences between the two girls and he appreciated them. Daisy had never felt "lesser than" in her dad's eyes.

As they ate ham and passed the green beans and scalloped potatoes, Camellia talked about new wines being developed, the plays she'd seen, the actors she'd spotted, the Halloween decorations in the city that never slept. Daisy thought they were over the hump tonight and that they could just enjoy each other's company. As her mother brought warm apple cobbler, topped with vanilla ice cream, to the table in dessert dishes, Daisy filled coffee cups.

She'd just settled beside Jazzi again, when Jazzi said, "I have some news."

Daisy's heart sped up. *She* had been planning to mention Jazzi's search for her birth parents, but it seemed Jazzi wanted to do it herself.

"What news, honey?" Rose asked with real interest.

Jazzi's gaze met Daisy's for a couple of seconds. Daisy knew all she could do was to stand by Jazzi and support her, trying to keep her own heartache from showing.

"I'm searching for my birth parents."

Rose's gaze targeted Daisy. "And you approve of this?"

"It's not a matter of approving, Mom. If this is something Jazzi needs to do, then I'll help her any way I can."

But Rose wasn't buying it. "Jazzi, do you know what this is going to do to your mother? She's raised you all these years, and now you just want to go find another mother?"

Daisy's father jumped in. "Rose, that's not what this is about. Is it, Jazzi?" he asked gently.

Jazzi's eyes were already misty. "No, Granddad. I just feel like there's a big hole in my history. I want to know about that hole. I know Mom loves me. I'm not looking for another mother. But I want to search for my origins."

Finally, Camellia joined in the discussion. "You know,

don't you, Jazzi, that this could get complicated, that your birth mother might not want anything to do with a daughter she gave up."

"There's no point borrowing trouble," Daisy interjected. "We'll just take this one step at a time."

"How are you going about it?" Camellia asked. She was a go-getter and a planner and always wanted all of her ducks in a row.

"Mom? How *are* we going to do it . . . to learn more, I mean?" Jazzi's eyes were beseeching. She needed an answer.

Daisy had one. "I'm thinking about asking help from Jonas Groft. Once upon a time, he was a detective in Philadelphia."

"I've heard good things about his store—Woods," her father said, obviously trying to lighten the atmosphere.

"You know this Jonas Groft because he's a store owner too?" her mother asked.

"Yes, that's right. He stops in for tea and scones now and then."

"Good," her father said. "He sounds like a viable resource." He patted Jazzi's hand. "Whatever happens and whatever you learn, just know that we love you."

"Thank you, Granddad," Jazzi said.

Thank you, Dad. Daisy didn't say it out loud, but she meant it from the bottom of her heart.

Chapter Eight

Daisy had quickly discovered the press could be bothersome. She'd been screening her calls since the murder, and so had her Aunt Iris. She understood the curiosity. After all, she and Iris were reopening the tea garden after a murder had been committed there. That was sensational news. But that morning, as she drove into the tea garden's back parking lot—both her van and Iris's car had been released by the police—she really hadn't expected eight different news outlets to bombard her.

Parking in the back was probably mistake number one. Professionally dressed anchors with microphones and cameras surrounded her. She couldn't even get out of the van. So this was what happened when you ignored their calls.

She was about to pick up her cell phone to call the police to see if there was anything *they* could do, when there was a rap on her driver's side window and she spotted Jonas. Not only Jonas; he was accompanied by a tall burly man built like a linebacker with a full beard hiding most of his face.

Daisy managed to open her van's door a few inches.

"Come on," Jonas said. "We'll get you inside."

She wasn't even sure she wanted to *go* inside, but she had a business to run.

"Iris and Tessa?" she asked.

"In the tea garden already," Jonas said. "They're fine. They're cooking up a storm. Let's get you in there too."

She grabbed her purse, pushed her door open a little further, and stepped down onto the asphalt.

The crowd of reporters surged in closer.

Jonas directed, "Back," in an authoritarian voice. "If you don't want to be prosecuted for causing a public disturbance, get back."

The reporters didn't move far, but they did move enough that Daisy could exit her van. Jonas closed the door. He and the other man practically surrounded her—at least it seemed that way. They had very long arms.

She caught sight of Trevor Lundquist, who shouted, "Remember our deal."

Another reporter asked, "What deal was that?"

Daisy tried to ignore the questions, tried not to be unnerved by Jonas's strong arm around her shoulders, tried to remember that her life had once been normal.

Once inside the tea garden, Jonas shut the back door to the kitchen. "You know, once you open your doors for business, you can't prevent the reporters from coming in."

"I don't know what to do," Daisy admitted. "I can't postpone the inevitable. How did you come to be here?"

"When I drove in to Woods this morning, I saw them crawling all over the back of your property, probably looking for signs that the murder had happened or the police had forgotten to take something away. I knew you were going to have trouble. I called Howie. He's an old friend and a retired cop."

Howie? This man did not look like a Howie. She extended her hand to him. "Thank you so much. I don't know what to say. I don't know how I would have gotten out without you."

"No problem, ma'am," Howie said. "Jonas suggested I stick around here after your tea garden opens."

"And be my security guard?" she asked with a weak smile. "I can't ask you to do that."

"No problem, ma'am. That's what I do now, security."

"Then I insist on paying you."

Howie and Jonas exchanged a look. "If you insist, ma'am. But I'll only charge you half my rates since Jonas is a good friend."

"Do you really think you can keep this under control when we open?"

"Between the two of us, we can," Jonas said. "I'll handle the front door, and Howie will handle the garden entrance. We'll just make sure everything stays calm in here and no one causes a ruckus."

"You have your own shop to run," she said to Jonas.

"I do, and I have a clerk who knows full well how to sell furniture. Just say *thank you*, Daisy, and you can get on with your day."

He'd used her first name as if that were the most natural thing in the world to do. She didn't know if he'd ever called her by name before. It was one of those things—until you knew a person well, you didn't really use their name. Names had power. Names conveyed meaning.

She was probably totally losing her mind.

Iris called from behind the counter, "The last scones

are coming out of the oven. We just have to brew the tea."

"Can I offer you gentlemen a cinnamon swirl scone before the real fun starts?" Daisy asked them.

"Tips are good," Howie said with a grin. "Starting the day with one is even better than waiting till the end of the day to get one. And I gotta admit, Mrs. Swanson, I'm not a tea drinker."

"I think I can rustle up a cup of coffee for you if you don't tell anybody."

He nodded. "Deal."

That's how Jonas and Howie ended up in her office, eating scones and drinking coffee while she, Tessa, and Iris prepared to open the tea garden. She wanted to ask questions of Jonas and his friend to find out exactly why they would do this for her, but there wasn't time for that right now.

Donning her yellow apron with the huge daisy printed on the bib, she filled the cases with scones, apple bread, lemon tea cakes, chocolate chip as well as oatmeal cookies, and buttermilk biscuits. By the time she'd checked the electric water kettles and added infusers to teapots so they were ready for brewing, she'd taken several deep breaths and hoped for the best. She was about to head to the front door to open it when Jonas appeared by her side.

"Let *us* open the doors for you. That will send the message."

"I don't want to scare customers away."

"I think your customers will be glad you have order in here rather than reporters stuffing microphones in their faces like they're doing out there."

When Daisy peered out the window, she saw that

the reporters were doing exactly that. Anyone who approached the shop ended up being interviewed.

"They're going to drive all my customers away," she complained.

"Not if your customers want a scone badly enough or a good cup of tea. Howie?" Jonas called.

And Howie was there, going to the garden door, his expression somber.

"We'll make sure your customers get in before the reporters do, and we'll only let two reporters in at a time. We almost have to let them in because this is a public place."

Daisy nodded. "I just hate the idea of my customers being disturbed. This is supposed to be a serene, calm, pleasant experience."

"And it will be. Maybe not for the first hour or so, but it will be after that. These journalists just want a sound bite they can run on the news, then they'll leave. Harvey's murder will be old news in a few days, if not before that. It's sad, but it's true," he said when he saw her expression.

Daisy was about to rush to the counter to get ready when she stopped and turned back to Jonas. "I don't know how to thank you for this."

"Just give me a rain check on a cup of your Daisy's Blend tea."

She suddenly felt choked up by his kindness. So he wouldn't see, she just waved her hand at him and went to join Iris behind the counter.

Jonas and Howie were dressed in jeans and flannel shirts like everyday people. Yet something about their bearing was different from your normal man on the street, and everyone seemed to sense that. The two men appeared to wear a mantle of authority on their broad shoulders. It was evident in their straight posture and their no-nonsense bearing.

In spite of what Daisy had thought about the reporters chasing her customers away, that didn't happen. It seemed the reporters being there attracted even more customers. Her staff couldn't seat everyone who appeared for a cup of tea and a cookie or scone. When the usual eat-in area as well as the afternoon tea room were both filled, the customers seemed to understand. They took along takeout, expressing an interest in coming back again when the tea garden was less crowded.

Fortunately, Daisy had extra scones and cookies stored in the freezer. When she saw how fast her supply was being depleted, she pulled them out. By eleven o'clock, they were almost out of baked goods. Tessa and Iris mixed up more batter, with Eva assisting, while Daisy, Cora Sue, and Karina handled the front. Security became less and less a concern. Even Howie and Jonas helped carry trays to the tables. It was almost funny, really, to see these burly men serving tea.

By noon, Daisy was ready with the luncheon selections, including beef barley soup, smoked salmon and cream cheese sandwiches, and carrot-grape-walnut salad. Her luncheon selections were similar to what she served with an afternoon tea service. Fortunately, this wasn't an afternoon tea service day. They never could have kept up. In fact, if business increased, and she was hopeful it might, now that more people had tasted what she had to offer, she'd have to hire more help. She felt guilty that she was profiting from Harvey's death.

It was almost two o'clock when the surge in business abated. Daisy had insisted Iris stay in the kitchen or behind the counter so she wouldn't run into a reporter asking an impertinent question. Most of all, she didn't have to deal with serving out in the garden area. That would still be traumatic for her.

With the afternoon business quieting, she thanked Jonas and Howie profusely. She could handle whatever happened next, she hoped.

After handing both men a bag filled with cookies and scones as well as a container of beef barley soup, she added, "The two of you can have a free cup of tea anytime you'd like. Just come in and ask." Then she focused on Howie. "You will taste tea one of these days, won't you? I can brew you up something really strong instead of fruity."

Howie smiled. "We'll see. Come summer I might be able to handle iced tea."

She laughed. "It's a deal."

As the men left the front porch, Howie went east, and Jonas went west toward his store. Daisy watched the way he walked and the tilt of his head. As the wind tossed his black hair, he didn't seem to care. There was nothing pretentious about Jonas, and she liked that.

She was thinking again about how easily he'd stepped in to help, how he'd called in reinforcements, when the door dinged and a new customer stepped over the threshold. Daisy had never seen the man before. He was about five foot nine or ten with pocked cheeks as though he'd had acne as a youth and hadn't had it treated. His gray hair was a bit wispy, and his wire-rimmed glasses were an outdated style. He was wearing a tweed sports jacket with suede patches on the elbows. Since he was overweight by twenty to thirty pounds, it hung open.

He glanced around the tea garden, then strode to

the garden door and looked outside. He didn't push the door open.

"Excuse me, sir," Daisy said. "Can I help you?"

"It's hard to imagine a murder happened in a place that's so serene. In your garden, right?"

What to do? She could be firm and ask him to leave if he was just another lookie-loo. If he was a journalist, she'd definitely ask him to leave. On the other hand, if he was a curiosity seeker who wanted a cup of tea . . .

She decided to be tactful and gain a customer instead of losing one.

"The garden is one of my favorite places. I don't know how long it will take to get over what happened there," she confessed.

Now the man faced her instead of the garden and came toward her. "I can't believe Harvey's gone."

Apparently, this wasn't a journalist or even a lookie-loo. He seemed to be genuinely sad that he'd lost someone he'd known. Just how well *had* he known Harvey Fitz?

"Would you like to sit down?" Daisy asked.

The man nodded. Then as if he were emerging from a great fog, he said, "Excuse my bad manners. My name is Guy Tremont."

Daisy extended her hand. "Daisy Swanson."

"You own the place."

"My aunt and I own the place. Is there anything I can get you?"

He lowered himself heavily into a chair at a table for two and picked up a menu that had been forgotten there. "Do you still have soup? I missed lunch, and a couple of those lemon tea cakes Harvey talked so much about would hit the right spot too."

"Tea?" Daisy asked.

Guy Tremont gave her a weak smile. "I'm a black

coffee or Scotch man. Harvey kept telling me I should try tea. I did that day you had confections in his store. It wasn't bad."

Daisy bit back a wry smile. "What kind did you have?"

"Something with pomegranate, I think."

When Daisy looked up at her aunt, Iris raised her hand and said, "I got the order—soup, lemon tea cakes, and pomegranate green tea. It will be there in five."

Iris could see that Daisy was maybe cultivating a customer, or maybe digging further into the investigation of Harvey's murder. Who knew? Not knowing what else to say, she started where the conversation had begun.

"Did you come to see where Harvey died?"

"Actually, I did. His funeral is Wednesday, and I just don't think I can go."

"I'll be there with my aunt. It will be a sad day for her too."

Guy looked over at Iris and then lowered his voice. "I've never met your aunt, but Harvey told me about her. He even told me that when his divorce was final, he was going to change his life and do it with Iris."

"It's good to know Harvey's intentions were pure."

"Harvey respected your aunt, Daisy. May I call you Daisy?"

"Sure you can, if I can call you Guy."

"A pretty young woman like you can call me almost anything you want." Then he flushed a bit. "That wasn't a come-on."

"I didn't take it as one, Guy. Thank you." Since they had a bit of time before his order arrived, she asked, "So you and Harvey were good friends?"

"We were, as good as men friends get, I guess. We

didn't talk much about private matters the first years we knew each other. Harvey just came to see me when he wanted to buy coins. But then, year by year, you see somebody a few times and you start to talk about other things. Suddenly one night a few years ago, Harvey asked if I wanted to come over to Men's Trends for a drink, and I did. He had a great selection of liquor in the back room of the store. Not many people knew about that."

"So you think he drank alone a lot?"

"I think he drank alone a lot until he decided to file for divorce. Then he developed a penchant for tea. When you and your aunt opened this place, he became even more of a connoisseur."

"I heard that Harvey had an extensive coin collection."

Just then Tessa appeared from the kitchen with a tray. It held a vintage two-cup teapot, a cup and saucer, a bowl of soup, and three lemon tea cakes. She arranged it all on the table in front of Guy, adding silverware wrapped in a napkin as well as a small plate of lemon slices and a miniature creamer.

Guy waved at the place setting. "Is this how you serve everyone . . . with this fancy china?" He pointed to the plate with the lemon slices. "My mother had a dish like that—that light pink, clear glass. Depression glass I think it was called."

"That's what it is," Daisy said. "I love the color pink. Since so many of our teapots have pink flowers, those dishes go with all of them."

Tessa asked him, "The tea is ready to pour. Would you like me to do it?"

"Go right ahead," he said with a smile, seemingly liking the idea of being served this way. Daisy wondered if he had many niceties in his life, or someone to serve him once in a while simply because they cared about him.

After Tessa departed, Daisy let Guy concentrate on his soup.

"This is good," he determined. "No wonder Harvey came in here so often."

"Tell me more about Harvey and his coins."

Tremont didn't hesitate. "The coin collection was a family tradition. That's why it was so important to him. Harvey's grandfather handed down a collection to his dad, and his dad left it to Harvey. Harvey added to it, and I think he would have done anything to protect it. That's why he gave his mansion to his wife, so he didn't have to sell the collection or split it."

A mansion versus a coin collection. Wow. They were talking about money Daisy could only imagine.

"So how much would this coin collection be worth?" she asked. "*If* you can say."

"I'm discreet. But I don't have confidentiality agreements with my clients and . . . Harvey's dead. The amount of the collection will come out soon anyway, I suppose. I appraised it for him just a few months ago. It's worth nearly six hundred thousand dollars."

When Daisy glanced over at the counter, her gaze met her aunt's. Iris's eyes had gone wide, and she looked a little pale. Had Aunt Iris just realized who she would be marrying if she had married Harvey Fitz? And how rich she would have become as his wife?

Chapter Nine

Daisy had served the last customer for the day. She'd been more than ready to turn around the CLOSED sign on the door when she spotted Jonas coming up the sidewalk.

"Dead on your feet?" he asked as he reached the door. Then he amended, "Sorry. Poor choice of words. Rough day?"

"It was an interesting day in many ways. Do you want a cup of tea?"

"Are you sure you wouldn't rather close the door, clean up, and put your feet up?"

"Maybe. But a cup of tea will fortify me for the evening. Come on."

"Are you alone?" he asked, surprised.

"Everyone else was beat too. Cora Sue, Eva, and Karina stayed beyond their shift to help. I sent Iris home a few minutes ago, and Tessa went upstairs. I've already swept the floors. I just have to grab my keys and lock up. I'm picking up Jazzi at Mom's. How about an orthodox tea from Nepal? I also baked blond brownies for something new. Do you want to taste test them?"

"Tea from Nepal sounds sophisticated, and I'll taste test any time. When did you have time to try a new recipe?"

"The flow of customers slowed down around two. We kept baking because we didn't know if we'd run out. The cookies and brownies freeze well, so we can pull them out whenever we need extra. I'll put a kettle on."

"Is there anything I can do to help?"

She could see Jonas didn't like to be idle, and she understood that. "Sure. You can fill the tea infuser while I cut the brownies."

"You'll let me into your kitchen?"

"I'll let anyone into my kitchen who wants to help."

He laughed. "I'd say that's a good philosophy. Jazzi didn't come at all today?"

"I dropped her off at Mom's this morning so she could attend church with them."

"How's she reacting to everything that happened?"

Daisy thought about Jazzi's confusion over the idea of murder so close to home and her concern over her great-aunt's sadness. Daisy considered again how she'd promised to help her daughter find her birth parents. They'd need help if they were serious about finding them. Was Jonas the person to ask for help?

She put that thought aside for the moment. "Harvey's murder shocked her. Thank goodness, she wasn't here when it happened. She understands how sad Iris is, but she didn't know Harvey."

She told Jonas which cupboard held the tea tins for the Nepal tea. He took it down, found a spoon in a drawer, and asked, "How many teaspoons?"

"Do you think you'll have one cup or two?"

"Maybe two, if there's time."

"I'll use the four-cup teapot. For that tea, measure eight teaspoons. It will have to steep for five minutes."

For the next few minutes, Daisy readied a plate with brownies, while Jonas filled the tea infuser. Her tea-kettle had signaled that the water was ready, and she poured it over the tea. Then she put the lid on the infuser and the James Sandler teapot with pink rose-buds decorating the cream porcelain.

She carried the teapot to one of the tables near the counter, and Jonas brought the brownies. They sat across from each other, and Daisy suddenly felt . . . un-nerved, maybe because she hadn't been alone with Jonas often. In the silence of the tea garden, she was so aware of him—of the way his black hair dipped over his brow line. There were lines around his eyes from squinting into the sun, laughing, or frowning. She didn't know him well enough to know which. Again, she noticed the scar on his left cheekbone that was about an inch long and looked as if it might have been left after stitches. But his face was so interesting that it didn't stand out . . . not for her at least. She suddenly realized his green eyes were studying her just as hard as she was studying him.

He cleared his throat, crossed his arms on the table, and asked, "So you think you might have done triple your business today?"

"Easily. I'm sure that won't keep up."

Jonas shrugged. "Hard to know. The tea garden could make some tourist list, and if it mentions the murder, you could get curiosity seekers."

"I want to think that business is business, but I do hate getting it this way."

"Customers won't return unless they like your tea

and baked goods. If they come back, you know you're doing something right."

"I did have a new customer today whom I talked to for a little while. He was a friend of Harvey's."

Jonas's brows arched, and he looked interested. "Did you talk to him long?"

"Long enough to learn interesting facts." As soon as she said it, she was afraid she'd hear some kind of warning from Jonas. *Stay away from the investigation.* But he didn't say that.

Instead he asked, "How did he know Harvey?"

"His name is Guy Tremont. He has a shop—Loose Change. He buys and sells coins. He filled me in on Harvey's history. Apparently, Harvey's grandfather built a collection and handed it down to his son, and then it went to Harvey. It was a family tradition and much cherished, from the way Mr. Tremont spoke of it. It seems that Harvey valued that coin collection more than his mansion, because in the divorce settlement, Monica would get the mansion and he would get the collection. Guy Tremont said it was worth six hundred thousand dollars."

Jonas whistled. "That's some collection."

"If they've been collecting for decades, imagine what's in it," Daisy mused. "I suspect there would be coins with historic value, coins with mint condition value, proof coins. And possibly gold coins. I wonder where the coin collection is now?"

"My best guess is that it's with Harvey's lawyer or in a safe deposit box. I can't imagine Harvey would leave something like that lying around, unless of course he had a safe in his condo."

"I'll have to ask Aunt Iris. Maybe she knows."

"Your aunt was too busy this morning for me to

observe her demeanor for very long, but how's she doing in quieter moments?"

Jonas sounded as if he might know what it was like to grieve in quieter moments. Daisy knew what it was like. Those were the tough times—when no one was around, when lethargy set in, when thinking time was the darkest.

"Since she's staying with my mom and dad, she has someone to talk to whenever she needs to. Though my mother isn't sympathetic about Aunt Iris's relationship with Harvey since he wasn't divorced. The funeral is going to be really hard for Iris."

"I heard it's on Wednesday."

Daisy had a feeling that Jonas's contacts in law enforcement kept him informed. "I thought about closing the tea garden in the morning, but I really can't afford to do that. Tessa is going to try to run it along with my part-time help. If they get into a bind, she's going to call me. I just want to be there for Aunt Iris. I doubt there will be anybody there she knows. It's not as if she'd become part of Harvey's social circle."

"And I imagine women in that crowd wouldn't be kind to outsiders," Jonas said perceptively.

"You know the crowd?" Daisy asked.

"I know the type. I've dealt with some society debutantes and matrons. They're a closed circle, and they don't like to let anybody else in."

"Do you think Willow Creek society is like that?"

"I guess I'm making a judgment, and I shouldn't. But whether you're born to money or come into it later in life, I think it changes aspects of your personality. When people have money, they have a cushion. That cushion can make them comfortable and enable them to do things normal people can't. Wealth is also a safeguard against bad things that happen. The rich can hire the best lawyers, engage private nurses, enjoy advantages regular people don't have. And they know that, so it gives them a superior attitude. At least that's been my experience."

Daisy wondered if that experience had come from Jonas's work or from his personal life. Thinking about everything Jonas had said, she realized Harvey had seemed to have a kindness about him. Though Monica did not.

"I'm not sure we can judge all society matrons based on Monica, but you never know. I don't like to have preconceptions," Daisy admitted.

She poured cups of tea for the two of them. "No lemon, sugar, or cream?" she asked.

"You remembered."

Yes, she did. She remembered almost everything Jonas had said to her. She also remembered that he didn't carry an umbrella in the rain or wear an overcoat in winter.

Something about Jonas encouraged her to sit and talk to him, and to ask him a question or two for Jazzi's sake.

As they munched on blond brownies, she studied him once more. "If I wanted to find someone, how hard would it be?"

He finished one brownie and started on another. After he wiped his fingers on a napkin, he took a few swigs of tea.

"Good tea," he said.

She nodded, adding a bit of sugar to hers.

"Do you want to find someone who has to do with the investigation?"

"Oh, no. This is personal."

His gaze met hers. "I have computer skills I learned on the job as well as in investigative training."

"I don't want to take advantage of you. I can pay you."

At that Jonas scowled. His brow crinkled, and the lines around his mouth cut deep. "No payment necessary. What do you need?" His worried expression told her he cared if she was in trouble.

"Jazzi's been out of sorts for the past month. I thought it was because Violet went to college and she missed her. But it wasn't that. I found out a few days ago exactly what it was."

She debated how to explain in the easiest and quickest way. "When Violet was two, Ryan and I decided we wanted another child. The problem was I'd had a miscarriage about a year after we had Violet. That miscarriage caused a uterine tear. It was highly unlikely I would carry a baby to term again."

"Oh, Daisy, I'm so sorry."

She could see that he was, and a lot of people were. She tried to remove herself from difficult memories as she said softly, "When a woman receives that diagnosis, her world is devastated if she wants to have more children. I was devastated. I had always thought I'd have a brood of five or six. But with that diagnosis, I'd known better, and so had my husband. We went through a rough patch in our marriage, as we let the news settle in. But eventually we turned to each other and decided if we wanted more children, we'd adopt."

As she told Jonas this, she tried to keep the emotion out of her voice. However, although it was out of her voice, it must have shown in her eyes. Without warning, a tear escaped and rolled down her cheek.

To her surprise, Jonas caught it.

The world stood still for those few seconds when his fingertip grazed her skin and they gazed at each other with an understanding that would bond two people who had lost something important, *someone* important.

She tore her gaze from his and looked down at her teacup, searching for answers there. Since she didn't know how to read tea leaves, she didn't find any.

Daisy said, "All I know about Jazzi's birth mother is that her first name is Portia." After taking a deep breath, she explained, "The lawyer we used for the adoption was located in Florida. That's where we were living then. Since Jazzi told me she wanted to search, I looked him up online, but I can't find anything recent about him. Nothing current popped up."

"That's something I can easily check out," Jonas assured her, leaning back in his chair. "I still have access to databases you wouldn't. The truth is, though, if the adoption is closed, the lawyer won't be able to tell us anything. But finding him would be a start. What's his name?"

"His name is Glenn Reeves."

"All right. Florida and the name give me a place to start. This is the first Jazzi talked about searching for her birth parents?"

"Yes. She registered on one of those sites that connects adoptees with birth families, hoping her birth mother or father would see her statistics and info there and contact her. That's always the hope."

Jonas turned his teacup in a circle, and she knew something was bothering him. What?

"If the mother or father or both don't want to be found, this won't be a positive experience for Jazzi. Does she realize that?"

"Does she realize how hurtful it will be? She can't possibly, and I don't think she'll listen if I try to tell her. My sister brought up the same point. Jazzi insists she just wants answers. Yet I know if she finds a birth parent, she'll want to build a relationship. That's just the way she is."

"Is that the way *you* are?"

"Are you asking me if it's a learned behavior?"

"My guess is that it is. If she's around a caring, loving woman who builds relationships, she'll be like that too."

Their gazes connected again, and Daisy felt a frisson of excitement in the way Jonas was looking at her.

Finally, he cleared his throat, breaking the moment. "I'll check this out and let you know what I find."

"Do you want a few brownies to take along?"

He narrowed his eyes. "Tea and baked goods for an information trade?"

She gave a shrug and a nod.

He chuckled and held out his hand for a shake. "It's a deal."

Daisy gave her hand to Jonas, feeling as if they were shaking on more than a business deal. A bond had formed between them. Daisy didn't know how she felt about that . . . at all.

Early Monday morning, Daisy made a stop on her way to the tea garden, wondering if today would be as hectic as yesterday. She wanted to pick up a few local supplies. The small market that offered products from farms in the area was one of Daisy's favorite places to shop. Apples, of course, were the popular produce item right now—from Honey Crisp to Stayman to Red and Golden Delicious, to Gala and Rome. She had suppliers from whom she bought produce, but she often liked to pick out her own.

Ruth Zook, a Mennonite woman managing the market, made divine products. Her homemade jam was the best, and Daisy used it at the tea garden. She picked up several jars—raspberry, strawberry, and peach. She also pointed to a basket of Stayman apples, which would be good in everything from apple tarts to applesauce. Ruth nodded that she'd ready them.

After telling Ruth she was going to take a quick look around, she headed to the potato section and found white sweet potatoes. She could whip up something, from sweet potato pie to sweet potato crisp. White sweet potatoes had a more delicate taste and were less fibrous than the orange variety. When she began poking a few into a plastic bag, she glanced across the top of the stand to the other side and spotted a friend of her aunt's, Edith Campbell. Edith played cards with Iris once a month. They'd been canasta buddies for years. In her fifties, Edith was still a math teacher at the local high school. She'd apparently decided to stop at the market before her day began.

Edith caught sight of Daisy at about the same time Daisy caught sight of her. Iris's friend smiled and waved and came around the stand to Daisy's side.

"What a mess you've got at the tea garden," Edith said.

Daisy didn't know if Edith meant the crime scene or the whole situation. "We're getting back on track."

"I told Iris no good would come of her dating a man whose divorce wasn't even final," Edith maintained.

That wasn't something Daisy wanted to discuss. She wouldn't gossip about her aunt.

But Edith apparently didn't catch her quick frown. "What kind of example is that for his children . . . or for yours, for that matter?"

"Violet and Jazzi just want Aunt Iris to be happy. They only considered whether Harvey was a nice man or not."

"Nice? I didn't know him, so I don't know about that, but as far as being a good father—"

Daisy wouldn't gossip about her aunt, but if Edith had information about Harvey, she'd be willing to listen to that. "Harvey wasn't a good father?"

"I taught his son and daughter," Edith explained. "They had their problems then, and they have their problems now. Harvey gave them too much. He and his wife argued constantly and weren't consistent with the kids. Marlene and Daniel both felt entitled to good grades simply because their father was rich and could give them whatever they wanted. They didn't think they had to earn them. Marlene has already been married twice, and she isn't twenty-five. Daniel has been charged with a DUI, and he can't hold a job. From what I understand, neither of them think a lot of their father. With him cutting them out of his will, who knows what could happen."

"Do you believe they're capable of murder?" That's what Edith seemed to be implying.

Edith shrugged. "I've seen it all, Daisy. Kids who are perfectly normal one minute and snap the next. Even in Willow Creek we have bullying. We have kids doing drugs. Not so long ago, one of the sophomore boys was caught bringing a switchblade to school. If you're asking me if they're capable of such a heinous deed, I can't rightly say. But I don't think we can rule it out, either. When spoiled kids get angry, they don't care who they hurt."

That might be true. But Daisy simply couldn't imagine a son or daughter murdering their father.

On Wednesday, Harvey Fitz's funeral drew even more people than his twenty-fifth store celebration had.

Fountain of Life Cemetery sat atop a rolling hill surrounded by pines and sycamores. The Fitz grave-site was large, with six-foot-tall monuments for Harvey's grandparents. An angel memorial almost as tall marked his parents' graves. Expecting a crowd, the cemetery director had ordered four canopies to be set up surrounding the grave site, with as many chairs as could fit under each one. Mourners had parked along the lane leading to different sections of the cemetery, and the surrounding area was filled with cars. Security guards, obvious in their suits and with Bluetooth equipment at their ears, made certain no reporters disrupted the service.

Daisy, her mom, and her aunt had driven there together. Her mom had insisted on coming to support her sister. They knew to arrive early and found chairs under one of the canopies. A loudspeaker system had been set up near a podium at the open grave site. Daisy had never seen a funeral quite like this. She spotted many people she knew, not only customers coming into the tea garden but Harvey's store staff as well as his almost ex-wife and his children. Detective Rappaport stood on the edge of the crowd, watching all with interest.

Fortunately, the October day held the hint of Indian summer. A cool breeze fanned Daisy's cheeks, but she hardly noticed as she caught sight of Cade under another canopy. There was no room around her or she would have waved to him and invited him to sit with them. Their last encounter had ended with tension, and that bothered her.

Putting those thoughts aside, she concentrated on Harvey's minister as he took his position at the podium and began speaking. The reverend talked mostly about Harvey's dedication to the community and the tradition of quality goods and services he'd carried on that had begun with his grandfather. He concluded with a sermonette about reward in the next life for good deeds done in this one, as well as Bible verses with a few words about each.

At the conclusion of the service, he motioned to the casket and the array of flowers that surrounded it, and asked everyone present to be respectful and line up quietly to pay their last respects. Daisy watched Monica and her children walk slowly up to the casket. Each pulled a red rose from the cascade that lay on top.

Daisy began to rise to her feet, but her aunt pulled on her arm. "I want to wait until most of the crowd has gone through."

Reseating herself, Daisy understood. Her aunt didn't want anyone to make comments about her.

As she glanced around, Daisy spied Bennett Topper standing by one of the canopy supports. Impeccably dressed as always in a black suit and taupe shirt and tie, with a kerchief that matched his shirt in his jacket pocket, he looked pained to be there, as if he too was waiting for the crowd to disperse.

Daisy patted her aunt's hand. "I'm going to speak to Harvey's store manager. I'll be right back."

After Iris nodded her consent, Daisy approached Bennett. When he saw her coming, he gave her a weak smile.

"I'm so sorry for your loss," she told him. "Harvey must have depended on you."

"Thank you for saying so. The past week has been the hardest of my life."

"I can only imagine."

"The police haven't made it any easier," he said with a sigh. "I know they're only doing their job, but they've questioned all of Harvey's employees more than once."

"They're trying to get to the bottom of what happened."

Bennett's eyes strayed to Iris. "How is your aunt holding up? I know Harvey enjoyed the time he spent with her."

"She's taking his death hard."

Together they watched the line that circled Harvey's casket as it lengthened. Monica and her children stayed right near the head of the casket, though, as if they couldn't bear to leave it.

Bennett wrinkled his nose. "She's such a hypocrite." Suddenly he turned away from those paying their respects as if the sight of Monica disgusted him. "I've been wanting to tell you that I think your tea garden is one of the best things to happen to Willow Creek in decades. The little bake shop that was there before had a nice following, but it didn't appeal to the residents of Willow Creek the same way your tea garden does."

"That's good to know, especially since you're involved in a downtown business. You probably hear what my customers think after they've left Daisy's."

"We do. Often, they'll be carrying bags with your cookies or scones or even munching on them when they come in the store, which is a no-no, as you know. No food or drink in our store, not unless we're serving it."

She gave him a smile of understanding.

He went on, "It's not only your products that they enjoy. They enjoy the tea garden atmosphere. It seems as if it's become a real community gathering place. That's the best way to sell any product. Word gets around."

"I think word *is* getting around," she agreed. "Business this week has been phenomenal. But this hasn't been the way I wanted success to happen."

"I certainly understand that. Harvey's store is the same way. Men's Trends has had an increase in traffic ever since he was murdered. But we certainly can't turn business away, can we?"

"No, we can't. How long have you been in the retail business?"

"I've worked in menswear boutiques ever since I was fresh out of high school and learning the ropes. My first position was a job in New York. But I've been with Harvey for fifteen years."

Daisy was ready to ask a few more questions when she saw Bennett frown. He was looking toward the casket at Harvey's son, Daniel.

Daniel wasn't standing at the casket, not anymore. He was weaving through the crowd. But the way he was weaving was a little odd. He looked shaky. He looked drunk.

Bennett shook his head and muttered, "I'm afraid to think what that boy has done. How *could* he come to his father's funeral *drunk?*"

"We don't know for sure that's what's wrong," Daisy offered. Maybe Daniel was overcome with loss.

"If it isn't booze, then it's weed or molly . . . or something worse. And it's the *worse* that concerns me the most. What if he was under the influence when he had an argument with his father? What if he met his father in the tea garden that night?"

"You don't believe he's the one who killed Harvey, do you?" The idea that a son could do that still shocked Daisy.

"Believe me, I don't want to think that. But I got the impression the police have put him on a short suspect list, just as they have your aunt." He looked embarrassed for saying it. "I'm sorry. That seems to be common knowledge as patrons gossip in the store and the detective asks more questions."

"Aunt Iris didn't have anything to do with Harvey's death. She believed she was going to marry him."

"I hope she's soon cleared of all suspicion."

Daisy hoped so too. With Bennett's comments, though, Daisy wondered if the entire town of Willow Creek believed her aunt was guilty.

Chapter Ten

After Daisy left her conversation with Bennett, she returned to her aunt's side.

Iris said, "We might as well join the line. I really can't stand to be here much longer."

Daisy's mother said, "We can just leave."

But Iris shook her head. "No. I have to pay my final respects."

Daisy was relieved when her mother didn't comment. Whether or not she disapproved of Iris's relationship with Harvey, her mom understood how much her sister was hurting today. With Rose on one side of her and Daisy on the other, Iris joined the line of mourners and waited for her turn to stand near the head of the casket.

Monica was still planted there, ramrod straight. When she spotted Iris approaching, she glared at her.

"Don't let her intimidate you," Daisy murmured to her aunt. "You didn't do anything wrong."

"Then why do I feel like the other woman?" Iris responded sadly. "Harvey told me his divorce was in the works when we started dating. He said the papers were all drawn up and it was just a matter of signing on the dotted line. But somehow Monica kept stalling."

All of a sudden, Harvey's daughter walked toward them, her head lowered. Daisy was afraid that Marlene as well as her mother would be vindictive and they'd all get caught up in a scandalous scene. However, that wasn't what happened. When Harvey's daughter approached them, she did so with a half smile.

After a glance at Monica, Marlene leaned closer to Iris. Right next to her, Daisy could hear Marlene say in a low voice, "I'm glad my father found you. For the month, he'd been happier than I've ever seen him."

"That's kind of you to say," Iris murmured. "I cared about your father deeply."

"I believe that. After he spent time with you, even just to have a cup of tea, he acted like a burden had been lifted from his shoulders."

Daisy cut Monica a quick glance and could see her scowl. It wasn't attractive.

While Iris thanked Marlene for expressing her sentiments about Harvey, Daisy wondered if Marlene took after her father, rather than her mother. And Daniel? At present, he was nowhere in sight.

Suddenly Marlene took Iris's arm and motioned to vacant chairs under one of the canopies. Daisy and her mother followed as Marlene led Iris in that direction. Once they were seated, Marlene took one of the chairs and spun it around so she was facing them. The gathering was breaking up, and most of the mourners who'd paid their respects were heading for their vehicles.

The look on Marlene's face told Daisy she needed to confide in someone. Apparently, that someone couldn't be her mother. She said to them, "The day before Daddy died, he brought me a book of his coins. He said he was changing his life and he wanted to change mine, no matter what my mother and brother did." She nodded to Iris. "I imagined that meant he was going to ask you to marry him."

She peered into the area behind the canopies. When she sighed, Daisy realized why. Her brother, who had been sitting hunched in the back row, stood. But as he made his way around the row of chairs, he wobbled. He looked as if he couldn't stand straight or walk steadily.

There was an irrefutable look of sadness in Marlene's eyes as she watched him. She practically whispered, "Daniel was once so close to Dad. When he and I were little, we spent hours sitting with Dad, sorting through coins. I'd be bored after a little while and would slip away, but Daniel didn't. He stayed right there. Dad always maintained he was teaching Daniel history. I don't know what happened between the two of them. Maybe someday Daniel will tell me. I'd better see if he needs me to take him home. I don't want him stopping at Bases on the way. He's been spending too much time there."

Daisy knew Bases was a sports bar and could understand Marlene's concern.

Marlene stood and briefly touched Iris's arm. "It was good talking to someone who really cared about Dad. Please excuse me."

As Marlene made her way to her brother, Daisy felt certain she wasn't the killer. However, when she looked over at Daniel she had her suspicions about him, right or wrong. In spite of his inebriated condition now, he was tall, muscled, and every bit capable of picking up a unicorn statue and smashing it into his father's head. Could a son have done that? Could Daniel Fitz have killed his father?

Daisy leaned toward her aunt. "Doesn't that make you feel better, knowing that Harvey was serious about you?"

"I suppose," Iris admitted, her gaze still on Harvey's daughter. "I'm surprised she told us what she did. Wouldn't she be on her mother's side? Her mother is all she has left now."

"Maybe when Harvey brought her that book of coins, she saw another side of him," Daisy suggested. "Maybe her mother had been filling her head with lies about her dad, and when he came to her himself, she saw the truth."

While they had been talking to Marlene, Daisy's attention had been diverted from the friends and neighbors who had been paying their respects at the casket. But now she spotted Cade walking toward them. In his hand, he held one of the roses from the spray on the casket.

He approached them all with a smile and a "hello," and then he held out the red rose to her aunt. "I thought you might like to have one of these."

Daisy could see her aunt became misty-eyed. "Thank you so much, Cade. That means a lot. I wanted to go up there and pluck it out myself, but I guess I just didn't have the courage with Harvey's wife standing right there."

"Nonsense," he said kindly. "You have courage. You also have common sense. I've heard rumors about Harvey Fitz's wife. She can be anything but pleasant. She's giving one of my associates a really hard time."

"She's thinking about selling the mansion?" Daisy asked.

"Apparently so. Though I think she's waiting to find out what's in Harvey's will."

Just what *had* Harvey Fitz put in his will? Had he changed it at the last minute?

Daisy's mom put her arm around Iris. "Come on, why don't we go to the car?"

Iris nodded. It seemed all the oomph had gone out of her.

All too easily, Daisy understood how grief could do that. She turned to Cade. "Thank you so much for thinking about my aunt that way. I know she wouldn't have taken a rose herself. She didn't consider herself immediate family, although if all the signs were right, she might have soon been part of Harvey's most intimate family."

Cade cast her a glance. "Would you have approved?"

"My approval didn't mean a thing. I just wanted . . . want . . . my aunt to be happy."

"You didn't answer my question. *Would* you have approved?"

Daisy thought about it, then responded, "I understand that Harvey and my aunt are older, and grabbing happy moments becomes even more important as you age. But he wasn't divorced yet, Cade. He shouldn't have been making any kind of promises. That says something about the integrity of a man, don't you think?"

"But what about love, Daisy? What if Harvey and your aunt were truly in love? Harvey following his heart should have meant something too."

Daisy understood what Cade meant. Maybe she'd always followed the rules a little too closely. "I hadn't thought of it that way, and you're right. A man following his heart should mean something."

"I don't think I told you how much I appreciated dinner at your house. Maybe we can do it again sometime. I'll give you a call, and I'll take you to Sarah Jane's diner. She has the best potpie and shoofly pie around."

Maybe Daisy had been wrong about Cade. She'd thought he didn't have a romantic interest in her. Possibly he did. Would she like to follow up on that? Wasn't it time she moved *her* life forward?

"I'd like to go to Sarah Jane's with you."

When Cade smiled at her, his smile was reminiscent of the boy who'd asked her to the prom. Potpie, Sarah Jane's, and Cade. It was a nice combination.

Everyone was exhausted by the end of the day. Daisy and Iris had returned to the tea garden to continue the busyness of the week. Daisy had asked Karina to stay until closing. Jazzi had come in after school, and they needed her help too. There was a rush on scones, not a drop of soup left in the pot, and Daisy had so many kinds of tea steeping she could hardly keep track. But she did. They all did a wonderful job. But if they were going to be this busy, she had to consider reorganization. It was the only way to keep up the standard of quality she needed to maintain.

Later, at home, she made a quick supper of barbecued beef, oven-roasted potatoes, and salad. Jazzi ate in her room as she worked on her homework. Daisy tidied up the kitchen, made her to-do list for the next day, then went upstairs to talk to her daughter.

When she entered the room, Jazzi was sitting at her desk with her laptop open before her. Pepper lay across her lap, and Marjoram, on the desk with her golden eyes following Jazzi's fingers, made sure Jazzi's keystrokes were the right ones.

"You have helpers tonight," Daisy commented.

Jazzi didn't look up, but Pepper meowed. She was the more vocal of the two cats and talked back often. She made her needs known, whether she was hungry or just wanted attention and affection. Stretching out, she reached one paw toward Daisy.

With a smile, Daisy ran her hand over her thick black coat and gently scratched her under the chin. Pepper's motorboat-like purr practically filled the room.

Jazzi gave a sigh and turned away from the computer. "She's louder than my music sometimes." She motioned to Marjoram. "And with her watching my every move, I feel like I have a bodyguard."

"They love you."

"They love you too. You just move around a lot more than I do when you're in the house. So they settle with me. Their company helps when I'm missing Violet."

So Jazzi finally admitted it. "You wish she was coming home before Thanksgiving."

"So do you," Jazzi accused defensively.

"Yes, I do. But I didn't tell her that. The first month or two of college is really important. She's settling in, and that's a good thing. Those first two months, when she makes new friends, can determine her social life while she's there."

"But you don't know if she's getting into the wrong crowd."

"No, I don't, but I have to trust her. I have to trust what I've taught her, what your dad and I taught her. And you have to trust her too."

Jazzi ducked her head and focused on Pepper. "I don't know what you mean."

Daisy wasn't buying it. "I think you do. You're afraid Vi will make new friends and forget all about you."

When Jazzi made eye contact with Daisy, an expression crossed her face that told Daisy she was right on target.

"It's okay to miss her, Jazzi. You're both going to move on. But your bond as sisters—that will always be there."

Once more Jazzi looked down at the cat and petted her. "What happens to that bond if I look for my birth parents?"

"Have you told Violet that you are?"

"No, not yet."

"I think she'll support whatever you need to do."

"She could feel I was being disloyal."

"She could. But you won't know until you talk to her about it."

"Maybe I'll think about it," Jazzi murmured. Then she asked the question Daisy knew she'd been wanting to ask. "Have you found anything more about my birth mother?"

"No."

The disappointed expression on her daughter's face broke Daisy's heart, so she sat on Jazzi's bed. "Because I couldn't find anything on my own, as I mentioned the other night, I decided to ask for help from Jonas."

"What's he going to do?"

"He has more than decent computer skills from his investigative years when he was a detective. For starters, he's going to try to find the lawyer who handled your adoption. He can be so much more effective at searching than I can. Than *we* can."

"Mom, you do understand why I have to do this, don't you?"

"I've got to admit the idea of you finding your birth mother scares me. But I don't want you to feel as if you have a hole in your heart because you don't know that part of yourself. So I'm behind you on this, Jazzi. Honestly, I am. I'll help you do whatever we can to find out something. I can't promise we'll find your birth mother or your birth father, but we're going to start, and maybe we'll get somewhere."

Jazzi's eyes glistened with tears. "Thank you."

Before Daisy started crying herself, she cleared her throat and said, "Now let me ask you a question."

"Uh oh. What?"

"How would you really feel if I went out to dinner with Cade sometime?"

"You mean like on a date?"

"I don't know if we'll call the first time that, but, yes, on a date."

"I can't think of you with anybody else but Dad."

Daisy suddenly felt deflated at the idea of moving on.

But then Jazzi continued. "I'll always remember you with Dad. I have all the memories of the things we did, the places we went, the four of us together. And I'll never forget them. I know you're thinking about what happens after Violet finishes college and maybe moves away from Willow Creek. And what happens when *I* go to college. I guess you don't want to be alone."

"I would never be with a man just because I don't want to be alone."

Jazzi thought about that, and then she nodded. "Okay. But I guess what I'm saying is—I don't want you to be alone either. You probably need more than these two fur babies to keep you company."

"I don't know. They might be a lot less complicated than dating."

Jazzi laughed. "You could be right about that. But I get it, Mom. If you want to date Cade, I'm okay with that. But what about Jonas?"

"What *about* Jonas?"

"Have you ever thought about dating him?"

"I . . . I—" She stopped and felt her cheeks redden.

Jazzi pointed at her. "You have."

"I don't know if Jonas is ready to date. I certainly don't know if he's interested in me."

"But if he is?"

"I'm not even going to think about it. Cade asked if I'd like to have dinner at Sarah Jane's some time, so I thought I'd talk to you about it. That way if he asks and I say *yes*, you won't be surprised."

"And if Jonas asks, and you say *yes*, I won't be surprised either."

Daisy just shook her head, rose to her feet, and went to the door. "Just so you know, dreams of Cinderella are still alive for you. But my dreams about being Cinderella—they're far in the past."

"Was Dad your Prince Charming?"

"No, he was my partner. We loved each other, Jazzi, and all we wanted was the best for you and Vi."

"I'm sorry I hid all this from you, Mom. I'm sorry I've been . . ."

"Difficult?" Daisy asked.

"Yeah, difficult. But I didn't know how to tell you, and I didn't know what to do."

"The next time that happens, just come talk to me." Instead of leaving the room, she went to her daughter and gave her a hug. It was the best way she knew to communicate what she wanted to tell her—that she loved her no matter what.

They were just leaning away from each other when Daisy heard her cell phone play from her pocket. "I'd better get that," she said to Jazzi. "It could be your Aunt Iris."

"Or Cade asking you for a definite date," Jazzi said slyly.

Daisy blew her daughter a kiss and checked her phone screen. She was surprised to see the Willow Creek Police Department number.

"Hello?" she asked tentatively.

Two minutes later, she'd gone downstairs to her bedroom and closed the door. Then she made a call. She hated to do it this late. Of course, some people wouldn't consider nine o'clock late. But she didn't feel she had a choice. She expected to reach voice mail, but she didn't.

Marshall Thompson answered himself. His deep baritone sounded distracted as he said, "Hello."

"Mr. Thompson, it's Daisy Swanson."

"I saw your name come across my caller ID. How can I help you?"

"I hope it's not too late—"

"Never too late for a client who needs my help. What's wrong, Mrs. Swanson?"

"Please call me Daisy. Detective Rappaport called me. He wants me to come in for questioning tomorrow afternoon at one o'clock."

"I see. Do you want me to go with you?"

Daisy thought about that. "I don't think that's necessary, but I just wanted your advice on how I should handle it."

"Mrs. Swanson"—he quickly amended—"Daisy, the only advice I can give you if I'm not with you is not to talk to the detective."

She was silent for a moment. "If I don't talk to him, he'll think I'm hiding something. He'll think I'm guilty of something."

"Possibly. But if you talk to him without my presence, you could say something you wish you hadn't. If it's my fee you're worried about, I'll remind you I'll charge you half of my hourly rate. You're a friend of Jonas."

"And the hourly rate is?"

"I'm billing at $300 an hour right now."

She gasped.

"If I'm with you, we won't be at that police station longer than an hour. That would be $150. Can you manage that?"

"Yes, I can manage that."

"Then I'll meet you at the Willow Creek PD at one o'clock."

"Do you think they're going to question me about something in my statement?"

"Possibly. Or else new information has come to light and Detective Rappaport wants to question you about that."

"But I don't know anything!"

"Oftentimes, you think you don't know something when you do. Try to get some sleep tonight, Daisy. I'll see you at the station tomorrow at one."

After Daisy ended the call, she slid her phone onto her dresser. She thought about calling her aunt to see if she had received a call from Detective Rappaport too. Then she decided against it. If her Aunt Iris had received a call, she would have phoned Daisy.

Jazzi rapped on Daisy's bedroom door.

Daisy said, "Come in, honey."

Sticking her head around the door, Jazzi asked, "Is anything wrong? You ran down here awful fast."

"No, nothing is wrong," she lied. Wasn't protecting Jazzi from angst her job? "I'm going to make myself a mug of hot chocolate. Do you want one?"

"Sure," Jazzi said. "I have to keep working now. I'm behind on reading this biology chapter."

"I understand. I'll bring you a mug. Then I'm going to turn in."

"You look worried, Mom. Are you sure there isn't something I should know about?"

Daisy's reply was immediate. "There's nothing for you to worry about." Then she gave Jazzi's arm a squeeze.

She sincerely hoped there wasn't anything for Jazzi to worry about—or anyone else, for that matter. But the stone-cold feeling in the pit of her stomach told her otherwise.

Chapter Eleven

The following morning, as Daisy, Tessa, and Aunt Iris readied the tea garden for customers, Daisy felt odd because she was holding something back. She'd debated with herself all night whether she should tell Iris that she was going to the police station. She didn't usually keep things from her family. And it was quite possible her aunt would get called in for questioning too. So she supposed it would be better if Aunt Iris was prepared.

Daisy told Tessa and Iris, "I'm going to be away from the tea garden for an hour or so this afternoon. Do you think you'll be able to cover it with Cora Sue and Eva? Or should I call Karina to come in again?"

Tessa and Iris exchanged a look. "We have a full afternoon tea service this afternoon," Iris reminded her. "The prep is finished. The two of us can handle serving. But I don't know if Cora Sue can handle the counter and serving customers in the green room too."

Daisy pushed up her bangs, as she was wont to do when she was anxious, nervous, or frustrated. "I'm so distracted, I forgot all about afternoon tea. How's that even possible?"

Tessa patted her shoulder kindly. "You've a lot to think about right now. Let me call Karina and Pamela Dorsey. They're both efficient, know how to brew tea, and how to balance a tray. I think we'll need two serving the afternoon tea, and two on the counter, with Eva in the kitchen."

Pamela Dorsey was a college student who'd helped them over the holidays last year and during the summer when tourist traffic had been at its height. She also helped out if someone on their regular staff called in sick. "That's probably a good idea, especially since I could get held up," Daisy ruminated. She really didn't *want* to get held up when she was paying Marshall Thompson $150 an hour.

"Your errand can't wait?" Iris asked with a probing look, knowing how budget-conscious Daisy was.

Blowing out a breath, Daisy shook her head. "I'm afraid not. Detective Rappaport wants to talk to me at one o'clock at the police station. Marshall Thompson is going with me."

Iris's hand went to her chest. "If you take Marshall Thompson along, won't you look guilty?"

"I asked Marshall that, but since we have no idea what the detective wants, he thinks it's best if he accompanies me. He's experienced, Aunt Iris. I have to trust his and Jonas's recommendation."

Her aunt's hands got all fluttery when she was nervous, and they fluttered now. "Don't you worry about anything here. We'll handle it. At the worst, we'll sell out of everything, brew all our tea, and have to stay until midnight to prep for the next day."

That was the most positive way of looking at it.

Daisy heard Karina, Eva, and Cora Sue come in the back door. After greetings all around, she checked the teapot clock on the wall and saw that it was exactly eight o'clock—opening time. She went to the front door, unlocked it, and switched the CLOSED sign to OPEN. A few customers were already standing on the porch by the colorful array of flowers. One lady was pointing to a decorative enameled scarecrow stake in a bright yellow ceramic pot.

When Daisy opened the door, she said hello to all of them, pretending she didn't have a care in the world and her outlook was always optimistic. That's what customers wanted to see. A fourth customer trailed in behind the others, and she recognized him. It was Guy Tremont. He was wearing a plaid sport coat, a wilder plaid than any of the men she knew would wear.

He said, "I decided to try you out again."

"I'm glad you did. Would you like our breakfast special? Tea and a scone. Or would you prefer something else?"

"Tea and a scone sounds good. What kind of scones?"

"This morning we have blueberry, apple, and chocolate raspberry."

"I'm a sucker for chocolate and raspberry, and I'll probably want to take six along."

She laughed. "What kind of tea? Our main selections are up on the board. But if you want something special, we can do that."

"Oh, all of it is just plain confusing. What would you suggest with the chocolate raspberry scone?"

"I have a tea called lemon soufflé. It has a green tea base, but it should complement the scone well."

"Lemon soufflé it is."

Since Guy Tremont had returned, Daisy wanted to take the opportunity to talk to him more thoroughly about Harvey and his coin collection. So she signaled

Cora Sue that she would serve the man herself. In about five minutes, she'd assembled a tray with a cobalt blue teapot with tea steeping inside. She'd placed a scone on a cobalt blue and white stoneware dish. Also on the tray, she'd included a white china sugar bowl with a serving spoon. With a smile, she set the teapot at Guy's right side.

"Another two minutes and that should be just right," she predicted.

"Tea has to be timed just perfectly, doesn't it?"

"It depends if you like your tea weak or strong. But, yes, each type of tea has its best steeping time."

He studied the scone with chocolate drizzled over the surface and brought his gaze up to Daisy's. "That looks almost too pretty to eat."

She laughed. "We have more, but if you just want to stare at it—"

He broke the scone in two. "Just look at that chocolate dough. And I can see raspberries."

"They're dried raspberries. They help the dough keep its consistency."

He tasted a bite, closed his eyes, and savored it. "Mmm, mmm, mmm. You do know how to bake. Is this your recipe or someone else's?"

"This one's mine."

"I declare you the best scone maker I've ever visited."

She laughed. "Mr. Tremont, you have a way with words. Thank you for the compliment."

"Well earned," he said, shaking half a scone at her. "Yep, I'm going to want a half dozen of these to take along."

Daisy looked across the counter at her aunt, and her aunt nodded and started packing a box.

"If you don't eat them all before tonight, consider

putting them in a Ziploc bag in the refrigerator. They'll keep better that way."

Guy nodded. "Somebody told me you're a widow. Is that right?"

She didn't talk about her personal life with her customers, but this man was a little different. If she wanted information, she might have to give some.

"I am a widow. Why?"

"Because a man would sure be glad to get someone like you with this kind of baking skill."

"My daughters appreciate my baking skills."

"I imagine they might."

Daisy decided the time was right to press for a little information. "Since you're here, do you mind if I ask you a question about Harvey's coin collection?"

"I don't mind."

"What all was in the collection?"

Guy thought about it, as if he were taking inventory of the collection in his mind. "Harvey's collection encompassed a wide range—from silver dollars that had value because they're in mint condition to silver dollars that are valuable because they're rare. There were coins with the original government packaging. His gold coin collection was spectacular, maybe more spectacular than anybody knows."

Just what could Guy mean by that? "Did you know about the book of coins he gave his daughter?"

Tremont looked genuinely surprised. "I didn't know he gave her a book."

"That's what she said. Harvey told her it was worth enough that she could change her life if she wanted to."

"That's odd. It was either one of his rare coin books or a gold coin book. Has she had it appraised?"

"No, I don't think she has. But certainly she'd come to you for your opinion, don't you think?"

"I would hope. Did she seem to appreciate the coins? Or is she just going to sell them?"

"We didn't get that far. I'm not sure she knows what she's going to do with them." Daisy poured tea into Guy's cup for him.

He stared at it, then added sugar from the white china bowl on the table. "Maybe I'll give her a call. She won't think that's unusual. She knows her father and I were good friends."

Another group of customers came in, and Daisy knew she'd be needed in the kitchen. She said to Tremont, "It was good to see you again. Iris has your scones at the counter when you're ready to leave. If you need more tea, just let us know."

After he mumbled, "Have a good day," around another bite of scone, she hurried to the back, thinking about silver dollars, gold coins, and a collection worth a mint.

"Recording this interview isn't necessary, is it?" Marshall Thompson asked Detective Rappaport shortly after one PM. "Mrs. Swanson already gave you a statement, and you recorded that. From what I understand, this is informal follow-up questioning. Am I correct?"

The detective looked disgruntled, but he grudgingly agreed. "That's right, informal additional questioning." He glared at Daisy, as if by bringing Marshall along she'd broken an important rule.

Marshall had advised her not to talk and to answer questions only minimally when Detective Rappaport asked them. So she just sat there calmly—though she wasn't calm inside at all—and waited.

They were in the room where she'd given her

statement, she and Marshall on one side of the table, Detective Rappaport on the other. The table had seen better days. Its laminated wood finish was scratched and scarred, and Daisy didn't even want to think about who might have sat here before her.

"You and your aunt opened Daisy's Tea Garden as partners. Is that correct?" the detective asked tersely.

"It is."

"Your aunt invested money, and you invested money."

Daisy didn't hear a question there, so she kept quiet.

Marshall gave her an approving glance.

Apparently, the detective wasn't happy with her non-response. "You comingled your funds, is that correct?"

"That's correct," she responded.

"Are you and your aunt close?" he pushed on.

"Yes, we are."

"Would you like to elaborate on that?" His tone was so even, Daisy suspected he was holding his temper.

When she looked at Marshall, he gave a nod.

With her lawyer's approval, she explained, "While I was growing up, Aunt Iris and I were always close. I think it's because we both like to work in the kitchen, making baked goods especially. We stayed close over the years, even when I lived in Florida."

"Would you say you're closer to your aunt than your mother?"

"Of course not," Daisy answered, annoyed with the detective's attitude. "Why would you ask that?"

Rappaport didn't answer, just gave her a sly smile. "That caused a reaction, didn't it? Do you think your mother's jealous of your relationship with your aunt?"

Marshall cut in. "Where is this going?"

Rappaport sat forward in his seat. "I'm just saying

if you and your aunt are close, the possibility is good that if you found out that Harvey was hurting her in some way, you'd want to do something about it."

Daisy didn't even know where to wade in on that. "Harvey wasn't hurting her. He was going to marry her."

"There's no evidence of that. She doesn't have a ring, does she?"

"No, but—"

Rappaport cut her off. "A man makes a promise and then reneges on that promise. I'd say that could get a woman pretty riled up."

What did Rappaport think? That Aunt Iris had gone outside that night and Harvey had told her . . . what? That he was breaking off his relationship with her? And because of that, she hauled off and socked him with a statue?

"What are you suggesting, Detective?" Daisy asked.

"I'm the one asking the questions."

"You're not exactly asking questions. You're setting up theories with no basis," she returned, not bothering to check with Marshall.

Detective Rappaport looked taken aback that she'd confronted him with logic. "I'm suggesting that you might have been just as angry as your aunt if Harvey Fitz was going to drop her. And the two of you might have colluded to kill him."

Daisy's mouth dropped open, but then she snapped it shut and asked, "To what end?"

"That's what I'm trying to find out. I heard a rumor that Harvey was going to sell his store and invest in the expansion of Daisy's Tea Garden, maybe even start a chain."

"Where did you hear something like that?"

Marshall gently tapped her arm. She was responding too much and, she guessed, saying too much. But she'd had enough of Rappaport's insinuations. He was the one keeping silent now.

Whether Marshall wanted her to be quiet or not, she couldn't be. "Let's say your theory is true, Detective. Let's say the gossip you heard was true. Just how would Iris and I benefit from Harvey's death? We'd be better off if he was alive. A chain of Daisy's Tea Gardens? That sounds like a gold mine. Why would we want to end the possibility of that?"

He jumped on what she'd said. "So you're saying it's true?"

"No, I'm not saying it's true. Nothing like that was ever in the works." She sat back in her chair, crossed her arms over her chest, and kept her gaze on his. She could feel Marshall's tension beside her, but there was nothing she could do about that. Being silent was one thing. Being silent in the face of bold-faced lies was quite another, especially when they involved her aunt.

The detective finally looked away, took a long time studying the notes in front of him, then shuffled the papers into a stack and stood. "We're done for today, Mrs. Swanson. You can go."

With her dander still up, she felt she needed to take a poke at him. She didn't like being bullied, and that's what he was doing.

"You should stop at the tea garden for orange pekoe tea sometime. It might improve your disposition."

The detective's face turned red. But before he could manufacture a response, Marshall ushered Daisy out of the room, down the hall, and out into the reception area.

"You can't goad him like that," Marshall said to her in a whisper.

"Goad him? What do you think *he* was doing to *me*?"

"That's his job, Daisy. He was trying to get a rise out of you so you'd confess to something."

"There's nothing to confess to," she returned with exasperation. She saw another officer look up from his desk to see what her raised voice was about.

Marshall just shook his head. "Come on. Before you say something that gets us both arrested."

By the time they reached Marshall's car, Daisy was feeling contrite. After all, Marshall was only trying to help.

Once they were inside his car, she said, "I'm sorry. He just made me so mad. Iris and I colluding to kill someone? That makes no sense at all."

"Daisy, you have to remember who Detective Rappaport deals with. Maybe not so much who he deals with now. Crime in Willow Creek is mostly limited to DUIs, jaywalking, and now and then a domestic violence issue. But he dealt with more than that in Pittsburgh. He's witnessed a seedy side of life, and that's what colors his thoughts and his memories. So when he sees a pretty blonde with blue eyes sitting before him, he believes you have to be making things up as you go."

"Because I'm blond and have blue eyes I'm lying?"

Marshall chuckled. "I didn't mean to make this a blond thing. I'm just saying he's probably seen a lot of pretty women hide sins. So cut him a little slack, and just try not to take it all so personally."

"Not take it personally? Mr. Thompson, you're not living on the same planet I am."

At that he chuckled. "Do you want me to come in with you to discuss this with your aunt?"

"Do you think I can't relate what happened back there?"

"You're getting defensive now. That's not good between lawyer and client."

She sighed. "Sorry. That whole scene, this whole murder, just seems like something out of a movie, and I shouldn't be living it."

"I know," Marshall sympathized. "But this is real, Daisy. Harvey was killed on your property. There is a murderer in Willow Creek, and you or your aunt might even know him or her. So when Detective Rappaport comes at you with what may seem like odd questions, just remember, he's trying to get to that murderer. He wants to make sure that murderer isn't you."

"You're making me feel as if I should apologize to him."

"I did not say that. You don't want to give him the upper hand if you can help it. But you do have to tell your aunt what he's thinking and where he's trying to go with the investigation."

"All right, I'll do that as soon as I can pull Iris aside."

A car left a space in front of the tea garden right before Marshall pulled up. He expertly slipped into the parking space. "I told you it would be less than an hour."

"You did. Do you want me to write you a check now?"

He shook his head. "No. Let's wait until the end of the month. Olivia will bill you. You never know if we could have another session or two. Detective Rappaport might come up with something else that could require my services."

"Or Aunt Iris could. Thank you for taking the time out to do this today."

"It's what I do, Daisy. Take care, and if anything else comes up, call me. Do not set foot in that police station without a lawyer."

Daisy nodded that she understood; then she climbed out of his car and closed the door. After she went inside, she saw the gray sedan pull away. Was she glad Marshall had gone along? Or because Marshall had gone along, had she set up an adversarial relationship with Rappaport? It was so hard to know the right thing to do.

As Daisy glanced around the tea garden's two rooms, she was glad they'd called in help. Aunt Iris was serving tea to her afternoon tea appointments. She was scurrying through the room, carrying a three-tiered dish of sandwiches, cookies, and scones to a table on the left in the yellow room. Everyone seemed to be having a good time.

In the green room, where they served their customers daily, every table was filled, even at this hour of the afternoon. Were tourists plentiful this year? They'd come to stay in the surrounding area and just decided to stop in for tea? There was a reason for all this business, and she had to find out what it was. It couldn't just be because of the news reports.

It was almost an hour later when Daisy had a few minutes to take Iris aside. They went into her office and Daisy filled her in on the "interview."

"I don't know where he got the idea that Harvey was going to sell his store and invest in an expansion of Daisy's."

Iris sat in front of the desk and twisted her hands in her lap. That was never a good sign. Either she was nervous or thinking way too much.

Daisy was totally surprised when her aunt said,

"Harvey and I did talk about him investing in Daisy's. We talked about expanding too. But only in a hypothetical way and not until after we were married."

"You never mentioned this to me."

"Maybe I thought I would jinx it. Maybe I thought I would jinx the whole idea of marrying Harvey. I mean, after all, he wasn't divorced yet. Even if he gave me a ring, we would have had to wait until the divorce came through."

"When you and Harvey discussed expanding the tea garden, was it coming out of your relationship? I mean, was it just a dream the two of you had together? Or is it possible that someone else might know about it?" Somehow Rappaport had found out about it.

"We were just thinking about things we might want to do in the future. His store took up a gargantuan amount of his time. Some weeks he put in eighty hours. He was in control of everything. He had to oversee everything. Going forward, I don't think he wanted that. If he would invest in Daisy's, *we* would be managing it. If we went to a chain or franchise idea, he could hire a business manager. It was just a project for the two of us. Of course, you were included, but you know what I mean. It was a brainchild we wanted to develop. But it wasn't real yet."

"It might have been more real than you think, Aunt Iris. Maybe it wasn't so hypothetical to Harvey. Maybe he confided in someone and asked a few questions of his banker, of an attorney, of even a financial adviser."

"What if he did?"

"Well, apparently he did or Detective Rappaport wouldn't know about it."

There was a knock at the back door of the kitchen.

Their suppliers often came to that door because they could enter the kitchen directly from the parking lot.

When Daisy answered the knock, she found Angus Bedford, their tea supplier.

He brought in the bags of tea and lined them up on the counter. "I have a new blend for you. It combines pineapple and peach. I've been told it's sublime."

Angus was a big man, maybe six foot two, with a full beard and heavy black glasses that his big nose held up easily. He always wore black. He wasn't Amish but seemed to believe a lot of what the Amish believed. Sublime just wasn't a word he usually used.

"Did you taste this one?" she asked with a smile.

"I did. I even liked it. I liked it iced. I liked it with a touch of honey. I liked it with some additional lemon. I tried it several different ways, and you can too before you serve it. It tastes versatile to me."

"Glad for the hints."

"It might be pretty popular with the new crowd."

"New crowd?"

Angus moved over to the doorway and into the green room. "I heard your business has picked up since Harvey Fitz's murder."

"It has," Daisy said with a sigh, still not liking the idea.

Angus could obviously see that. "You have a pure heart, Mrs. Daisy, and you don't want someone's misfortune to be your gain. But maybe you should just latch onto the idea and go with it."

Before she could protest, he went on, "Daisy's Tea Garden is getting media attention because of the murder. The tea garden is mentioned anytime the murder is cited on the news and on the Internet."

"The Internet," Daisy murmured. She hadn't thought much about that. Whenever she did think about the Internet, Jazzi's adoption site came to mind.

"You do know there are tea bloggers," Angus said.

Yes, she knew there were tea bloggers—all different kinds. Some touted the taste of a particular tea. Others talked more about the process—the tradition of brewing tea the correct way. Many others delved into the health benefits.

Angus continued, "Every one of those bloggers are connecting to your tea garden website because they think you're famous now. If I were you, I'd check the number of page views you've received since the murder. Check your comments section. Check how many more followers you have. That could be where a lot of your new business is coming from, and you should be aware of it as a good manager."

As a good manager. Right now, she wasn't sure she was managing *anything* properly.

Chapter Twelve

At almost six PM, Daisy was ready to close. She was removing her apron, ready to look over the menu for the following day, when Jonas came in.

He looked as if he'd had a busy day too and needed dinner.

"I have a bowl of beef barley soup left," she said. "Are you interested?"

"You're determined to keep me away from a fast-food burger, aren't you?"

"I am. It's my civic duty," she teased.

"How about orange pekoe tea to go with that?"

"Coming right up." She went to the door and flipped the sign to CLOSED before she crossed to the kitchen.

Minutes later, after Daisy brought the soup to Jonas in a white ironstone bowl and the tea in a black cast-iron teapot, she sat across from him and slipped off her shoes.

He must have heard them clatter to the floor because he looked under the table. "Rough day?"

"A draining day."

"Is Jazzi around?"

"No. She had a meeting after school. I have to pick her up in half an hour."

"I wanted to give you a progress report."

She felt her shoulders tense, and he must have seen that.

"I don't have much to report," he assured her quickly. "I'm still searching public records for Jazzi's birth. You and your husband named her, which makes the search more difficult. Not impossible, just more difficult."

He stirred his soup, letting the steam rise so it would cool off. "I'm also trying to trace down your lawyer's records. I expect to have more luck with that, but that's where I am. Have you told Jazzi I'm looking into it?"

"Yes, I have. She's pleased. I told her your background, so she also realizes you know what you're doing."

He dipped his spoon into the soup bowl. "It's not a matter of knowing what I'm doing as much as knowing what databases to use in order to search. But it's tedious, Daisy. What I haven't told you is that your lawyer died."

She blinked. "Then how are you going to find the records?"

"I found information on him in the Florida newspaper. There was an ad about private adoptions. It listed his secretary's name, so I'm trying to track her down. I'll get something. It's just going to take time."

"I'll tell Jazzi that, though teenagers aren't the most patient beings on earth."

He took a spoonful of soup, blew on it, then ate it. "This is good. I shouldn't be surprised. Everything you make is good."

The compliment felt nice. Ever since Ryan had died,

she'd kept her guard up around men. It had been her way of protecting her love for Ryan, keeping her grief private, not giving off any signals so that a man would get the wrong idea. But with Jonas, she didn't feel a need to have that guard in place.

So when he asked, "How was the funeral?" she felt comfortable discussing it with him.

"It was an ordinary funeral," she began. "If you don't count the security keeping the reporters out. Harvey's wife gave Aunt Iris scathing looks, but his daughter actually came up to us and talked. She told Aunt Iris that she'd been good for Harvey. I think it made Iris feel a little better. Marlene also mentioned that her dad had brought her one of his coin books. He told her he wanted her to have it, that he wanted them to make a new start."

"That's interesting."

"What's even more interesting is that Detective Rappaport called me down to the police station again. That's where I was this afternoon."

"Alone?"

"No. Marshall Thompson went with me. I was glad he did. Detective Rappaport is proposing the theory that Aunt Iris and I colluded to kill Harvey."

Jonas laid his spoon down, sat back, and just stared at her. "You are *not* serious."

"Oh, I'm very serious. I'm not exactly sure what to do. Do I just sit back and let him suspect me?"

Jonas took another spoonful of soup, then poured a mug of tea. "Maybe I should talk to him."

"About me?"

"No, not about you. Not directly anyway. As a former cop, maybe I can get a sense of the investigation because Rappaport might be more open with me. I wouldn't mention your name. Maybe he'll tell me what his next move is."

"I suppose that would be all right. He scares me, almost as much as Marshall does."

"Marshall? He acts tough, but he's an old softie."

"An expensive softie."

Jonas nodded, "That's because he's good. Did he cut his rate for you?"

"Yes, he did. Thank you. That was *your* doing."

Jonas finished his bowl of soup and then sipped at the mug of tea. "Has business still been on an up-swing?"

"It has, and I think I know why. Bloggers who write about tea have gotten hold of this story. When they mention the murder, they mention the tea garden or vice versa. I checked on my phone and our website for page views, and they've ratcheted up by about a thou-sand in the past few days. But this isn't the way I want the tea garden's name to get around."

Looking thoughtful, Jonas rubbed his thumb along the handle of the teapot; then he motioned to his mug. "If you really want to garner more business, you need to attack your social media following while the iron's hot, so to speak. Or while the teapot's hot. You should make a podcast on how to brew tea correctly and put it on YouTube and your website."

When Daisy wrinkled up her nose as if the thought made her cringe, Jonas laughed. "You don't want all that attention?"

"Not on your life."

"Just because you don't want to do it, doesn't mean you can't have Tessa do it, or even your Aunt Iris."

"Jazzi would probably love to be on camera, but I'm not going there. It's possible Tessa might want to. You really think that would bring us more customers?"

"It could, especially if your YouTube video goes viral."

"And how would I make that happen?"

"*You* know how you can make that happen—give a tour of your garden where the murder took place."

"Jonas! I would never do that."

He reached across the table as if he were going to pat her hand, but his fingertips didn't quite reach hers, and he pulled his hand back. "I didn't think you would. So just stick to brewing tea, and I'm sure you'll attract loyal followers. But, Daisy, this tea garden is named after you, so you're really the one who should do the video. And you might want to enlist Jazzi's help. Teenagers are great at shooting videos. Their smartphones have made them experts."

As she thought about it, he took a last swallow of tea and set down his mug. Then he pushed back his chair and rose to his feet. "I don't want to keep you any longer. And I have to tally the day's receipts at Woods and close up. I'll let you know if anything turns up in my searches. I promise I'll keep you informed."

She stood now too. "I'll take your idea about making a video seriously, and not only for business's sake. It's something Jazzi and I can do together. Maybe we can get closer again."

He didn't ask why she and Jazzi had grown apart, and she didn't volunteer the information. Maybe because she still did have her guard up. Maybe because she didn't want to confide in Jonas too much. If she did, they'd be starting a friendship, and she didn't know if mere friendship was all she wanted from Jonas Groft.

* * *

The following morning, Iris and Daisy were mixing cookie dough when Joachim Adler delivered produce at the kitchen's back door. Daisy peered into the plastic bins of lettuce, broccoli, yellow and purple cauliflower, leeks, carrots, and celery, and gave him a wide smile.

"It all looks good, Joachim."

He had a heavy beard and sideburns that showed mostly gray. He repositioned his felt hat and said, "You know mine's the best."

"I sure do. I wouldn't buy it otherwise."

"The bill will be coming next week for September. In the New Year, I'll be sending out e-mails as bills instead of using the post office."

"Stepping into the tech age?"

"What choice do I have? My daughter says it's the only way to keep the business efficient."

Daisy again said, "Thank you" and waved as he exited the kitchen. Then she and Eva started wrapping the produce to store it. She heard the front bell ring but didn't pay any attention. Tessa was manning the front counter until Cora Sue arrived.

Tessa called to Daisy, "Can you come out front?"

Daisy hoped a reporter hadn't barged in.

When she approached the counter, she spotted a young man talking to Tessa. He looked to be in his late teens or early twenties. He could be a reporter, though she imagined he could also be a blogger. Anybody could be a blogger.

The young man, who was wind-tossed with russet brown hair and rimless glasses, immediately held his hand out to Daisy. "Foster Cranshaw. You're Mrs. Swanson?"

"I am. You wanted to see me?"

"I'd like to know if you're hiring any help."

Daisy and Tessa exchanged a glance. They were both sizing up Foster Cranshaw. Yes, they'd seriously thought about hiring temporary help, but did he fit the bill? Daisy decided she wouldn't know unless she asked him a few interview-type questions.

She was honest with him. "With everything that has happened, we do have more customers. I don't know if we'll keep them, so I'm thinking about hiring more temporary help. But anybody who works here needs to be familiar with types of teas and how they're brewed. Granted, we can teach you what you need to know, but it's better if you have a basic foundation. Do you have any experience with tea?"

His smile was boyishly engaging. "You're thinking I'm one of those college kids who go to Starbucks and order a latté. Yeah, I do that sometimes. But my mom had a pure appreciation for tea. She had a whole cupboard designated just for it, everything from cans of tea to bags of loose tea to tea bags. She even had those little metal tea balls, infusers, and filters. I helped her make her tea since I was about ten."

"Do you drink tea?"

"I do now and then. I'm not a connoisseur, but I know the difference between white tea, black tea, and green tea. And tisanes too."

Again Tessa and Daisy exchanged a look. "Are you in school?" Daisy asked.

"I'm a sophomore at Millersville. Many of my classes are in the evening or online. I can even work your afternoon tea shift if you need help then. And I'd be available all day on Saturdays and Sundays."

His schedule sounded flexible to work around, and they really could use the help.

Foster gave her another ingratiating grin. "The

holidays will be coming up before you know it. I'm sure you'll need even more help then."

"Your hours could fluctuate," she warned him. "I might need you twenty hours one week and forty the next."

He shrugged. "I don't have any other commitments. Between school and this job, that would be it. I can be focused and single-minded when I need to be."

That brought her around to the necessary component of this interview. "Do you have a résumé and references?"

Foster pulled a thumb drive from his windbreaker pocket. "Here you go," he said. "Everything you need is on there. I gave you three references and their numbers, but if you need more, I have more."

"I'll examine the information tonight, and I'll be in touch with you, one way or the other."

"One way or the other?" he asked. "Jobs I've applied for and didn't get . . ." He trailed off. "Those employers never contact me."

"I'll let you know. I promise."

Foster took a look around the tea garden again, seeming to note the tables of men and women having conversations. He spotted the vintage china displayed on shelves on the walls. His gaze lingered on the knitted tea cozies that were handcrafted by residents of Willow Creek and were for sale.

"I know what happened here," he said, "and I don't care. I think it would be a great place to work."

Did her customers feel the same way he did? Or would the new customers come back a second or third time? She saw repeat faces, but it was hard to keep track.

"I'll be giving you a call, Foster. Thanks for dropping

in. How about a cup of tea before you go back out again? Pick your pleasure."

He looked delighted at the idea, and she had the feeling he didn't have extra money for baked goods or cups of tea. He checked the board with the specials.

"The pineapple ginger green tea sounds good."

"And I imagine you might like oatmeal cookies?" Daisy asked.

"Oh, I do."

"All right. Find a seat, and Tessa will serve you."

"Thank you, Mrs. Swanson."

As Foster seated himself at a table near the front window, Tessa said, "I'll brew his tea if you want to finish putting the produce away. Do you think he's a good candidate for help?"

"I'll know when I check his thumb drive and his references. He probably has teachers listed who can provide recommendations. They'll tell me the truth."

At least, she certainly hoped they would.

On Friday night, Daisy picked up takeout for dinner on the way home. She'd called Sarah Jane's and ordered turkey potpie and the shoofly pie Cade had mentioned. Sometimes she and her girls appreciated the expertise of local bakers.

As she and Jazzi sat at the kitchen island with glasses of apple cider to accompany their meal, Jazzi talked about her classes and friends. Daisy was about to broach the idea of making the video Jonas recommended when her landline rang. Pushing away from the island, she stood and crossed to the counter. She picked up the cordless phone. Caller ID told her it was her Aunt Iris calling. This evening, after dinner with Daisy's mom and dad, her aunt had intended to go back to her own place. Maybe she'd changed her mind.

"Aunt Iris. Are you back home?"

"Oh, Daisy. I don't know what to do." Her aunt's voice shook, and she sounded panicked.

"What's wrong?"

"My house was broken into. And not just broken into. It's been ransacked. I didn't know who to call. Can you come? I didn't call the police or do anything yet. I just don't know what to do."

"I'll be there as soon as I can. Lock your doors."

"Apparently that didn't do much good before," Iris said dryly.

As soon as Daisy ended the call, she said to Jazzi, "Aunt Iris's place has been broken into. I hate to take you with me because I don't know what I'll be walking into. On the other hand, I don't know if you should stay here alone either."

"Mom, I stay here alone a lot."

"Yes, but—"

"No buts. I'm fifteen. Our house has an alarm."

"I don't know, Jazzi. I don't like everything that's been going on."

"Mom, somebody murdered Harvey Fitz. They didn't want to hurt *you*."

"But they might want to hurt your Aunt Iris. What if she'd been at home?"

"Go help her. I'll set the alarm. I promise. I'll keep my cell phone right beside me. Pepper and Marjoram will be here too. I'll be fine." Pepper suddenly appeared and brushed against Jazzi's foot with a soft meow as if agreeing to be a guard cat.

"You've got to start treating me like an adult," her younger daughter insisted. "There are kids my age who are out on the street fending for themselves—"

Daisy held up her hand. "All right. You've convinced me. I might bring Aunt Iris back here with me."

"That's fine. Go help her."

So Daisy did. The thing was, however, she didn't know what help she was going to be.

Ten minutes later, she parked her PT Cruiser at the curb in front of Iris's house. It was a charming little stone bungalow with about a thousand square feet of living space. It was located in an older section of town on a street with mature trees, other bungalows, ranch houses, and modest two-story homes. The single-car garage was located on the west side. A gable with a tall Palladian window was located on the east. Iris particularly gushed over the pretty oval window with stained glass that decorated the entrance, along with two white pillars and a gabled overhang.

Iris opened the door as soon as Daisy rang the bell. Her face was red, which meant her blood pressure was up.

"You just won't believe this," she said, "You won't."

Daisy walked into the foyer onto its ceramic tile floor. A doorway on the left led to the garage. She walked straight in, crossing in front of another door that led to the basement.

"Just look at this mess," Iris said, waving to the master bedroom located on the right and the living room that was straight ahead.

The place *was* a disaster. When Daisy peeked into the bedroom, with its pretty lilac bedspread and curtains, she saw the dresser drawers all pulled out and dumped. The mattress had been slid to one side, and the bedroom chair cushion had been sliced open.

In the living room, the disarray was worse. Her aunt's sofa cushions in a pretty green and yellow leaf pattern had been sliced open. Everything on the shelf under the coffee table had been swiped to the floor, and one of Iris's crystal vases had been broken. Books had been tossed off the bookshelf, and photo frames lay flat and crooked on the bookshelves. Fortunately, the lamps hadn't been touched, and none were broken. But peering into the small dining room, Daisy could see the doors to the hutch standing open and shards of broken cups inside. The kitchen was small, only about eight by twelve. Even there, all the cupboard doors hung open. Food and glassware had been tossed out. The same with the pantry closet beside the refrigerator. The second bedroom near the kitchen had seen the same angry ransacking.

"Someone even looked through my medicine cabinet," Iris exclaimed with outrage. "All my medication bottles are on the floor."

"Don't touch anything. I'm going to call Jonas and then Detective Rappaport."

"You're going to call Jonas?"

"He told me to call him if I needed him, and I can certainly use his cop's eye."

Iris looked at all of it, and tears came to her eyes. She began to cry.

Daisy put her arms around her and gave her a huge hug. "It's going to be okay. I'll help you clear all this up. We'll put everything back the way it was."

"We can't, Daisy. Some of those cups and saucers were irreplaceable. Oh, sure, I can get a new sofa, but am I ever going to be able to forget what this looked like?"

Daisy patted her aunt's back. "Let me call Jonas and the detective, and we'll go from there.

Iris had collapsed into one of the dining room chairs when Jonas arrived barely ten minutes after Daisy's call. He gave a low whistle as he came inside.

"Someone was looking for something, and they got really angry when they couldn't find it."

"But I don't *have* anything," Iris said.

The words were barely out of her mouth when Detective Rappaport was at the door. They'd left it open, and he walked right in.

"You're *all* contaminating this crime scene."

"He's right," Jonas said. "If he wants to call in the forensics team, our hair, fibers, and DNA could be here too."

"We didn't touch anything," Daisy told the detective, almost defensively. And my fingerprints and DNA are everywhere because I come here often." She really didn't like his attitude.

"Great to know," the detective said. "But you'd better step outside.

"Shouldn't my aunt look around and see if anything's missing?"

"I imagine you've already done that since you were here before me. Or—" He gave his pause emphasis with arched fuzzy brows.

"Or?" Jonas asked.

"Or . . . Miss Albright could have done this herself."

Chapter Thirteen

At Detective Rappaport's preposterous accusation, Daisy felt her blood boil. She was going to make this detective see reason, no matter what she had to do.

Despite contaminating the crime scene, she stepped into the kitchen and picked up a chunk of porcelain that had once been her aunt's favorite teapot.

"Look at this, Detective," she ordered, waving it in front of his nose. "This is one of my aunt's favorite teapots, handed down to her by her mother. Do you really think she would do this?"

He gave a shrug that was supposed to be nonchalant. "Persons of interest do unbelievable things to escape a murder charge."

Jonas placed a hand on Daisy's shoulder. She supposed he did it to keep her from erupting. In a gentle voice, he advised, "Why don't you and your aunt step outside. Let me talk to the detective."

Detective Rappaport was looking around now. Before Daisy took a broom from the broom closet and swatted him with it, she decided Jonas's suggestion was best.

She tugged on her aunt's elbow. "Come on. Let's wait on the porch."

What she wanted to do was eavesdrop. Instead, she and Iris exited the house and stood on the porch. Not long after, a patrol car pulled into the driveway. Two officers climbed from the vehicle, nodded to Daisy and Iris, and went inside.

Jonas came out. "I tried to talk sense into him," he said.

"You mean telling him that Iris isn't guilty?"

Jonas frowned. "No. That would just make him even more determined to prove she is. I suggested other possibilities. They have to decide where the point of entry was, if the lock was jimmied, or if possibly someone could have crawled in a basement window, maybe in the back."

The detective suddenly appeared on the porch. Hearing what Jonas said, he addressed the women. "I called in our evidence tech." He focused on Iris. "You, of course, can't stay here tonight."

"I wouldn't want to," she said.

"Did you have anything of Harvey Fitz's in your bungalow?" he asked brusquely.

"No, I didn't."

"Was Mr. Fitz ever *inside* your bungalow?"

Her aunt's face reddened. "A few times."

"He didn't leave any belongings here?"

"No, of course not. We were dating, not sleeping together."

Daisy had never seen her aunt so outraged, and she felt sorry for her.

"Miss Albright, you must realize I need to ask you these questions. If Mr. Fitz didn't leave any of his belongings here, if you weren't keeping anything for him, then how would anyone get the idea that you had something that they might want?"

"If I knew that, Detective, we all wouldn't be standing here like this," her aunt shot back.

Jonas, in a voice filled with reason, interjected, "Iris, I know you and Harvey were just dating. But outside perceptions of that might be different. Someone could think your relationship was different than it was, without old-fashioned values. If Harvey told anyone he intended to marry you, an outsider could think he was sleeping here or dividing his time between your house and his condo. Isn't that possible?"

Iris looked deflated when she realized that was entirely possible. She said, "I suppose you're right."

Detective Rappaport gave Jonas an odd look as if he respected his skills but didn't appreciate having his interview hijacked. He said to them, "Mrs. Swanson, Miss Albright, I have your fingerprints in the AFIS database. As I said, I'll send out my tech and see what we can find. I'll give you a call when they're finished."

Daisy felt dismissed, and she hated feeling dismissed. Jonas must have seen that in her expression because he offered, "Why don't I go back to your place with you? We can talk about this, maybe come up with ideas and information that could help the detective. What do you think?"

Though Daisy was feeling a little "handled" by Jonas, she knew she probably needed handling right now or she'd say something she shouldn't or encourage Iris to say something she shouldn't. They were both tired and upset and didn't like Detective Rappaport.

She gave Jonas an "I know what you're doing" look, but she said, "That's a good idea. Aunt Iris, you can stay with me tonight. Let's go back to the house and talk about all this. Jonas might be able to give us perspective that we can't gain on our own."

And that's how the three of them ended up on the stoop of Daisy's house. She'd called Jazzi to tell her they were coming.

Jazzi opened the door to them, and after they'd stepped inside, she gave her Aunt Iris a hug. "I'm so sorry all this is happening to you."

"I am too, sweetie," Iris said. "I just wish I knew why."

"We're going to talk about it and try to figure it out," Jonas told Jazzi.

Pepper came to the top of the steps and meowed at them all.

"I promised her I'd give her and Marjoram treats," Jazzi said. "I'd better go do that."

Daisy was just as glad to see Jazzi climb the stairs to her bedroom. She wanted her daughter to be far away from anything connected with this murder.

As soon as Jazzi was at the top of the stairs and picked up Pepper, Iris asked, "Any progress finding her birth parents?"

"Not yet. But Jonas is helping."

Jonas was looking around the living room and peered into the kitchen. "This house is really neat. It was an old barn?"

Daisy nodded. "I saw it and the possibilities."

Iris said, "I need tea while we talk. I'll make it." When Daisy started after her, she said, "No, stay and talk to Jonas. I can certainly brew tea on my own, and I know where you keep yours."

As she went into the kitchen, Jonas continued to study the walls, the chandelier, the way Daisy had decorated the space.

She motioned to the sofa, and they both went there to sit.

"Did you furnish and decorate this yourself?" he asked.

"I did, with Jazzi and Vi's help. We wanted it to be our taste. Ryan's insurance money enabled me to come back here and make a brand-new start. I'm so grateful for that."

After a moment's hesitation, as if he was debating with himself, he asked, "Do you have good memories from your marriage?"

"I do," she answered, leaning back into the sofa, becoming more comfortable. "No marriage is perfect. Ryan and I had bumps, like every married couple does. But somehow we always managed to work through them. Sometimes I wondered if we did it for the girls' sake more than we did it for ours. We didn't want them living with tension. We wanted them to have a solid understanding of what a relationship should be."

Jonas got a faraway look in his eyes, and Daisy could see he was remembering something too. She wondered what or who. Nothing ventured, nothing gained. "Do you mind if I ask you a personal question?"

"I don't mind, but I reserve the right to give you a yes or no answer."

"You sound more like a lawyer than a former cop," she said dryly.

"Some of the same qualities are necessary for both."

"Can you tell me why you left the police force?"

With his silence, Jonas communicated that this wasn't a question he answered lightly or often. Finally, he revealed, "My partner and I received a notice that a witness in a murder investigation had been found. We were sent to question him. Long story short, the witness shot and killed my partner and injured me."

Daisy couldn't help but reach out and touch his arm. "I'm so sorry."

He didn't shrug or brush off her condolences, like many men might have. He just looked her straight in the eye, and she could see the pain his history had caused him. She sensed there was so much more to his story than what he'd just told her. But his story was his to tell. If in time they became closer friends, maybe he'd reveal more.

The teakettle whistled. That whistle was like a signal, a signal to think about what was happening between her and Jonas. They were sitting close on that sofa, her leg against his. They were looking at each other as if . . . as if they had more on their minds than past history.

Without warning, Jonas reached up and touched Daisy's face. He simply said, "Memories are hard to handle sometimes, aren't they?"

She found her mouth was dry, and she couldn't speak. She nodded. They seemed to sit there suspended in time as his fingers brushed her cheek, as she breathed in the scent of his soap, noticed the beard stubble on his jaw, wondered how soft his hair was. She suddenly imagined herself running her fingers through it.

No! Those feelings didn't belong in this conversation. They didn't go with the memories of Ryan and the life they'd shared together. Those feelings didn't go with raising two teenage girls without their father, running her tea garden, and organizing her life.

Iris called from the kitchen, "Oatmeal cookies with the tea or lemon tea cakes?"

"Up to you," Daisy called back, knowing what her aunt would pick. Iris would choose lemon tea cakes because those had been Harvey's favorite.

Daisy shifted a bit so she and Jonas weren't so close as Iris set the tea tray on the coffee table. She'd used one of Daisy's favorite enamel teapots with pretty blue and silver flowered cups and saucers. She'd arranged the cookies on a plate to match.

Jonas cleared his throat and studied the tray. "You ladies know how to serve a snack."

"I learned from my mom and Aunt Iris," Daisy said.

"Those lemon tea cakes are fabulous. I can see why they were Harvey's favorite," Jonas remarked, as if it were the most natural thing in the world to do.

Iris ducked her head for a moment. "He surely did like them."

"Have you thought more about what the intruder might have wanted at your bungalow?"

"I've thought and thought and thought, and I just can't imagine what it would have been."

"From the places he or she looked and the way he or she looked, I'd say whoever it was was searching for something small—a key, maybe. A gem. A piece of jewelry. It had to be small enough to hide in a cushion or a drawer," Jonas noted.

Daisy hadn't thought about that. She'd just seen all the damage.

"Like an engagement ring?" she asked.

"Possibly."

He studied Iris. "Was Harvey ever in your bungalow alone so that he could have hidden something without you knowing it?"

Iris's face showed pure concentration. She finally responded, "He was certainly in a room alone, like if I went to the kitchen to make tea or if I went into the bedroom to change." Her face reddened. "I don't mean anything intimate by that, I just mean after work

I liked to get into something more comfortable than the clothes I'd worn all day to serve."

Daisy gave her a gentle smile. "We understand, Aunt Iris. Really we do."

"I don't think that detective believed me," Iris said dejectedly.

"So Harvey *could* have hidden something." Jonas got the conversation back on track.

"I suppose he could have."

"The question is," Daisy interrupted, "did the intruder find what he or she was looking for?"

Jonas shook his head and picked up one of the lemon tea cakes. "Isn't that the million-dollar question?"

Chapter Fourteen

Saturdays in October were busy tourist days at the tea garden. Fall in Pennsylvania was a beautiful time with the leaves turning. Tour buses that stopped in historic Gettysburg also came through Lancaster County. They would park in Willow Creek's public lot, and sightseers would stroll up and down the streets, stopping in at the shops. Many came to the tea garden for refreshment or to give their feet a rest.

One busload had come and gone, and Daisy believed they'd handled the service fairly well. However, a group of senior couples came in immediately afterward. There were eight in all. Apparently, they'd driven down from Carlisle for the day—at least that's what one of the women had told Daisy when she'd placed her order.

Tessa brewed the tea, and Eva readied the individual orders, while Cora Sue handled sales at the counter. Iris carried tea and baked goods to the tables and served each person. But unlike her usual precise attention to detail, she somehow mixed up the orders. Not just two of them, but four or five. They were all scrambled. The next thing Daisy knew, a cup of tea had spilled at that table, and their customer looked horrified as she dabbed at her skirt.

"If this is the kind of service we're going to get, we might as well go to the donut shop up the road," a matronly woman with a white hair-sprayed hairdo grumbled.

"Or the fast-food place at the edge of town," the man with her added.

Iris was red-faced, looking ashamed, trying to clean up the mess and straighten out the orders. Daisy felt sorry for her aunt, who'd gone through so much lately. Because of all the stress, Iris just wasn't thinking as straight as she usually did, and Daisy knew what she had to do.

She plucked out coupons she kept under the counter for just this purpose and went over to the table. The woman who'd had tea spilled on her glared at her. "Are you the manager?"

"My aunt and I are the owners. This is my aunt, Iris Albright, and my name is Daisy Swanson. I'm sorry there's been a spill and mix-up here." She handed each person at the table a coupon. "The next time you're in the area and stop in, you can use that for a free service of tea. But, right now, I want to make sure you all have what you want. Let me go through your orders again, and I'll even add a free scone for each of you to make up for what happened here. If you send me the bill for your skirt, I'd be glad to pay for the dry cleaning."

With Daisy's apologizing manner and her determination to make her customers happy, all the bluster went out of the woman. She stopped dabbing at her skirt and laid the napkin on the table. "We certainly can't complain about any of that. Can we take the scones along? We can nibble on them later."

"Of course, you can. How about chocolate raspberry scones?"

"They sound delicious," one of the women said.

Iris had retreated to the office, and that wasn't like her either. Normally she would have helped Daisy straighten everything out.

After Daisy went to the baked goods counter for the scones and took them to the table, she also made sure her customers had refills on their tea and were happily sipping, drinking, and chatting by the time she went back to the kitchen.

When Daisy saw Tessa had moved to the counter in case anyone new came in, she knew Tessa was sensitive to the situation and realized Daisy needed to talk to her aunt privately. Her aunt was standing by the office window, peering out. Daisy doubted she was seeing anything out there.

"I'm sorry," her aunt said when Daisy entered the office.

Daisy went over to the window with her aunt, her elbow touching Iris's. "There's nothing to be sorry for. Anyone can mix up an order."

"But I don't usually do that. I'm just not . . . myself."

"Of course, you're not. You lost a man who was soon to be your fiancé. The police have been grilling you, and they even accused you of messing up your own place. Who would be themselves? I think you should take a few days off."

"I wouldn't know what to do with myself with that messed-up bungalow, or even at your mother's, if I stayed there. This is a busy time of year for them with the holidays coming—garlands and hay bales, Halloween and Thanksgiving decorations, trees to plant before winter sets in. I'd just be in the way.

Besides, with the extra customers, you need my help here."

"I always need your help. But I think I found someone to hire. His references panned out. He could cover for you while you're gone. I can take over the baking or just buy apple streusels from Emma Stoltz this week. This time of year, apple is a favorite anyway."

Iris seemed to consider what she'd said. "When do you think this person can start?"

"I have his phone number. Let me give him a call. Maybe he can even come in this afternoon, and we can see how he works out. Then you can take the next few days off."

Iris blew out a big breath. "Call him, but I only need a day. I'll go out driving tomorrow, maybe up to Caledonia to see the leaves turning. But if this person you want to hire is busy, can't come in, or doesn't work out, I'll get my head on straight. I promise."

Daisy knew her aunt composing herself wasn't a matter of determination. It might be a matter of time. She went to the desk and picked up the phone to call Foster.

When Foster arrived promptly at three, he was dressed in black slacks and a white shirt. That was perfect, as far as Daisy was concerned. He'd passed the wardrobe test, and now onto others.

He immediately came to Daisy and said, "I understand this is a test run. What would you like me to do first?"

Eagerness would chalk up points for him too.

"Let's meet the rest of the staff, and then you can brew us a cup of tea."

When Daisy introduced Foster to Aunt Iris, he

shook her hand. "I hope to learn from you. Running a business, any business, isn't easy."

Iris smiled at him, and Daisy could tell her aunt already liked him.

"You'll see every aspect of business while you're here, if you last," Daisy assured him. "You'll watch us buy from distributers and tea suppliers and learn the nuts and bolts of serving the public. I hope you're ready for that because sometimes they're as hard to handle as two-year-olds."

Foster smiled. "I have a younger brother and sister, so I can certainly relate to that. I also know that people don't like to feel they're being handled, so I try not to do that."

Daisy herself hated to be "handled" and knew he was right. Whenever she went into an establishment and felt she was being manipulated or sold a bill of goods she didn't want, she simply wanted to leave.

Tessa was working in the kitchen with Eva. When Daisy introduced Foster to them, Tessa's hands were wrist-deep in dough for scones.

He said, "It's good to meet you both. Those look like cinnamon scones."

Tessa's brows arched. "At least you know one of your spices."

His face reddened a little. "I hope I know more than one, but cinnamon is my favorite. It reminds me of Mom baking Christmas cookies."

"So your mom bakes?" Daisy asked.

"We lost her two years ago," Foster explained, sadness in his eyes. "She caught a virus, and it went to her heart."

"I'm so sorry, Foster," Daisy said immediately. Tessa, Eva, and Iris said the same.

Afterward, never one to stand on formality or to hold back, Tessa asked, "How's your dad coping?"

Foster shrugged. "He's doing okay. He never complains. Sometimes I wish he would. I think he holds it all inside. I don't want him to have a heart attack or something."

"It's hard to lose a life partner or a parent," Daisy empathized. "When my husband died, I didn't know how I was going to raise my two girls. But, somehow, that parental love kicks in and shows you the way. Children can be a lifeline."

"I think that's what we are for Dad," Foster said. He shook his head. "I don't know why I told you all that. I don't usually talk about it."

"Like your dad?" Tessa asked. "The strong silent type?"

"Touché," Foster said. "Now show me where your tea is. What kind do you want me to brew?"

"How about black tea?" Daisy suggested and showed him the tea cupboard.

He whistled low. "Wow, you do have teas."

Daisy showed him the shelf with the black tea and where the bags and labels were located for those customers who wanted to buy loose tea. Foster took a canister of black tea and went to the kitchen counter. Teapots were lined up on shelves along one wall. He chose one that would brew six cups, and Daisy was impressed. Not just anybody knew a two-cup from a six-cup pot.

Aunt Iris went to the counter as the bell above the door rang and she had customers to help. Foster scooped tea into the infuser—just the right amount, Daisy noted. Then he let the hot water from the urn gently wash over the tea into the pot. After he was finished, he set it on the counter and set the nearby timer for five minutes. He nodded to the scones that Tessa was cutting into sections.

"I'm not much of a baker, but Franco's Pizza is on my résumé. I learned to toss a good one, so I could probably learn whatever you want to teach me about scones too."

"I think you're angling for more than a service position," Daisy teased.

"I'm taking business courses at college. Who knows, you might want to hire me to do your books or manage your supplies or something other than service. In two years when I graduate, I want to be ready for the business world."

Daisy imagined he would be.

Still waiting for the timer to go off, he asked Daisy, "Have you ventured into social media?"

"I tweet, but I really don't know what I'm doing. I've been at it about six months and only have two hundred followers."

"I bet I could get you more followers. What else are you doing?"

"Tessa set up a website for us, but we didn't get a whole lot of traffic until . . . lately."

"Do you check it daily and respond to comments?"

"I don't pay much attention to it," Daisy admitted.

"We can bring it up and see what's happening while you sip a cup of tea. You really ought to have a page on Trends."

"Trends?" Tessa asked, her brows raised.

"Yeah. It's a whole new social network. It's not just for chatting and telling what you had for supper or posting a picture of it. There are groups for businesses and how to make them popular. Tea is really on an upswing. Set up a page on Trends. You'll have more customers, more discussions, more visits to your website."

"Is it hard to do?" Daisy asked.

"I know how to do it," Foster said with a sly smile.

She shook her finger at him. "You *are* angling for more than a service position."

When Foster pronounced the tea perfectly brewed, he asked how each of them wanted it. Tessa took a little milk for herself, and Daisy added a dab of honey. Aunt Iris liked a touch of lemon, and Eva took hers straight.

After their first sips, they all nodded at Foster.

"You passed," Daisy said. "If you can carry a tray with two teapots and six cups and saucers, you're hired," she proclaimed with a grin. Then she looked at her aunt. "And you can take a vacation."

"I'll drive to Caledonia tomorrow. Are you sure you don't mind working on Sunday? That's your usual day off."

Daisy liked to spend the day going to church, then making brunch for Jazzi and hanging out with her. But she knew her aunt needed this day off. "I don't mind."

An influx of customers suddenly swept into the store. That's the way it went sometimes.

Foster settled right in, coordinating with Tessa and Eva and serving with Aunt Iris. Daisy and Cora Sue took orders at the counter and passed them along to Tessa. They all worked together well, as if they'd been doing it for a long time.

It was almost closing time when Foster took out his phone and studied something on the screen. Daisy had gone to the refrigerator to check on the supplies for the next day.

He brought his phone to her. "I want you to see something."

When Daisy glanced at his phone, she noticed he'd brought up the tea garden website. "There are comments from this week," he said. "You ought to read them."

To Daisy's surprise, few of the comments had to do with what had happened there, the sensationalism about it, or the reporters being present. The comments were mostly about slow service.

"This isn't good," she murmured. "A tea garden has to be a haven, a place for discussion, a place of comfort. Customers can't be comfortable if they're disgruntled because they have to wait for service."

"You ought to tell them that. You should comment there too."

"How honest should I be?"

"Just be positive. Tell them you're getting more help, and they should come in and try you again."

"All right. I'll do that now. Thanks, Foster. Let me know if you find anybody else who wants a part-time position. But they have to be as motivated as you."

"I'll check around," he said. "I can always put a notice up on the bulletin board at the Student Memorial Center."

Daisy considered where else she could get help. "I often buy supplies from a farmers market. Some of the stand owners might know of someone who wants to work part-time too."

"This all happened fast didn't it . . . with Mr. Fitz's murder," Foster said.

"Yes, it did. I never expected business to boom because of something like this."

"Something good from something bad. My brother and sister and I are closer since Mom died. That's one good thing that came from something bad. You have to look really hard sometimes, but if you do, you can find it."

Daisy liked Foster. She liked him a lot. She hoped his association with the tea garden would be good for everyone.

The following day, Daisy missed her aunt at the tea garden, but she had to admit, Foster did a terrific job. He knew how to serve. He knew how to brew tea. He knew how to make the customers feel comfortable. She couldn't have asked for more. He was definitely a keeper, and she'd be willing to work around his schedule at school. He had done so well today that soon she might put him in charge of the afternoon tea sit-down service. She was seriously thinking about paying his hourly wage for off-site work too—setting up a page on Trends, for example, and monitoring it. That and the comments on the website. If he could do that, his help would take a burden from her. With the increased customer base, she could afford to pay him.

A little worrisome voice in her head reminded her—*that's if you keep growing your customer base.*

So true, she reflected.

Jazzi had decided to come in with her today to help, and she seemed to like Foster too. Win-win all around. Jazzi's attitude had improved a hundredfold since she'd revealed the search for her birth parents. Daisy just hoped Jonas was getting somewhere.

At five o'clock, Foster had left for the day, and Tessa was on her way out when Daisy's phone in her pocket played. Seeing her Aunt Iris's ID, she answered the call. "How was your day?"

"The leaves were beautiful on the drive up to Caledonia, and I think the day away really helped. But now—"

"Now what?"

"Detective Rappaport called me this morning to tell me I can go back to my house. They finished there. So I came home to this mess I need to straighten up. Do you and Jazzi want to come over? We can order a pizza."

Daisy called to Jazzi, who was wiping down the counters in the kitchen. "How about pizza for supper over at Aunt Iris's?"

"That's okay with me."

After telling her aunt they'd be over shortly, she ended the call. She also grabbed a container of a cleaner that could help wipe up fingerprint dust. The service had left it when they'd finished cleaning up the tea garden.

When Daisy and Jazzi arrived at her aunt's, they went inside. Daisy saw that Iris had made a little headway. Even though the sofa cushions were ripped open, she'd put them back on the sofa and laid a crocheted afghan on top to hide the torn fabric. She'd been working on placing books back on the bookshelves when they arrived. But there was a mess with rags and fingerprint dust.

"I'm not sure what to keep and what to throw away," Iris said, shaking her head. "I'm going to have to get a new sofa for sure, and possibly a recliner too. Look at that tear in the seat and in the back."

Daisy took off her sweater coat and opened the door to the small closet just inside the door. But there she noticed all Iris's coats were on the floor, the pockets turned inside out.

"I can hang those back up," Jazzi said.

They worked for an hour, straightening, replacing,

wiping, washing, and sympathizing. Finally, Jazzi said, "I'm starved, Mom. Can we order that pizza?"

"Sure, honey. The number's on the fridge. Do you want to call?"

"Half plain and half with pepperoni?" she asked the two older women.

"Yep," Daisy said. "No broccoli tonight."

"Get an order of wings too," her aunt said. "We'll really live it up."

Daisy laughed, and it felt good to do it. It had been a long, tough week.

Iris glanced around the living room, which was beginning to resemble its former orderliness. "Franco's usually delivers promptly. Why don't I brew tea to go with the pizza?"

After Jazzi placed the call to Franco's, she wandered over to Aunt Iris's bookshelves and pulled down a volume.

"You have three Nancy Drew mysteries here that look really old. Are they first editions?"

"I bought them with my own money when they came out. I waited with bated breath at the department store, eager for the next volume, sort of like the way you waited for the next Harry Potter. What kind of tea would you like, honey?"

"I don't care," Jazzi said with a shrug.

"I can't stop thinking about Harvey," Iris said as she opened a top cupboard door.

Daisy had been in charge of the kitchen, and she'd replaced the tea tins and coffee mugs back in the cupboard. Now her aunt took out the tea tin that Harvey had given her with its painted sunflower lid and its perky yellow bow.

"Instead of trying to forget, maybe I should remember," she decided. "How about if we all have cups of white tea in tribute to Harvey."

"I think that's a great idea, Aunt Iris," Jazzi encouraged her. "After Dad died, I used to go into his and Mom's room and just pick up the things he'd left on the dresser. Somehow, I felt closer to him. Maybe you'll feel that way when you drink the tea."

Daisy was so proud of her daughter. She herself didn't realize Jazzi's depths. She'd never known about her daughter's excursions into her bedroom. And if she had—maybe they would have talked and hugged more. Maybe she wouldn't have felt Jazzi begin to pull away. But she couldn't redo the past. All she could do was stay connected to Jazzi now and in the future.

Since Aunt Iris was a tea aficionado, she'd had a filtering system put on the municipal water faucets in her house. So Daisy was able to fill the teakettle with that water and put it on the stove to heat. In the meantime, Aunt Iris pulled down one of her teapots that hadn't been broken in the ransacking. It was red with a white polka dot design.

"Harvey liked this one," she said. "It feels right to use it."

Setting the teapot in the center of the table, she found the metal infuser and set it inside the rim. Then she brought over the tin of tea and a measuring spoon and sat at the table.

Daisy could see how sad her aunt felt . . . how much she wished everything was different, how she wished she could rewind time. But no one could. Daisy could remember the day exactly when Harvey had given her aunt the tea tin. Her aunt had been so happy.

Now she watched Iris pull on the bow and open it.

It had kept the lid secure, so even in the ransacking, no tea had spilled out.

The lid fit tightly on the tea tin and Iris spent a minute or two working it free. After she did, she took her teaspoon and dug it into the loose tea. She needed six full teaspoons to make the white, mild tea full-bodied. This was White Symphony, the lightest of the white teas. It had a wonderful taste without honey, sugar, or milk. Even Aunt Iris didn't add lemon to this one.

Her aunt scooped out three spoonfuls and let the tea sift into the infuser. Then she went back for another spoonful. But when she did, her spoon clanked against something.

Daisy heard it too. "Was that the side of the tin?"

"No, it wasn't. I scooped from the middle." She stirred the tea around and clanked against something again. Dipping her fingers into the tin, she pulled out what looked like a gold coin. "What's this doing in here? Do you think Harvey knew it was there?" Iris asked.

"He gave you this tin. He *must* have known." Daisy took the coin in her hand and turned it over, studying it. "It looks like gold, Aunt Iris. I'm not sure what happens next, but I think maybe we should call Marshall and ask him what to do," Daisy advised her as she carefully set the coin on a dish on the table.

None of them wanted to make a misstep with the murder investigation going on and Detective Rappaport suspecting her and her aunt. So Daisy dialed Marshall's number. Unfortunately, she reached his voice mail.

She shook her head at Iris and Jazzi. "We're going to have to wait until he calls back to know what to do."

"We might have to wait," Jazzi said, "but we can google the coin and maybe find out exactly what it is."

Leave it to Jazzi to find a solution using the tech age. Of course, they should google it.

"Search *woman's profile on gold coin?*" Daisy asked.

Jazzi grinned at her. "You're learning, Mom."

All three women sat at the table in the dining room. Iris just stared at the gold coin while Jazzi and Daisy hunched over their smartphones.

"I found it, Mom," Jazzi suddenly said. "At least I think I did. Look."

The women crowded around Jazzi's phone. The photo she found indeed did look like the coin lying on the table. The headline read—*Rare four-dollar gold coin worth over a million dollars.*

"A million dollars," Iris exclaimed. "They can't be serious. That can't be what we found."

"It looks like it, Aunt Iris." Jazzi pointed to every detail of the coin; they were all the same on the photo and on the round dish on the table. "This says it's a four dollar, Coiled Hair Stella gold coin from eighteen eighty. It's six grams of gold and was never released to the public."

Daisy took Jazzi's phone to study the article. She summed it up for Iris. "Apparently the coin had been designed to match money from countries like France and Switzerland, but it never received official support. It became a political issue, and extremely rare. Only ten or twelve were known to be in public institutions or private collections."

"Wow," Aunt Iris said, disbelievingly.

Daisy's phone sounded, and she quickly picked it up. "Marshall, you won't believe what we found." She went on to tell him.

"A million dollars, you say?" Marshall's tone was thoughtful. "Whether the coin is worth that or not, it could be evidence. Call Detective Rappaport at once. Leave a message if you can't reach him. I don't want the detective to think we're hiding anything from him. Don't handle the coin again."

Rappaport wasn't at the police station, though Daisy did leave a message on his voice mail telling him exactly what she wanted. She gave him details of how they'd found the coin and described it.

After she ended the call, pizza arrived. Without disturbing the coin sitting on the table, they ate their pizza in the living room, not talking much, just thinking about that million-dollar piece of gold not so far away.

Iris didn't know whether to brew the white tea or not, so she let the tin sit too. They made do with soda with their pizza and wings. All three were about halfway through when the doorbell rang.

Iris went to open it and found Detective Rappaport standing there.

"Mrs. Swanson left a message for me," he said.

"I didn't think you'd be over tonight." Iris stepped back so he could enter.

"This is a murder investigation, Miss Albright. I don't waste time. I hope you're not wasting my time right now. Let me see what you found."

"Good evening to you too," Daisy said sweetly as she joined her aunt, and they all went to the table.

Rappaport scowled at her, maybe not liking the idea she'd called his manners into question. He took a plastic evidence bag from his pocket and a set of tweezers. Using the tweezers, he pushed the coin around on the dish, then flipped it, studying it hard.

"Iris took it out of the tea tin Harvey gave her. I can show you what I found on the Internet about it."

"I already looked it up. I'll have to verify if it's authentic. You're not to tell anyone about this, not anyone. Do you understand?"

"Marshall knows," Daisy quickly told him. "I called him first to see what we should do."

"Marshall Thompson knows how to keep his mouth shut."

"Can I tell Jonas?" Daisy asked.

Rappaport gave her a hard look. He thought about it and then he sighed. "Jonas Groft knows not to let information out too. All right, but no one else." He studied Iris. "How long have you had this?"

"Harvey gave it to me the day of his twenty-fifth anniversary celebration. He said we'd brew the white tea together on the day his divorce was final."

It passed through Daisy's mind that Marshall was going to think Iris was giving the detective too much information, but it was too late now.

"And you hadn't opened the tin since then?"

"No, sir," Iris said with certainty. "After Harvey died, I didn't know if I was ever going to open it."

"So what made you open it tonight?"

"My place was a mess, and we cleaned up. We were just going to drink the tea in tribute to Harvey."

The detective studied the three women, the teapot sitting on the counter, the teakettle on the stove burner. He must have remembered what the place had looked like the day before.

He'd been taking notes in his notebook. Now he snapped it shut. "I'll have to take the tin of tea along too."

"That doesn't surprise me," Aunt Iris murmured.

"Take whatever you have to, Detective, but I would like you to return it to me if at all possible."

"If it's true Harvey gave you the coin before he died, then it's yours. I have to wonder why he did that. Or maybe he was going to retrieve it after the two of you opened the tin of tea. Then he wouldn't have to make it a matter in his divorce settlement. It would be a great way to hide an asset and cash in on it later. Did you say the two of you were planning a trip?"

"I did not, Detective. Harvey and I hadn't planned anything."

"Except hiding a million-dollar gold coin," Rappaport mumbled.

Daisy knew this turn of events had just dipped her aunt into deeper water. What had Harvey Fitz been thinking?

Chapter Fifteen

The next morning, Daisy set off for the tea garden early because she wanted to stop in at Jonas's shop and tell him what she and Iris had found. His establishment wasn't open yet, but she saw him moving around inside, placing a new chair at one of the tables. She rapped on the front door.

When Jonas came to the door, he peered out, saw her, and smiled. Then he unlocked the door and let her in. "You're early this morning."

"I wanted to talk to you. Is anyone else here?"

"Dave doesn't come in until a minute before the dot of nine. What did you want to see me about?"

When she gazed into his green eyes, she almost forgot. But then she found her composure again. "I was helping Aunt Iris put her place back in order last night. We decided to have a cup of tea."

"Needed a boost to finish?" he asked.

"Something like that. But we decided to use the White Symphony tea in the can of tea that Harvey had given Aunt Iris. We were going to have a tribute to him."

Jonas nodded. "Understandable. Your aunt has

been so caught up in the investigation. She hasn't had time to grieve."

Daisy nodded. "Exactly. So we were going to drink tea and talk about Harvey. But as Aunt Iris scooped out the tea, we found a gold coin, and we looked it up on the Internet. We discovered it's supposed to be worth over a million dollars!"

Jonas gave a low whistle. "I hope you called Marshall and Rappaport."

"We did. Rappaport suggested Aunt Iris may have hidden it there herself. Honestly, I just want to sock him sometimes."

"Not a great idea," Jonas advised her. "Do you think Harvey was hiding his asset from his wife? Is that why he wanted to share the tea with Iris when his divorce was final, so he could get it back? With or without your aunt knowing?"

"Any of those scenarios are possible," she agreed. "Was Harvey that conniving?"

"Anyone as successful as he was had to be a bit conniving, maybe a little ruthless too. When it comes to divorce, the parties involved can be bitter, revengeful, and greedy."

"How do you know this?" Maybe Jonas had been divorced.

"Not from personal experience, if that's what you're thinking. But in police work we see it all—murder, theft, assault, and all the reasons that go with them. When you think about how much planning goes into a divorce, how much analyzing, how much the lawyers cost, it's only natural each party wants to keep as much as they possibly can. Sometimes they find unlawful ways to do that."

Daisy shook her head, imagining the bitterness and

regrets between two people who no longer wanted to be married.

"Let's go over the suspects for Harvey's murder," Jonas suggested. "If Harvey's son knew about that coin, and he might have seen it as a kid going through the coins, maybe he found out it wasn't appraised with the rest of the collection. Maybe he somehow knew his dad had hidden that asset. Maybe he was drunk and so angry about his father's new life that he killed him in a rage."

"Daniel is one suspect. Then there's Harvey's wife," Daisy offered. "If she knew Harvey was trying to cheat her, maybe she was determined she wouldn't let him. If she knew about the coin, and that it was hidden somewhere, she might have badgered him about it. If he wouldn't tell her what she wanted to know, she could have murdered him in a rage."

"She could have," Jonas added, "and then ransacked your aunt's bungalow. It doesn't take a man to do that."

"What about Guy Tremont?" Daisy asked. "The coin dealer. Could he have had a stake in that coin somehow? Maybe the coin had nothing to do with the murder. What if Guy found out that Harvey gave Iris the coin to hold for him. But he hadn't known how Harvey packaged it. It was only luck that the tin had fallen sideways on the back of the shelf and the intruder missed it. Or else he saw the pretty bow and just didn't imagine the coin would be inside."

"Or he was interrupted. Was any of the tea spilled?"

"Yes, two of the other tins were emptied out."

"There you go. Maybe he just didn't get to those last tins. Maybe a car drove up, or someone walked by, or he or she feared they'd be seen. The possibilities are endless."

"We're not any closer to knowing who did this than when it happened."

Jonas nodded to his office in the back. "Would you like a cup of coffee? I know it could be treason if you drink coffee instead of tea, but it gets me started in the morning."

"No crime there," she said with a laugh. "But . . ." She checked her watch. "I'd better get over to the tea garden."

When she looked into Jonas's eyes, she felt a little quiver in her stomach. The idea of having coffee with him in his office increased the velocity of that quiver. She didn't think she was ready for that. She didn't know if *he* was ready for anything more than being a friend in an investigation. Were they even friends?

"At lunchtime today I want to duck out to a dress shop," she explained.

"Important event?" He seemed mildly curious. Did he think she was going out on a date?

"Tessa's gallery showing is on Wednesday evening. I haven't bought anything new for a while, and I'd like to pretty up."

He hesitated a moment, but then he said, "You don't need to buy something new to be pretty."

She didn't know what to say to that as her mouth suddenly went dry.

He cleared his throat and then said, "I'm still going through records looking for Jazzi's mom—or rather birth mother, since you're her mom."

"If she finds her birth mother, she might have two moms."

"I hope you both have faced the reality of a re-union. In general, people don't like to have their lives disrupted. A child they gave up for adoption suddenly coming around is a huge disruption."

"I know, and I'll try to prepare Jazzi better if we find out anything. I think she's excited about it now, and nothing I say is going to sink in."

"You're probably right. Thanks for keeping me informed about the coin."

"I asked Detective Rappaport if I could tell you, and he said I could. But please keep it confidential."

"Of course."

They were back on that "friends together in an investigation" footing, and Daisy was more comfortable with that. She expected that he was too.

She made a move toward the door. "Whenever you want another cup of tea and a scone, just stop in."

"I'll take you up on that offer soon."

As she left Jonas's store, she could feel his gaze on her back. It was a nice feeling. An exciting feeling. Did she need a little excitement in her life?

At one-thirty, Daisy took her break, deciding to skip lunch in favor of dress shopping. At least she thought she wanted a dress. For some reason, she considered what Jonas's reaction might be if he saw her in a new dress. That was just crazy. He didn't seem the type to go to an art gallery showing. Besides, she'd never dressed for men before. She dressed in what she liked, clothes she felt good and comfortable in. Advice to do just that had come from her Aunt Iris.

She headed north toward her favorite dress shop. At least the Rainbow Flamingo was her favorite *window-shopping* dress shop. They carried everything from an L.L.Bean type of look to a Serengeti style, and she could usually find something reasonable. When she walked in, she waved to the clerk, Heidi Korn, who often patronized the tea garden.

Heidi asked, "Are you looking for anything special?"

"I am. Something versatile that I could multi-purpose with. I want to wear it to the art gallery showing this week."

"Tessa's showing. I bet she's excited."

"Oh, she is."

Heidi motioned to the rack to the left. "I just got in new coordinates that might suit you—skirts and slacks and jackets and blouses. You can mix and match. Or . . ." She pointed to a rack on the other side. "New arrivals and dresses for the holidays."

"I'll take a look at all of it. I have about an hour."

"If you need any help, just give a yell."

Heidi apparently suspected that Daisy liked to do her own mixing and matching, and her own choosing.

She pulled out two skirts, one in plum and one in raspberry, and was choosing blouses that went with each when the door to the shop opened and the entrance bell rang. It was habit for Daisy to look up and see who the new customer was.

She was surprised to recognize Caroline, the employee from Men's Trends. As soon as Caroline stepped into the shop, she recognized Daisy too and gave a wave.

Daisy hung the clothes she'd selected on a nearby rack and approached Caroline. "How are you?"

"That's a good question," the young woman answered. "I'm no longer with Men's Trends. Bennett let me go. He's downsizing already. Since I was only part-time, I just didn't have the sales slips some of the others did."

"What are you going to do?"

"I have an interview with a men's shop in York—Gents. It's the store that's rumored to be interested in buying Men's Trends. I heard negotiations have been in the works for a while. I don't know how everyone kept it such a secret."

"But Bennett's in charge until the sale goes through?"

"That's right. He wants to keep the shop high-end, and he wants to keep the receipts up. Maybe he thinks that by doing that he'll have something to bargain with and can get the managerial spot if Gents buys the place. I'm trying to dress for success for this interview. How do you think I should go? It's a men's shop. Should I take a risk and dress in menswear? Like a lady-style tuxedo jacket, slim trousers, cool tie? Or should I go the usual business suit that shows off a woman's figure, in red or maybe yellow so I stand out?"

"Do you know the clientele at Gents?"

"I've been in the store. It's about the same as Men's Trends, though maybe not quite as pretentious."

Daisy laughed. "I know what you mean. Do you know what the owner's like? Staid, conservative, open to new trends?"

"No more open to new trends than Harvey, though Harvey had gone a little wild with those faux fur vests."

"So wear middle of the road. Not a traditional suit, but maybe your own kind of suit—slim pants, silk tank, jacket in a complementary color. You know, not all black, not all camel, something a little different. I don't know. You have to do what you feel comfortable with."

Caroline, who was a pretty girl with just a touch of mascara and wide lips that took lipstick well, said, "I think you could be right. I'll mix and match until I get the look I want. Thank you, Daisy."

"I make scones for a living. Don't take my fashion advice too seriously."

"I won't," Caroline said with a little laugh.

Daisy and Caroline ended up trying on clothes together. They turned up their noses at each other's outfits or gave thumbs-up signs. Although what Daisy tried on was satisfactory, it didn't wow her. Whenever she thought about Vi's college expenses, and eventually Jazzi's, that put a damper on her buying anything for herself. Along with the never-ending worry about business at the tea garden, she tried to be frugal. That's why whatever she bought had to have more than one use.

On another turn around the shop, she went to the rack in the back and stopped when she spotted a dress that reminded her of one she might wear with Ryan on a Florida night as they went out to dinner. It had a jacket and a halter top. The material was swirls of deep purple and sapphire blue. Ryan would have liked it. She could remember Ryan and many of the details about him—from the color of his eyes to the width of his smile to the way he walked and the sound of his laughter. However, some of the details and memories were growing dimmer, and it was hard for her to recall them. She didn't want to let go of them, but she didn't know how to keep them vivid either.

Caroline emerged from the dressing room in chocolate-brown slim slacks, an ivory silk shirt, and a cropped leather jacket. It was a put-together outfit for a younger woman, and it looked terrific.

"I'd hire you in that ensemble," Daisy told her honestly.

Caroline laughed. "The jacket's a little more than I want to spend, but I think the outfit will be a good investment. Thanks for your opinion. How about you?"

"I'm running out of time. I have three more dresses

I want to try, and then that will be it. If none of them are right, I'll find something old to use."

She took three selections from the rack, including the one that made her think of Ryan. In the dressing room, she quickly slipped on one and then the second and the third. She'd known right away which one she'd take, but she had to make sure by seeing them with her coloring. She chose the one with the halter top. The dress had a fairly open back, which was something she didn't usually wear. Was she too modest, or not adventurous enough?

The fact that the dress had an open back didn't mean a lot because there was also a jacket with it. The jacket was a soft, fluid material, like the dress, but was fitted and looked as if it belonged. With bold gold fashion jewelry and her hair swept to one side or mounded on top of her head, she'd look dressed up, feminine, and put together enough to be the up-and-coming business owner she was.

When she took the dress to the counter, Caroline was just checking out and paying her bill. "That will be beautiful on you," she said sincerely. "It will bring out the blond of your hair and complement your eyes, and if you wear fuchsia nail polish, you'll be hot."

"I don't know if I want to look hot, but I do want to look dressed up." She studied the wall of shoes across the room.

"Don't go with practical," Caroline said. "Choose something strappy, maybe with a wedge. If you really want to go big, buy purple. If you want to stay more classic, then black will do."

Should she go with purple? There was a pair on display that was designed with straps around the front and little gold buckles holding the straps together.

The heels were about two inches high, and they were doable. She wouldn't break her neck walking in them.

Daisy left the Rainbow Flamingo ten minutes later, unreasonably pleased with what she'd bought. It had been a couple of years since she'd splurged like this. She knew she'd probably regret it when she sat down with the bills for the month, but she'd worry about it then. She usually put her needs aside in favor of what her daughters needed. That's the way it should be. But now she felt she was earning a position in the town, and she needed to dress for success as well as for her own self-esteem. Maybe if she had time, she could get an appointment at Curly Cues. It was a highly regarded hair salon in town, but Daisy had never been there. She and Jazzi and Violet usually cut each other's hair.

Still, for once, just once, maybe she could get a good cut and style for Thursday night. With Foster covering more hours, it was possible. He'd done an excellent job yesterday, and she was hoping he'd do the same today. Afternoon tea from two to five would tell the tale. This was Bring a Friend to Tea Day at the tea garden, and all their tea room reservations were filled. Not a one left. Customers could come and go from the counter and tables in the serving area as well as outside. But the yellow tea room would be off-limits to anyone who didn't have a reservation.

Daisy stopped at her PT Cruiser and hung the dress inside, then lay the shoes on the seat. She'd bought a purse too, so nothing looked as if she'd borrowed it from her teenage daughter or confiscated it from her mom, who believed purses from twenty years ago were still perfectly acceptable because they were made so well. Normally, Daisy didn't give a thought to a purse one way or the other, but today, she just wanted to feel as if everything went together as it should.

She went through the back door of the tea garden into the kitchen. Tessa was taking a tray of cookies from the oven. She had ten multi-tiered serving trays lined up. Some were already filled with a shelf of madeleines. They were a new recipe, with maple flakes and a hint of orange zest. The chocolate raspberry scones would go on the second tier. The third tier would hold sandwiches—smoked salmon and cream cheese today, along with miniature turkey and Swiss paninis. Foster was helping Tessa ready the serving trays.

"There's someone here to see you," Tessa told Daisy. "Detective Rappaport."

Daisy wanted to groan, but she didn't.

Foster interjected, "He already has your Aunt Iris in the office. She wasn't looking happy."

"How long have they been in there?"

"About ten minutes," Foster said.

"I'm going in."

Foster called after her, "You might want to knock first."

But Daisy just waved her hand and went to her office. She could see through the glass that Iris was frowning. She didn't look particularly upset, yet she didn't look like her jovial self either.

Daisy opened the office door. "Good afternoon, Detective Rappaport. I hope we can make this short. We have a busy tea service to serve this afternoon. This is one of our afternoon tea days."

"Don't you serve tea every day?"

"This is a little different. We do it by reservation only. If you buy a ticket for afternoon tea—some people call it high tea, but it really isn't—we have a sit-down experience. We don't just serve a couple of scones and tea. We serve soup. Each table also receives a tray with savory goodies and desserts. It's more like a tiny meal. We have sittings like this twice a week, and it's a lot more difficult to serve than the general public in the front room. There's a timing involved. All the servers have to be coordinated and know exactly what they're doing as well as what they're serving."

Rappaport was wearing a tan fedora. He pushed it back on his head. "Whoever thought tea could be so complicated."

"Not as complicated as murder," Daisy said. "Tessa and Foster said you have questions for us?"

"I guess nothing's private when you all work together."

"Not much," Daisy agreed. "What did you want to ask us?"

"Did you see anyone near your aunt's house, anyone at all?"

"Before, during, or after the break-in?" Iris asked.

"Anytime," the detective stated. "Anyone who looked like he didn't belong could be the person we're looking for. Beforehand, he could have been casing your bungalow. Afterward, he might have hung around to watch everyone's reactions. There's just no knowing. That's why I need to know if you've seen anybody or heard of a neighbor seeing someone."

Iris shook her head. "I didn't see anyone. When I come home at night, it's dark, and I need downtime. I haven't talked to my neighbors since the murder because I didn't want to answer nosy questions. After the break-in, I went to stay with my sister. I only came back to straighten up. I wasn't focused on anything but that."

"One of your neighbors saw someone."

Daisy and Iris's eyes went directly to the detective. "Do they know who they saw?"

"No. Before Iris came home to clean up, your neighbor on the right, Lois Westin, saw someone skulking away from her house. They skulked up, and then they ran. She said he or she was wearing a windbreaker and a baseball cap. He or she was tall, but it was hard to tell how tall. Most of the fingerprints at Iris's are Iris's. But we found Harvey's and those of family members too. Was anything missing?"

"Some of my things were broken, but I didn't find anything missing."

"No, you just found a coin that could fund a lifetime. Why did you call me about it? Why didn't you just keep it?"

"Because it wasn't mine," Iris blurted out.

"It might have been meant for you. It might have been an engagement gift."

"If it was, then Harvey had a big heart. If it wasn't, and he just wanted to hide it until the papers were signed, then he wasn't the man I thought he was. But I can assure you, Detective, I went through my bungalow, and as you could see, it isn't that big. Nothing else was missing."

Detective Rappaport noticed that the customers who had made tea reservations were starting to stream in. The noise level was going up. Foster emerged from the kitchen to direct patrons to their tables.

Rappaport stepped out of Daisy's office and peered into the green tea room. "It looks as though you're going to have a full house. This murder must have done something for your business."

His voice was loud enough that, if customers had been standing close by, they could have heard him.

Daisy was incensed. She tried to insert calm into her voice. "We had full houses on tea room days *before* the murder, Detective. Now if you don't have anything else to ask us, we have business to conduct."

He looked a little surprised at her forcefulness, but he gave a small nod and left.

Iris elbowed her. "You'd better be careful."

"No, *he'd* better be careful what he says. I won't put up with him slandering us or the business. I'll sic Marshall on him."

Iris gave a little chuckle. "That *is* one strategy. Let's take care of our guests."

On afternoon tea service days, Daisy and her aunt considered their patrons guests. They served them the same way they would serve guests in their homes, taking special care with each person. Almost all of their patrons were seated. Karina and Foster had begun taking orders for the type of tea their customers preferred.

Suddenly, someone was standing beside Daisy, and she looked up to see . . . Trevor Lundquist. He pointed to the red-haired man beside him with the freckles and tortoiseshell glasses.

"I signed up for your Bring a Friend Day. This is David Ruiz. He's a writer for the *On the Road in PA Travel Guide.*"

Oh, my gosh, Daisy thought. If their tea garden were to be listed in a travel guide, they'd be assured of year-round business, and she'd definitely need more staff. But then, as she saw David Ruiz looking around, studying the china, the linens on the tables, and Foster and Karina, panic assailed her. What if he didn't like what they had to offer?

After she shook hands with David Ruiz, she said

genially, "Come on. I'll be glad to seat you myself. You can tell me what kind of tea and soup you'd like, and we'll get you started on enjoying what we have to offer here." She motioned to a table with two vacant chairs.

After a quick consultation with Tessa and Foster, she told them she'd be serving that table herself.

Foster just raised his eyebrows.

She explained, "These are important patrons who can win us more business." She didn't have to explain. After all, Foster worked for her. But it was better if they were all on the same page and had the same focus.

An hour later, although Daisy had been nervous, she'd been glad that her shaky hands hadn't fumbled when she'd served David Ruiz and Trevor. From the serving station across the room—she didn't want to be too obvious—she watched Trevor and David as they enjoyed tea, soup, salad, and the sandwich and dessert courses. Once, Trevor caught her glancing his way, and he winked.

She didn't know if she should feel buoyed by that or just attribute the gesture to his gregarious personality.

Other customers, mostly women, were lingering over their tea, madeleines, and conversation, and Trevor and David were among the first to finish.

She crossed the room to them and escorted them to the door. She said to David, "It was good to have you here." He just smiled. He went out the door first, and she asked Trevor, "Well?"

"He didn't say what he thought. You'll find out when he writes it up. Does this seal the deal?"

He meant their exclusive interview. After all, he

had brought in a food critic who could very well enhance their business.

What could she say except, "Yes, it does," even though that meant she could come to regret her alliance with Trevor Lundquist.

Chapter Sixteen

The customer stream at the tea garden ended for the day, and Daisy prepped with Tessa, Iris, and Eva for the following morning. While she did, she thought about Harvey's murder and the gold coin. She remembered something Marlene, Harvey's daughter, had said after the funeral service. She'd revealed to Daisy that her brother spent a lot of time at Bases, the sports bar downtown.

Since Jazzi had debate practice, Daisy didn't have to pick her up at school until later. She was going to make a detour to Bases on the off chance that Daniel would be there. After all, he wouldn't know that she never stopped for a drink after work.

Dusk had fallen by the time Daisy arrived at Bases. If he wasn't in the sports bar, Daisy would have only lost about five minutes of her time.

The bar and restaurant served mostly burgers and fries, pickles, and peanuts. The aroma of sizzling burgers, usually topped with bacon, wafted out the front door as she opened it.

As its name purported, the restaurant was about

bases—baseball bases. Inside, the establishment displayed photos of Fenway Park, Camden Yards, Yankee Stadium, and Wrigley Field along one wall. They'd been enlarged to poster size and framed in narrow black plastic frames. She noticed signed photos of players in their uniforms, along with shots of avid baseball fans, maybe those who were patrons of this bar. She didn't know.

Unlike lots of bars, this one wasn't dark. Track lighting gleamed from the ceiling at the edges of the room, so it was easy to see customers sitting at the tables along the outskirts as well as those sitting at the long wooden bar. A mirror on the wall at the back of the bar reflected faces. She studied each one. There was lots of chatter in the room, along with the low tones of three flat-screen TVs. Restaurant patrons at any table or at the bar could get a glimpse of a screen. Football game replays were on the TVs now, and that seemed ironic considering the theme of the bar.

Standing just inside the doorway, she glanced around, quickly looking for the face she'd studied at the funeral. It took her a minute to recognize Daniel. He wasn't wearing a suit but rather worn jeans, a sweatshirt with a hoodie, and a baseball cap with the Orioles team logo. Not a Phillies fan, she thought. After all, she did know a little something about baseball.

Fortunately, the stool next to Daniel was vacant. This seemed to be a slow evening at the bar because only three out of the ten stools were occupied. She guessed she'd missed happy hour, and it was still early for night owls.

As she approached the bar area where Daniel was seated, she saw the bartender shake his head, then say to Harvey's son, "I think you've had enough."

"I've only st . . . st . . . started," Daniel stuttered, slurring his words. Apparently, he was already sloshed. If happy hour had started at five, he'd had two hours to down drinks. Maybe he'd been there even longer.

Inhaling one huge deep breath for courage, Daisy squared her shoulders, pasted on a smile, and sat on the barstool next to him. She pretended not to notice him at first.

The bartender nodded at her. "A white wine spritzer, please." The drink would be a good investment.

When the bartender brought her a glass and sat it in front of her, Daniel looked her way as if he'd just realized somebody was sitting beside him.

She acted as if she'd just noticed him too. As pretended recognition dawned, she asked, "Aren't you Daniel Fitz?"

He responded without smiling in return. "The one and only."

"I'm Daisy Swanson. I hosted your father's party at Daisy's Tea Garden."

Daniel narrowed his eyes at her as if he was trying to remember. "You should have had Jack Daniels in some of those teacups." He called to the bartender. "Come on, Billy. One more shot."

"You're at your limit," Billy said firmly. Billy looked to be in his forties, husky and with tattoos down both arms. He wasn't anybody to mess with.

"My father's not around to dictate what I should and shouldn't do, or what you should or shouldn't *let* me do."

The bartender just shook his head and walked down to the register at the other end of the bar.

"I'm so sorry about your father," Daisy said.

Daniel gave a shrug. "He and my sister were close. He resented me because I took up for my mother."

That had to be the liquor talking. She couldn't imagine Daniel would willingly give out that information. She wondered how long she could keep him talking and how much she could learn. She took another sip of her drink.

After she pulled a bill from her handbag, she laid it on the counter. "I liked your dad," she said. "He was dating my aunt."

Daniel swung his gaze to her again and attempted to focus. "That older broad who didn't have any money," he said with a nod. "Yeah, I heard about that."

Daisy tried not to react to his statement. Then, as nonchalantly as she could, she asked, "Would you like a lift somewhere? Or is somebody picking you up?"

He gave a humorless laugh. "Nobody's picking me up. A friend dropped me off, but he left after two drinks." He looked Daisy up and down and then gave a shrug. "Sure, I'd appreciate a lift. You can take me to my mom's house. I'll get dinner there."

Right into the viper's den, Daisy thought. Why not?

Five minutes later, she showed Daniel to her car. His gait was unsteady, but he was upright and could put one foot in front of the other, so she didn't offer assistance. At her car, she used the remote to unlock it.

He looked at the purple PT Cruiser and gave a wry grimace. "Interesting wheels."

She guessed he might be used to driving a Maserati or a Porsche. They settled in the car, and he managed to fasten his seat belt. After she backed out of the parking space, she said, "You'll have to give me directions."

"You don't know where the Fitz mansion is located?"

"I never had occasion to visit there," she said reasonably, realizing Daniel's world mostly revolved around himself.

He motioned to the east. "Go through town. There's a development about a mile out called Palladian Arms. It's one of the biggest houses there."

He said that with pride, as if he'd built it himself.

Although darkness had fallen, streetlights illuminated the shop fronts. The first block of side streets were lit by those lamps too. Instead of taking the direct route, thinking Daniel might not even notice in his inebriated state, she turned right and proceeded to drive down the street where Guy's coin shop—Loose Change—was located.

Daniel appeared unaware until she slowed at the light near Loose Change instead of trying to race through the yellow signal. When it turned red, she gave Daniel a glance.

He stared at the signal right in front of them for a while, then swiveled his focus out the side window. When he saw the coin shop, he said, "My father collected lots and lots of coins. He went into Loose Change a lot."

As the light turned green, Daisy lifted her foot from the brake and asked, "What kind of coins did he have?"

Daniel fluttered his hand through the air. "All kinds—silver, gold, big and little, old and new. All kinds."

"Gold ones, huh? There must have been valuable ones there."

He turned his hat frontward on his head so the bill was covering his eyes. "Plenty valuable."

She waited for more, but he didn't go on, and she was afraid to push. She didn't want him to clam up or, even worse, tell her to stop the car so he could get out. It was something that someone in his condition might possibly do.

Harvey Fitz's former house, his widow's house now, was magazine-quality beautiful. Near the Willow Creek Country Club, it sat atop a hill overlooking the eighteenth hole of the golf course. Floodlights and post lamps illuminated the other houses in the area. Along with security systems and Halloween decorations that were done in the utmost good taste, Daisy peered at manicured lawns, precisely trimmed shrubs, and trees that might have seen a few decades worth of growth. Daniel directed her up a drive that led to the house. Parking before the three-car garage, Daisy wondered if Harvey's almost ex-wife appreciated her surroundings.

When she switched off the ignition, Daniel just sat there looking out the front windshield. She might have wondered if he'd dozed off, but in the light of the motion detector device on the garage, she could see his eyes were open. He was either spacing out, still dealing with grief, or thinking about something that bothered him greatly. She didn't know him, so she couldn't tell.

"Daniel?" she asked quietly.

It took him a moment, but then he turned and looked at her. "I guess we're home," he said in a resigned voice, and she had the feeling that "home" didn't mean the same thing to him as it did to her or her children.

"Are you okay?" she asked.

"Other than being hammered, you mean? I'm just dandy." Then he seemed to remember his manners. "But thanks for bringing me here." With that, he unfastened his seat belt and opened his door.

Daniel wasn't quite steady as he walked to the front door and Daisy followed him. The curved path was lined with ornamental grasses, and he stepped off of it twice, but he righted himself again and was soon at the front door, ringing the bell.

Ringing the doorbell at his own home? At his childhood home?

As if he'd heard Daisy's unasked question, he said, "Mother's vigilant about security. Everybody has to ring the doorbell." He pointed to a security camera above the door.

Daisy half-expected a maid to greet them, but Monica herself opened the oak barricade. It was high and wide.

Daniel said, "Hi, Mother," and walked past Monica through the foyer.

Monica was obviously surprised to see Daisy, and recognition dawned in her eyes. "You're that waitress at the tea garden."

"I'm Daisy Swanson," she reminded Monica. "My aunt and I own the tea garden." After she let that sink in, Daisy went on to say, "I ran into Daniel, and he needed a ride home." She didn't say she found him at Bases. That was up to Daniel to tell his mother.

"I could smell the alcohol. He's been drinking." She motioned Daisy inside as if it were the proper thing to do, though she didn't look especially happy about it. Daisy didn't particularly want to make nice with this woman, but if she could find out more about her, she'd do it.

The inside of the house was as impressive as the outside. Daisy could see into a spacious living room with luxurious draperies, oriental carpets, and furniture pricier than what Jonas sold. There were collectibles like Lladró figurines on one shelf, and what looked like a Waterford crystal vase on another.

"You have a beautiful home," Daisy said because it seemed to be in order.

"Yes, I do. I wasn't about to give it up because

Harvey fancied two separate lives instead of one. Thanks for bringing Daniel home. I don't know what to do with him right now. He acts as if he doesn't mind that his father's dead, but he does."

"Losing a parent is difficult," Daisy agreed.

"Losing a husband is too," Monica said. She checked her watch. "I hate to seem ungrateful, but Candace will be putting dinner on the table in about five minutes."

"Of course," Daisy allowed, knowing she wasn't about to get anything out of this woman, not without a tug of war or a fight. She wasn't going to engage in either.

She'd started to step outside again when Monica called, "You know your aunt was beneath Harvey. He was using her for something. He used everyone."

Daisy wondered why Monica wanted to insult her Aunt Iris. To see if Daisy would rise to the bait?

Before she could, Monica asked, "Wasn't Iris's house broken into?"

It wasn't a secret that her Aunt Iris's house had been burglarized. After all, there had been police cars all around it the night it happened. But just how did Monica know when the break-in hadn't been on the news? Detective Rappaport had tried to keep the event as quiet as he could.

When Daisy didn't answer, Monica offered, "You know, Harvey's killer is still out there. I, of course, have a state-of-the-art security system on my house. Do you?"

Was that a warning? Could Monica be the murderer? Whether she was or wasn't, it wouldn't hurt for her to know the truth.

"Yes, I have an alarm system on my home. I wouldn't do without it, not with children in the house. Although my girls are teenagers, I always like to go that special bit further to protect their well-being. Mothers can be tigresses when their children are put into danger, don't you think?"

Two could play at the warning game.

"Yes, they can," Monica maintained. "Thanks again for bringing my son home."

Daisy nodded and then left. Alarm system or not, she wouldn't leave Jazzi at the barn home alone until this case was solved.

When Daisy entered Men's Trends the next day over her lunch break, she was surprised by the changes. The store had seen an interior makeover, and she realized instantly why. Harvey's concept for Men's Trends had been traditionally classic, expensive, and luxurious. The clothes definitely targeted high-end clients. This makeover spoke to a different man than Harvey's Men's Trends had.

Spotting Bennett near the cashier's desk, she started that way but couldn't help but stop by a small boutique section that had been set up. It carried men's cosmetics, lotions, and hair supplies. When she detoured into the small area, she even found coffee-table-like books of men's hairdos and styling concepts.

Was Harvey turning over in his grave at this change?

The paisley carpet remained the same. The arrangement of the styling racks was much different. Harvey hadn't been one for placards. Apparently, Bennett was. One announced a new designer section, another unisex fashion. As she studied that advertisement, she recognized the designer's name from one of the TV fashion shows that Jazzi watched. The designer created sports clothes, mostly knitwear. Either a man or a woman could wear it. This was one way to bring in more business if a man's wife or girlfriend trailed along. Smart, wasn't it?

Bennett watched Daisy approach him and smiled. "What do you think?"

"I think you're targeting a younger customer along with the clientele that Harvey built up."

"You're right. I want to make this place as attractive and business savvy as it can be, so that anyone who buys from us will want us to keep going in the same direction. But I don't want to lose our return customers or the older generation."

"You mean like my father."

"Exactly." He waved to the west side of the store. "That section of the store will remain the same—suits, ties, dress shirts, brand names these men trust, custom suits too, of course."

She spotted a small placard on the desk—REGISTER FOR YOUR PERSONAL STYLIST. She waved at it. "What's that all about?"

"That's a new trend too—personalized service. I have a friend who's a stylist and works in New York. He's actually volunteering his time to get me started in this, and I've hired a Web person—a virtual assistant, so to speak—to oversee it all. You know about bridal registries, correct?"

"Yes, I do."

"Many types of stores have those registries now, including baby stores. Even the chains do. So it's time we join the fray. Our customers can have a profile page and a wish list, with all the things they might want for Christmas or birthdays or anniversaries. Friends and relatives can just go to their page, then either come into the store or eventually buy online."

"Wow, Bennett, you've put a lot of thought into this. A lot of time too."

"I've had these ideas for years, but Harvey would never let me run with them. Now I'm running. We've already seen a difference in sales, just with that unisex sportswear collection alone. Back to the stylist—he'll go over a survey with customers online and then suggest particular clothes within their budget."

She pointed to a denim collection. "That's focusing on late teens to twenty-plus buyers, right?"

"From jeans and vests to jackets to flannel-lined outerwear. Denim will never go out of style. Just check out that ombre denim."

The two of them walked over to the rack, and Daisy paged through, noting the indigo, slate, and almost light blue garments. Some of the jeans bore shredded holes, some didn't. Some looked worn, some didn't. Her hand went to an indigo-dyed wool peacoat. When she checked the price tag, she swallowed hard, and she was sure her eyes popped.

"I've sold two of those already," Bennett said with a smug expression.

She just shook her head. As she glanced across the store, from that new boutique to the classic section to cashmere sweaters in yellow and mesh bomber jackets, she saw Bennett's dream of what menswear should be. It was fascinating, really. The store was interesting and eye-catching.

"I don't think you have a place for a tea cart."

For a moment, he looked nonplussed, then he laughed. "Tell me something, Daisy. How would you make tea relevant for all generations? How could you convince Gen Xers or millennials that brewing tea was just the hottest thing on the planet, pardon the pun."

She laughed this time. Then she thought about it. "I'd probably go down your road and personalize what I sell. I'd have a station with a selection of teas, and the customer could mix or match for their particular brew. I'm not sure in practicality just how that would work, but I think it would be possible. I've visited sites online that do it."

Bennett nodded. "I see your point. You could be the new Starbucks, only for tea."

"Possibly," she agreed. "But I don't know if younger customers would go for the idea when spring and summer set in. Hot teas are more of a tradition, and I don't know how many young people are into tradition. Iced teas would be a lot easier to serve. I could set up a tea cart with different flavors already brewed. We could serve cups of iced teas for them to taste." She was liking the concept more and more.

"That might not be a bad idea. But I'm also thinking—go with me here, even though you may want to say no at first—brewed teas in urns, just like you serve coffee. They just push the spout and out comes blackberry black tea, or Earl Grey tea, or Darjeeling."

"Tea connoisseurs would be scandalized."

He shrugged. "Possibly. But come winter, I can see setting up a bar that served hot chocolate and tea."

"That's an interesting concept, Bennett. Let me think about it."

"So what can I help you with today? You aren't buying Christmas presents yet, are you? I have beautiful cashmere sweaters that would make a great gift for your dad, and unisex knitwear your mom might like."

She laughed. "You're the consummate salesman, and I will think about that. I don't believe my dad ever owned a cashmere sweater. He might possibly enjoy one. No, today I didn't come to shop. I'd like to know more about Harvey's son, Daniel."

Bennett looked thoughtful. "He's living at home with his mother after his last stint in rehab."

Daisy nodded, hoping Bennett would go on. Instead, he asked her, "Why do you want to gather information about Daniel?"

"To see if there are stronger suspects than my aunt," she said honestly.

Bennett shook his head. "I thought that was simply gossip about your aunt. The police don't seriously consider her a suspect, do they?"

"They do. We've consulted a lawyer because they took her in for questioning more than once."

"Your aunt is the sweetest person. She'd never hurt anyone."

"I know that, and maybe you know that, but Detective Rappaport doesn't. Let me ask you: Do you think Daniel is capable of killing?"

Bennett looked troubled. "Harvey cut Daniel out of his will because he thought it would teach him a lesson. Daniel isn't responsible, maybe at times not trustworthy, but I don't believe he could have hurt his father. I'd look in another direction."

"What direction?" Daisy asked.

Bennett hesitated. "Are you familiar with the store next door?"

"Sporty Digs?"

"Yes. I guess you can't help but notice it when you walk or drive down the street."

That was certainly true. Sporty Digs had opened up in that location about a year ago. When it did, the storefront had been redone. The marquee that ran across the front was painted garishly in yellow and green. Besides that, there was an orange neon sign that read SPORTY DIGS. The windows were never filled with displays, though there were signs plastered on them with the specials of the week.

"I don't know who owns Sporty Digs. I've never been inside," she admitted.

"Just as well for you," Bennett said. "The man's real name is Ron Milkin, but his nickname is Sporty Milkin. Everyone calls him Sporty, hence the name of his store. Sporty and Harvey didn't get along from the moment Sporty opened his store. Harvey was appalled by the man's gaucheness, lack of etiquette, and downright plebian taste. Harvey suggested more than once that Sporty at least take down the neon sign. I think Harvey would have just tried to keep the peace, except Sporty would come in here in his camouflage gear and high-topped boots and recommend that Harvey's store patrons stop on over to his store. The last time that happened was about a month ago. Harvey ran the man out himself and told Sporty if he didn't get his boots off of Men's Trends' carpet, Harvey would take his revolver out of the safe and use it."

"So Harvey threatened him?"

With a sigh, Bennett looked toward the office . . . toward the safe. "I think it was more bluster than a threat. But who knows how Sporty took it. Who knows if Sporty confronted Harvey and then killed him."

Daisy was going to have to think about all that. She wouldn't mind talking to Sporty herself. That could be foolish, or she could just pretend she was a clueless woman looking for a present for her father.

"I didn't mean to take up so much of your time. Thank you for talking with me. Did you tell Detective Rappaport about Sporty?"

"Actually, no. That whole episode slipped my mind. But maybe I'll give him a call and let him know about that confrontation. It might help. It also might take the heat off your aunt."

Daisy hoped that was true. Her Aunt Iris could use a little stress relief.

Daisy took one more look around the store. "I think you're on to something here, Bennett. After all, my two girls are into trendy. I think your store portrays that vibe now. Good luck with it."

"Thank you." He lowered his voice. "And if you do ever go next door to see Sporty, make sure you carry pepper spray."

Daisy didn't own pepper spray, but maybe she could buy a canister at Sporty Digs.

Chapter Seventeen

Revelations was one of those galleries that carried everything from Amish folk art to landscapes of Lancaster County to impressionistic paintings of cats to abstract art that didn't make much sense to Daisy. Tessa's art fell into the mood-making and feline art categories, realistic yet impressionistic. Daisy loved Tessa's paintings and always had. Tonight was a wonderful opportunity for her.

The gallery was located in an old Victorian that might have been one hundred fifty years old. The gallery itself was divided into several rooms. The rooms had been renovated with gallery specifications in mind. The lighting along the walls and in tracks on the ceiling cast a glow in just the right places. Reese Masemer lived upstairs.

Daisy felt good in her new dress and high heels, which she didn't wear much anymore. She'd swept her hair up on top of her head and wore gold dangly earrings that Ryan had given her. Jazzi had decided to come with her and had dressed up a bit too. She looked so grown-up in a bateau-neck sweater dress in her favorite shade of blue. She didn't realize yet that she was going to grow into a beautiful woman.

She tugged on Daisy's arm as they entered the main gallery. "Wow, look at all the people. There's Aunt Iris." Jazzi waved to her, and Iris waved back.

Daisy had convinced Iris that coming to the showing could take her mind off of everything else. She was glad her aunt had taken her advice.

Returning to Jazzi's comment, she responded to her daughter, "Tessa sent an e-mail blast to everyone she knew professionally as well as family and friends. It looks as if it worked."

As Daisy and Jazzi migrated toward Tessa's paintings, suddenly Jazzi pointed to a painting. "Look, Mom. That's Pepper!"

Daisy had to smile when she saw the painting of a black cat with white markings on its chest sitting in the middle of an herb garden.

"It's wonderful, isn't it? It's probably out of our price range or I'd buy it."

As she looked down the row to study the other paintings, a man waved to her. It was Trevor. She wasn't sure whether she should wave back, but she shouldn't have worried. He made his way through the crowd to approach her.

He smiled. "I should have known you'd be here. Besides being her employer, you and Tessa Miller went to school together, didn't you?"

"Something tells me you've been doing a background check."

"Everything for the story. I'm here tonight for the same reason. I cover these shows, not only here but in Lancaster and York too. See who else is here?"

Following the direction of Trevor's chin, Daisy was surprised when she spied Monica Fitz. "Does Monica often attend these shows?" She knew Revelations had two or three a year.

Trevor nodded vigorously. "She's often in attendance. She's an important patron of this gallery."

Suddenly Daisy felt a hand on her shoulder. When she turned, she faced Cade Bankert. It was good to see him again. He was looking as handsome as usual in a gray pinstripe suit, white shirt, and gray striped tie.

"Hi, Cade. Thinking of buying one of Tessa's paintings?"

"I might, though her work is a little too soft for me." He nodded toward the other room. "I like some of those abstracts."

A man who liked to interpret paintings. She could be intrigued by that.

Trevor said, "I'd better mingle. It was good to see you again, Daisy."

After Trevor moved on, Jazzi said, "I see one of my friends with her mom over there. I'm going to mingle too."

That left Cade and Daisy standing alone, at least for the moment. Cade asked, "So why were you asking about Monica Fitz?"

Apparently, he'd overheard her conversation with Trevor. "I wanted to know because I wondered if Monica was following me or my aunt around."

Cade look puzzled. "Why would Monica do that?"

Daisy didn't answer. She didn't think it was wise to tell Cade that she'd picked up Daniel and taken him home.

But he must have sensed something because he asked, "Are you snooping where you shouldn't?"

That question offended Daisy, whether it should or shouldn't have. "Cade, you're not my keeper." She turned away. "I'm going to take a look at Tessa's other paintings."

As she started to cross the room, he caught her elbow. "Wait."

She did.

"I'm worried about you. I don't want anything to happen to you."

She felt her annoyance vanish in the midst of his concern. "Nothing's going to happen to me simply because I ask a few questions. Knowledge is power, remember?"

"Yes, I remember. I use the concept all the time in my business dealings. Look. How would you like to go to dinner tomorrow night? Then you can tell me what you've been up to."

Telling him what she'd been up to probably wasn't a good idea, but dinner with him— "You might not want to know what I've been up to, but dinner sounds good."

"Instead of eating at Sara Jane's, why don't we drive into York? There's a new restaurant there I'd like to try, the Red Derby. It's gotten great reviews. I hear they even have candlelight."

Was he hinting that this was going to be a romantic dinner?

"So I should dress up?"

"You can wear what you're wearing tonight. You look gorgeous."

She felt her cheeks redden. It seemed she couldn't remember how to accept compliments. "Oh, I think I can manage to not wear the same dress two nights in a row. It's a date."

"Good. I'll make reservations for eight and pick you up at seven. You don't mind leaving Jazzi alone?"

"I'll make sure she's not alone. She's been talking about staying overnight with a friend to work on a history project. Maybe she can arrange that for tomorrow night. Win-win for both of us."

"Win-win for all three of us," he said. "I just saw the gallery owner add red dots to two of the paintings. That means Tessa sold them."

"She'll be thrilled."

As they turned to make their way across the gallery to see which paintings had sold, Daisy noticed the person who was coming in the front door. Detective Rappaport. Just what was *he* doing here?

Checking up on her aunt? Checking up on *her*? Maybe wanting to rub elbows with Monica Fitz in a different atmosphere?

As she felt Cade's arm brush hers, she tried to forget about Detective Rappaport by thinking about Cade's invitation for tomorrow night. She hoped he wasn't going to warn her away from the investigation again. It would be good to talk about it with him. On the other hand, she couldn't tell him about Harvey's coin.

She didn't want to start out on the wrong foot with Cade. Keeping secrets wasn't her style. Yet she had to obey Detective Rappaport's orders, didn't she?

Daisy was deep into preparations at the tea garden on Thursday morning when Tessa came in absolutely glowing. "I sold six paintings last night," she said happily and threw her arms around Daisy.

"That's wonderful. Was Reese pleased with the way the show went?"

"He seemed to be. I asked him how many paintings a new artist usually sells, and he said that depends.

We have reserved notices on two more. I was a little surprised at the prices that he wanted to ask for the paintings, but he said I can't sell myself short. He doesn't run an arts and crafts fair—it's a gallery. So when customers come in, they expect to pay gallery prices."

"Lots of people admired your paintings. You could possibly earn commissions from the show too, right?"

"Actually, I had an inquiry—a woman who wanted me to paint her two cats."

"Are you going to do it?"

"I'm not sure. I don't want my paintings to be a paint-from-a-photograph kind of art. I'd like to conceptualize the whole scene and then paint it, not always with an animal, though I do like doing them. I have her contact information. I'm going to see what happens with the show and how much time I have. We're going to get a lot busier here over the holidays, and I might be working extra hours, right?"

"If you want the hours, you can have them. How do you think Foster's working out?"

"Much more smoothly than I expected. He comes in again this afternoon, doesn't he?"

"He does. He seems responsible, picks up information quickly, and likes talking to the customers. What more could we want? I'm trying to figure out the best way to look for someone else because I think we'll need the extra help over the holidays, as you said."

"Part-time position?"

"I'm thinking maybe someone who can work thirty hours a week."

"What about putting the tea garden info up at one of the job sites? Or have Foster put a notice on our Trends page. After all, social media is where it's at. Isn't that what he says?"

"And he's doing a good job of it too. When I hired him, I wondered if he was too good to be true. But he's working out, and that's what matters."

She returned to the subject of Tessa's art. "Will your paintings stay at the gallery over the holidays?"

"Reese will move them around. But, yes, he'll keep them there until January anyway. Hopefully more will sell. If I get good reviews—and they haven't come out yet today—he thinks another gallery could pick me up. I suppose I should start preparing for another show."

"You're going to be one busy woman."

"It's not as if I have anything else going on in my life."

"Speaking of. Can I borrow one of your scarves? Cade asked me to go to dinner with him tonight in York at the Red Derby."

"Wow. I've heard that place is highfalutin. Crystal, silver, and white tablecloths. You rate."

Daisy felt a little flustered at the idea. "I don't know about that, but I do know I want to dress up a bit again. I have a black dress that I think will do, but it needs some color. One of your scarves should do it."

"On my lunch break, I'll run up and collect a few. You can take your pick."

"You're the best."

"We've been friends a long time, Daisy. We know each other's past as well as the present."

Yes, they did know each other's past. Tessa hadn't had an easy time growing up, though the impression she gave now was easy-breezy. She was an artist, and there was a reason for that. Her childhood had been an unhappy one, with parents who fought constantly and a dad who hit her mom when he drank too much. Tessa had needed an outlet for emotions she couldn't share or didn't know what to do with. That outlet had been her painting. Another outlet had also been her friendship with Daisy. They'd been pinky-swearing friends since third grade, when Tessa's family had moved into the area. It was satisfying working with her now and still building on their friendship. Adult women needed best friends just as much as third-graders.

Maybe that was one reason Tessa felt free to say to her now, "Let yourself go tonight with Cade, okay?"

"What do you mean?"

"I know you loved Ryan deeply. No one can ever replace him. You'll never forget him. But I'm sure he'd move over in your heart a little bit so that you can love someone else."

"And you think Cade's that person?"

"I don't know. Do you?"

"I've known Cade since high school, but we never crossed over that barrier of surface conversation. Do you know what I mean?"

"I think I do. When you were in high school, you had a crush on him, so it was hard to talk to him, especially about anything meaningful. And the same was probably true for him. When you moved back here, the conversation was all about real estate and finding you the properties you needed."

"Exactly. So it just feels kind of strange to be getting all dressed up, going to some swanky place, and sitting across the table from him."

"Try to just let whatever happens happen. It's not more complicated than that."

"This is the voice of experience speaking?"

Tessa shrugged her shoulders. "I didn't have role models to fill me with confidence about finding a life partner, at least one I wanted to spend my entire life with. So dating is not a high priority for me. I've got to admit, though, I really like Reese. And not because he's the gallery owner. He's just got that 'it' I like in men. He's tall and lean with sandy-brown hair that's longer than most men in Willow Creek wear theirs. We can talk art all day long and all night long too. But we're not past talking art yet, and maybe we never will be."

Iris peeked her head into the kitchen. "The tables are ready, and the cases are full. I'm about ready to turn over the OPEN sign. Are you okay back here?"

"We're good," Daisy said, meaning it. "Did Karina arrive yet?"

Karina had agreed to work a full set of hours today. In her twenties, she lived with her mom and had a two-year-old at home. She was a little avant-garde for the tea garden, sometimes dying her hair purple or blue or, this month, fuchsia. But she was a dependable employee, and she worked hard.

Iris answered her question. "She left a voice mail on the tea garden answering machine that she'd be late. She said she tried to phone you last night, but you didn't call her back."

Daisy shut her eyes and sighed. "That's my own fault. I was so tired when we got home, I didn't even check my phone. I had it turned off during the showing."

"What if Vi had called?" Iris asked.

"I knew if she couldn't get me, she'd call Jazzi. But I think she's too busy to call anybody. Go ahead and open. We'll just hope we don't get too busy before Karina arrives."

They were in the swing of service, Tessa plating, Daisy and Iris serving, Cora Sue selling at the counter, and Eva aiding in all, when Karina rushed in, all apologetic smiles. "I'm so sorry." Her blue eyes looked it. She went on to explain, "The battery went dead in my car. My dad had to get me a new one this morning. I'm so sorry."

"Emergencies happen to everyone," Daisy said. "No worries. You can start preparing the spread for lunch. Make sure the soup is seasoned correctly, and then help Tessa plate. We're good out front."

Cora Sue had just rung up another customer at the counter when Daisy skirted it to check on the customers at the tables. One woman raised her hand that she needed more tea. Daisy saw to that quickly. She also brought another scone plate to a table of four and replenished a pot of raspberry curd at another table. She'd hardly noticed who was coming and going until she approached a table with one man sitting at it, with his back to her. She thought she recognized the shape of the head, the set of the shoulders—

When she rounded the table, she saw Marshall. "Hi! What are you doing here?"

"I thought I'd take you up on your offer for a cup of tea and a scone."

"Terrific. This morning our specialty scones are apple cinnamon." She pointed to a small placard on the table. "And those are the teas. Pick one, and I'll make sure it's brewed perfectly."

"I'll go with the Earl Grey this morning."

"Good choice. I'll be right back."

And she was, with one of the vintage teapots that held two cups of tea as well as a plate with three scones. For Marshall, the order was on the house. No arguing about that.

As he motioned to the tea and scones, he asked, "Can you sit with me for a few minutes?"

She took a quick look around, and seeing that

everything was in order and everyone was served, she motioned to Iris that she was going to sit at the table. Her aunt gave a nod that she understood and would cover, or else Karina or Tessa would.

"How's the tea?" she asked.

"As you said it would be. Perfectly brewed. And the scones are delicious. I might have to take some of these along."

"That's our aim. It's called secondary marketing. You eat one here, and you take home a dozen."

He laughed. "You're doing a good job at this. I'll have to come in more often." Then he grew serious. "But today, I came to give you information as well as to see how your aunt is faring. How is she?"

They both looked toward the counter, where Iris was speaking with a customer.

"She's pretending she's fine, but I know she's deeply affected by all of this, especially finding that coin. She doesn't know if Harvey meant it for her or if it was just a ploy and he was using her. That's hard to accept."

"Yes, it is. I'll speak with her before I leave and reassure her that Harvey's feelings must have been genuine. She deserves to think that."

Each time Daisy had dealings with Marshall, she realized he was a kind man. She liked that. "You said you had information for us. What is it?"

"You've met Guy Tremont?"

"Yes, I have."

"Apparently he's been under suspicion for running shady auctions or . . . keeping valuable items out of an appraisal to keep assets hidden. It's quite possible he knew all about what Harvey had given Iris to hold for him. And if he did know, then Guy is a viable suspect too. You can think about him in two ways. Maybe he's not the murderer. But if he knew about that coin, a million dollars is a lot of money to overlook. He could have easily broken into your aunt's to try to find it. On the other hand, if he and Harvey had some kind of falling out, he could have had a motive for the murder."

"Rappaport told me I can't tell anyone about the coin except for Jonas. Rappaport seems to trust him."

"Jonas does know how to keep his mouth shut, and Rappaport understands that. It's essential that word about the coin not get out."

"I understand that. It's just hard for me not to talk about it with people I'm close to. When we talk about the investigation . . ." She trailed off.

"When you talk about the investigation, you leave out the coin. You pretend that night didn't exist. It's as simple as that."

That night never existed. She'd have to remember Marshall's words when she had dinner with Cade tonight.

Chapter Eighteen

When Cade picked up Daisy for dinner on Thursday evening, she'd wrapped a silver-flecked shawl around the shoulders of her black dress—she and Tessa had decided the shawl would look better than a scarf—and got into his car. But the atmosphere was odd. It was almost as if they were strangers instead of old friends from high school.

New relationship, new vibes?

On the drive, they began talking, and the atmosphere changed from awkward to more comfortable. Cade's profession as a real estate agent took him to interesting places, and he spoke with a wide range of people. In no time at all, they were pulling into the parking lot of the Red Derby in the east end of York.

Daisy didn't wait for him to come around the car but climbed out on her own, and they walked to the front entrance. The maître d' checked his reservation sheet, then showed them to a table for two along the side of the restaurant near the windows. The white tablecloth was pristine. A bud vase on the table held real mums. It was a classy place.

That was emphasized again when the waiter brought

an extensive wine list. Cade chose one without consulting her, and then they turned to their tall leather-bound menus. Daisy studied the selections and couldn't help but notice the inflated prices. She was tempted to tell Cade she was a potpie and shoofly pie kind of girl, but he seemed comfortable here, as if he did this often.

Cade said, "This would be a great place to wine and dine clients. I'm glad we came."

So he could get a look at the restaurant? Or because he wanted to be with her?

Their knees didn't touch under the table, and she didn't know if she was sorry or relieved. She chose a chicken marsala entrée, while Cade ordered a rib-eye steak. After the waiter had taken their orders, Cade said, "I understand you're looking to hire more help at the tea garden."

"I am. Do you know anybody who's interested— who's responsible, honest, and likes tea?"

He laughed. "Not offhand. But I'll keep my eyes out and my ears open. Are you looking for someone full-time?"

"I'm not sure yet. Maybe part-time at first. Part-timers are more economical for me than full-timers with benefit packages."

"Can your business sustain another salary?"

Cade was a numbers person. She'd found that out when they were looking for houses for her and for the business. So she didn't find his question intrusive.

"With the increase in business, we certainly can. I'm hoping they'll all be repeat customers, not just curiosity seekers who try what we have because Harvey was murdered there."

Cade's expression was uncertain for a few moments, and that was unusual. So she waited for him to resume the conversation.

"I'm sorry about my attitude last night . . . if you felt I was trying to tell you what to do," he apologized. "I only want the best for you."

"I know you do. I'm just asking questions to see if I can get Aunt Iris off the hook. Detective Rappaport seems to want to pin this on her!"

"What have you come up with?"

"So far only the obvious suspects. I suppose Harvey's wife is the main one. Can you see her wielding something and conking him?"

Cade shrugged. "I heard she barged in on his twenty-fifth anniversary celebration at your tea garden and created quite a stir. If she could do that, she might have enough venom to have socked him." After a brief, pensive silence, Cade said, "I suppose no one wants to think about it, but Harvey Fitz's children could be suspects too, especially Daniel. He has a temper and feels entitled. Cut out of the will, he could have been angry enough to get into a fight with his dad."

"Whoever did it would have to have known Harvey was going to meet Aunt Iris at the tea garden, or else they would have had to follow him there."

"So you believe it was someone he knew?"

"Most likely. I don't think this was random; it wasn't a mugging gone wrong. There was an employee he let go because she was flirting with customers. I suppose he could have enemies because of his business dealings. The police have their work cut out for them."

"So you aren't really trying to solve this?"

"Just get some questions answered."

"Why do you think Iris's house was broken into?"

She decided to be honest with him. "I do know

some facts that Detective Rappaport wants to keep under wraps. I'm not supposed to say anything."

Cade cocked his head and studied her. Then he nodded. "Fair enough. A murder investigation isn't something to tamper with."

Was that another subtle warning? If it was, they didn't dwell on it, but rather changed the topic of conversation to the upcoming activities in Willow Creek for the holidays.

They rounded out their meal with coffee and crème brûlée. As Cade drove Daisy home, their conversation came and went comfortably.

At her house, he walked her to her door.

"Would you like to come in?" she asked.

He hesitated for a few moments, but then he shook his head. "I have showings in the morning and need to go over the stats. Besides . . . I think we should go slowly. We both have pasts to put behind us."

Just what was Cade's romantic past? Daisy knew he was right about venturing into new territory slowly. But she felt faintly disappointed as he drove away.

On Friday afternoon, Daisy took advantage of a lull in customers to spend her lunch break exploring Sporty Digs. Every once in a while, as she had poured tea for her morning patrons, she had considered her date last night with Cade. There hadn't been anything romantic about it really. So had it been a date?

Deciding her break time would be better served answering a few questions about Sporty Milkin's supposed feud with Harvey, she walked quickly to Men's Trends and passed by it.

She didn't know what to expect when she entered

Sporty Digs. It looked like a Halloween decoration explosion outside the store, with a skeleton, a fake spider crawling on the marquee, and orange twinkle lights bordering the inside of the windows. Daisy could see why the owner's approach to business promotion didn't fit in with Harvey Fitz's idea of decorum.

Inside the store, she found a discount warehouse kind of atmosphere. There were racks stuffed with hunter's jackets, shelves clogged with hiking boots and galoshes, cubbies stuffed with T-shirts and bill caps. Peering into the back of the store, which was darker, she spotted rifles lined up on the wall. A chill ran down her spine. This wasn't her kind of place, and she could see why it hadn't been Harvey's.

A tall, lean man with lank, brown hair combed over his balding pate stood at one of the glass-covered counters peering into the case filled with knives. Just because those knives were fashioned with beautiful elk-antler handles or enameled cases, didn't make her like them any better. He was dressed in a camouflage T-shirt and cargo pants. After a deep breath, she approached him with a smile, her cover story intact.

"Looking for something in particular?" the man asked her, without meeting her gaze.

"I am," she assured him. "An outerwear jacket for my dad. I'm Christmas shopping early. He owns a nursery, so I want something durable that will withstand the weather. It would be helpful if it's washable too because when he's carrying trees around he often gets his jackets dirty."

Whether her specifics warmed the man up, or whether he could see a sale in his future, he gave her a small smile. "I'm sure we can help you with that. Just come over here." He motioned her toward a rack of weather-proof jackets.

Daisy shuffled through them, pushing the hangers closer together on the rack. Some jackets were lined with flannel, some with fleece. She took a price tag in her hand and checked it out.

"These are reasonable," she said.

"I try to keep my prices competitive."

"I looked at a jacket in the store next door—Men's Trends. The price would pay my groceries for a month."

The man actually winked at her. "Awful, ain't they?" He scowled. "Harvey Fitz thought he knew best for everyone. He didn't."

"You knew the man who was murdered?"

"Couldn't help but know him. I had to deal with him, both of us being business owners and all."

"And members of the Chamber of Commerce, I suppose."

Sporty snorted. "That's a laugh. They only want people there who think the same as everybody else."

"Don't they have to take each business owner's opinion into account?"

"Maybe they should, but they don't. Fitz tried to cut me out more than once."

"Cut you out?"

"Yeah. Special promotions. Goings-on I should know about. He was a bigwig in the chamber, so he often controlled the list of the names of people who should get notices, e-mails, that kind of thing."

"I see," she said, understanding now what Bennett had mentioned as far as this man being Harvey's enemy.

"But surely you could find out information from other store owners," she prompted.

"Yeah, I could. So Fitz was more of a nuisance than anything. Until . . ." He stopped abruptly.

Daisy didn't want to seem too interested, so she pulled out a navy blue jacket that her father just might appreciate for a Christmas present. It was a large, his size, and the garment was roomy enough that he could move easily in it when he was lifting, carrying, or simply managing.

She said to Sporty, "I'll take this," and went over to the counter with it.

He came around the other side and rang up the sale. As she pulled a credit card from her purse and handed it to him, she said, "So Harvey Fitz did more than keep information from you?"

"He was planning to," Sporty mumbled. Then, as if he wanted to unburden himself, he went on, "He was trying to get me out of here."

"But you have a lease, don't you?"

"Sure do. The thing was, he was trying to convince the owner of this property to sell it to *him*. Then the lease wouldn't apply anymore and he could kick me out. Nasty business."

Yes, it was a nasty business.

Nasty enough to be a motivation for murder?

Daisy had just kneaded dough for cinnamon bread late Saturday morning when she heard a voice she recognized coming from the tea garden's general serving area. It was Violet! And she was talking animatedly with Foster at the sales counter.

Daisy quickly washed her hands and rushed right over to give Vi a hug. Then with her hands on her daughter's shoulders, Daisy studied her intently. Vi had gotten her hair cut into a swingy style that curved around her face. It looked as if she'd had her light-brown hair highlighted too. She was pretty and looked well.

"This is a surprise. What are you doing here?" She had resigned herself to the fact that she wouldn't see Vi until Thanksgiving because her activities at college were going so well.

"I was homesick. And I was worried about all of you," Vi answered. "Jazzi called me last night to tell me she's searching for her birth parents. Are you on board with that?"

Reflexively, Daisy checked both tea rooms and saw that everyone was taken care of. "Come in to my office with me, and we can chat."

Violet might be concerned about her family, but she was giving Foster a look as if she wanted to stay and talk to him. Hmmm. Then again, maybe Daisy was seeing something that wasn't there because her daughter responded, "A chat sounds good."

On the way to her office, Daisy snagged a few chocolate chip cookies from a cooling rack in the kitchen. Once she and Vi were seated, Daisy asked her, "Is everything okay at school?"

"Everything's fine. I just came home to pick up warmer clothes and check in with you."

"You know we're fine here, too."

"A murder in the tea garden, Mom? How did that happen?"

"The way any murder happens, I guess. Willow Creek is quiet, but not immune to crime."

"You've hired extra help, I see." Vi glanced out the glass partition to where Foster stood.

"The police are working on solving this crime. And business has been good."

"Because of the murder?" Vi looked horrified.

"Possibly," Daisy admitted. "But I'm hoping that everyone who tastes what we have to offer will come back. It seems they are doing just that. We even had a food critic come in for afternoon sit-down tea service. I haven't seen his review yet. I certainly hope he warns us before he publishes it." Or, she added to herself, hopefully Trevor would let her know what was in the review.

"A food critic. Not a tea critic?"

"I'm not sure," Daisy answered truthfully. Not dwelling on that, she informed Vi, "We have a busy day today. I'm serving tea and cookies at your grandparents' nursery this afternoon. They're having their fall sale, and it seemed like a good idea. Do you want to come along?"

Vi looked toward the other room. "Will Foster be helping?"

"No, he'll be staying here with Tessa and Cora Sue this afternoon. Aunt Iris will be with me at the nursery. I think she needs to get away from the tea garden now and then. I am worried about her. She was in love with Harvey, and his death has hit her hard."

"Jazzi told me the police have questioned her more than once."

"They have, and that's worrisome. We've consulted with a lawyer."

"I can help here this afternoon. I can see Gram and Gramps tomorrow." She looked in Foster's direction. "How long are you staying?"

"I don't have classes on Monday, so I don't have to go back until late Monday evening or Tuesday morning. That will give us all time to talk. I can help out here all day Monday if you need me. Foster said he's here in the afternoon."

Vi had a whole college campus full of guys to choose from, yet it seemed Foster had caught her eye. That was the way it went sometimes. Not that Daisy wanted to question her daughter's willingness to help her, but she suspected Violet's eagerness to serve tea had more to do with Foster than scones and Darjeeling.

Chapter Nineteen

Daisy had set up her tea cart at Gallagher's Garden Corner near the front entrance of the building, where her parents and staff had arranged houseplants, garden statues, planters, pots, and seasonal gifts. Her tea cart for this display was an old flower cart that she'd found at a secondhand shop. Once used to sell flowers along the road, it was cute, with three shelves, wheels, and a canopy. She'd had it refurbished, of course, painting it yellow and having the canopy redone in a flowered vinyl. For an event like this, it was perfect.

She'd set up a table nearby covered with a pale pink cloth for the electric urns for tea water, the teapots and cups with saucers. Iris mingled with customers, directing them to the tea cart. Daisy was glad to see many of her regulars from the tea garden buying colorful arrangements for the fall, along with glazed pots with mums and decorative plant stakes similar to those she had arranged on the tea garden's front porch. Other customers were considering fire pits, which were popular this time of year in Pennsylvania, and purchasing trees from the nursery outside to plant before winter set in. Her mom and dad were busy with customers, and one of their assistants manned the cashier's desk. The place was hopping, and Daisy was glad about that for herself, for the free publicity, and for Gallagher's Garden Corner. She was also happy Iris was mingling and away from the site of Harvey's murder. Daisy had broached the subject of her aunt seeing a counselor, but Iris had pooh-poohed the idea. She'd wait and see how her aunt reacted over the next week or so before she brought it up again.

Daisy had carried in trays of cookies and scones and stored them in the nursery's office so she could just bring out what she needed when she needed it. The same way with her cans of tea. She'd made a trip to the office and was carrying a tray of petite cinnamon scones and chocolate butter wafers to a group of customers when she spotted Detective Rappaport. She wasn't going to ignore him. He'd say she had something to hide if she did. Instead, when she finished making the rounds of the group in her corner, she went straight to him.

"How about a cookie, Detective?" She motioned to the tea cart. "You might try a cup of tea too."

He eyed the cookies and then actually took one of the chocolate wafers. After a bite, he nodded. "Did you make these?"

"My assistant, Tessa, made those. Do you like them?"

He nodded again. "They're great. They'd go with coffee at breakfast."

Daisy shook her head. "Add yogurt and you might get a bit of health benefit out of that."

He screwed up his face at the idea of yogurt. "Sugar and caffeine. That's what keeps me going."

Until it doesn't, Daisy thought. "What are you doing here?" she asked bluntly.

He didn't respond to her bluntness. Instead, he glanced toward Iris.

"Are you keeping an eye on my aunt and following her around?"

He met her gaze. "Harvey Fitz's killer could still think Miss Albright has something he or she wants."

"So my aunt isn't your number one suspect anymore?"

"No comment on that."

Daisy didn't like the idea that her aunt could be in danger. Could she *really* be in harm's way?

Before she had time to consider that, and what to do about it, a friend of her aunt's came over to Daisy and Detective Rappaport. Aggie Weiss greeted Daisy and then said, "It's good to see you again, Morris. Are you looking for a tree to plant?"

So Morris was Detective Rappaport's first name. Everyone knew that Aggie got around, and she seemed to know everything there was to know about everybody.

"I might be looking for a fast-growing tree to take the place of one I had to have cut down after last winter."

"A shade tree?" Daisy asked.

"Yes, that would keep the house cooler."

"Silver maples grow fast and give good shade. That would be one to consider." If he really *was* considering buying a tree.

Aggie turned to Daisy then. "I heard something about you."

"You did?"

Aggie made it sound as if what she'd heard was

scandalous. Daisy hadn't done anything scandalous in a very long time.

Aggie went on. "I heard you were seen at Bases talking to Harvey Fitz's son. Since when do you frequent a sports bar?"

Of all times for Aggie to bring that up . . . when Detective Rappaport was all ears. Not only all ears, but one big scowl too.

Daisy could feel her face flushing, and she wished she could stuff Aggie into one of the compost barrels that were for sale right outside. Thinking quickly and wanting to get Aggie off the subject, she replied, "I had an errand at Bases, and sometimes a person needs something stronger than tea."

Aggie looked shocked at that summation, made an excuse about having to get back home, and then rushed over to talk to Iris again. Daisy could only imagine *that* conversation. She hadn't told anyone but Marshall that she had talked to Daniel. That had seemed best.

After Aggie had scurried away, Rappaport asked Daisy, "What do you think you're doing?"

She kept her voice low. "I wanted to know if Daniel had a motive, or if he was the type of person who could commit murder. I'm just trying to protect my aunt by getting to the bottom of it."

"That is *not* your job."

"Protecting my aunt is."

"If you want to protect her, hire her a bodyguard. Do *not* get involved in this investigation, or I could file charges against you. I'm warning you, Mrs. Swanson. Stay away from anyone associated with Harvey Fitz."

Just then one of the customers, a woman who looked to be in her fifties, came up to Daisy and said, "I hear you're brewing blueberry pineapple tea."

"I am. It has a Rooibos base. I'd be glad to steep you a cup. Come on. I think we have mini blueberry muffins left to go with it. Are you interested?"

"I certainly am. This is a wonderful idea, you being here. Do you do this often?"

"A few times a year, usually with the change of seasons."

"It's a very inventive thing to do. It makes everyone more sociable and happy, and to tell you the truth, I'm going to buy my tree here because of it."

"What kind of tree do you want to buy?"

"I think an Alaskan cedar. I love the way their branches are weepy, and the pine needles are lace-like."

"I have several of those on my property, and you're right, they're very beautiful. Let's find you tea and a muffin, then I'll direct you to my mom, and she can show you the selection of Alaskan cedars that she has on the lot."

"A wonderful idea."

But as she did just that, she spotted Detective Rappaport's gaze on her, watching her closely. She really should watch her step or she could be in more trouble than she wanted to handle.

"Mom," Violet called from upstairs Saturday evening. "There's a police car in the driveway and somebody else too."

Daisy had been pulling ground beef, tomatoes, lettuce, and tortillas out of the refrigerator to make tacos. But at Vi's words, she hurriedly rushed to the front door and opened it.

To her total astonishment, Detective Rappaport stood there with her Aunt Iris. Oh my gosh, had he arrested her? Her brain finally kicked into gear. If he'd arrested her, he wouldn't have brought her here. What had happened?

As the detective and her aunt stepped inside, Jazzi and Vi ran down the steps, Marjoram and Pepper at their heels, and waited expectantly to find out what was going on.

Detective Rappaport gingerly held Iris's elbow as he helped her to the sofa, and she sat heavily on it. Used to Iris, maybe sensing she was in distress, Marjoram and Pepper hopped onto the sofa, Marjoram on the back and Pepper on Iris's lap.

Daisy couldn't wait for an explanation any longer. "What happened?" She sat down next to her aunt but looked up at Detective Rappaport, while Jazzi and Vi stood beside the sofa watching and waiting.

The detective's voice was brisk as he related what had happened. "Your aunt thought she was being followed. I'd given her my cell number, and she called me. I happened to be in the vicinity. I sent a patrol officer to meet her at a convenience store. I met up with her there, and now here we are. I drove in front of her, and the patrol car stayed in back of her until we got here."

"I'm sorry to bring this to you, Daisy," her aunt said, her voice cracking a bit. "But I didn't know where else to go."

"We weren't followed here," Rappaport said. "We made sure of that. I'm still not sure your aunt was followed."

Daisy patted her aunt's hand. "Tell me what happened."

Rappaport impatiently crossed his arms over his chest.

Her aunt stroked Pepper's shiny, blue-black fur.

"You left your mom's nursery before me. I followed you out, but then I turned onto Pine Street, and you headed home." Iris paused a moment. "These two headlights were in back of me. At least, that's how I thought of them. It was a dark car. It had those headlights that are almost bright white."

Daisy nodded that she understood what her aunt was telling her. Pepper gave a soft meow as if she understood too.

Iris continued, "He . . . or she . . . was tailgating me a little too close, so I sped up. But whoever was in the car sped up too. I decided to experiment a little, so I turned right, and the car turned right. Then I turned left, and the other car turned left. That's when I got worried. I really didn't know what to do. Detective Rappaport had given me his number, so I called him."

"Were there any security cameras on her route that you could check?" Daisy asked the detective.

"Willow Creek doesn't have the money for security cameras, Mrs. Swanson. Sure, we have speed traps, but that's not the same."

"What happened when you turned in at the convenience store?" Daisy asked her aunt.

"The car went around the block. I hurried inside the store, but I saw those same white headlights come around again and then again until the patrol car got there. Then I didn't see them anymore."

Daisy looked up at Rappaport. "And you think she's making this up? Someone ransacked her house, and someone definitely killed Harvey Fitz."

"I'm mindful of that every minute of every day." He let out a sigh and uncrossed his arms. "No one knows that we have that coin. Someone could still think your aunt has it, maybe on her person, maybe in her car, maybe in her house."

"Then *maybe* you should put out the word that the police have it."

Rappaport shook his head. "Not yet."

"And what's my aunt supposed to do in the meantime? She could be in danger."

"As long as she's with you, or with a group of people, she should be fine. I suggest that for the next week or so she not drive herself anywhere alone. We *are* closing in on suspects."

"But she's still one of them."

Again, he sighed. "I can't discuss the investigation, you know that. So just take my advice. If she stays here with you, she can go back and forth to work every day with you."

Iris looked at Daisy. "I don't want to impose, and with Vi here, you don't have room—"

"I always have room. The sofa opens up into a bed. I can sleep out here, and you can have my room. It's fine, Aunt Iris."

"But my clothes—"

Rappaport just rolled his eyes. "Women."

Now Vi stepped in. "Detective, don't tell me you don't care if you have a clean shirt to wear the next day."

The detective studied Violet. "I suppose you're the daughter who's in college?"

Daisy quickly introduced them.

After a nod, the detective said, "The patrol car's out in your driveway. I've got to let him go, and I've got to go. No point putting in more overtime for either of us." He studied Daisy. "Keep your alarm on whether you're here or not, and don't take any chances. Enjoy your time with your daughters, and no more visits to Bases."

"Are you ordering me around?" Daisy asked, having had enough of his attitude.

"I'm not ordering you. I'm making strong recommendations. If I were you, I would take them." He headed toward the door, opened it, and left.

"Isn't he a sweetheart?" Violet asked sarcastically.

Now Jazzi came around the sofa and sat with her aunt too. "Mom says he's just doing his job, Vi. The problem is—I don't know if he knows how to do it. Willow Creek hasn't seen many murders or investigations of any kind."

"He's right about one thing, though," Daisy said. "Let me switch on the alarm before we do anything else. Then I'll put supper together."

"We'll all help," Vi said.

Jazzi asked Iris, "Are you okay? You look a little pale."

"I'm fine. But, Daisy, do you have any spirits. A swig or two of wine might help."

"I bought white wine for that chicken recipe I make. I might still have some in the refrigerator. Come on, let's go to the kitchen, and I'll check."

Pepper protested when Iris stood but soon circled and kneaded the middle sofa cushion where she sat under Marjoram's watchful golden eyes.

Once in the kitchen, they all took a job. Aunt Iris insisted on browning the ground beef. Vi and Jazzi chopped up vegetables to layer in their tacos. Daisy peeled pears, placed them in a baking dish with a small amount of water, added butter and cinnamon, and slipped them into the oven to poach.

Jazzi said, "Speaking of investigations, Mom, has

Jonas said anything about what he's found about my birth parents?"

Iris's eyes targeted Daisy. "How do you really feel about Jazzi doing this?"

"I'll be honest," she said to Iris. "I didn't know how I felt about it at the beginning. But if it's what Jazzi wants, then I'm all for it. I'm still her mom, whether she finds her birth mother or not. Nothing will ever change that." She turned to Jazzi. "Jonas hasn't said anything more yet, but I'm sure he will as soon as he connects with the lawyer's secretary. You've got to realize searching takes time."

Jazzi looked disappointed, but she seemed to understand. Waiting was difficult for everyone.

Daisy had set up a buffet line to assemble their tacos. Then they took their dishes to the table.

After eating in silence for a few minutes, Daisy asked Vi, "Did you pack up warmer clothes to take back to school?"

Violet finished a bite of her taco. "I did. I'm glad I came home this weekend. I *was* homesick, and I couldn't wait until Thanksgiving to see you. I miss Jazzi, and I miss you, and I miss the cats. Oh, and I miss you too, Aunt Iris."

Daisy realized part of her little girl was still with her, even though Vi was becoming an accomplished, grown-up woman.

Jazzi elbowed her sister. "You might be missing Foster when you're back at school."

Vi ducked her head and mumbled, "Don't be silly."

Daisy glanced at Jazzi. "Missing Foster?"

"They talked every chance they could when customers weren't keeping us busy."

Violet's gaze met Daisy's. Her daughter looked

hesitant for a moment, then asked, "So what do you really think about Foster?"

Iris answered immediately. "He's a personable young man and a fine worker. Is Jazzi right? Might you miss him when you return to Lehigh?" In spite of what had happened tonight, there was a twinkle in Iris's eye.

Violet seemed a bit flustered when she answered, "He's great. We have a lot in common. Maybe, just maybe, I'll come home more often and help you out at the tea garden."

"Help me out at the tea garden, or hope he asks you out on a date?" Daisy teased.

"Don't you like any of the boys at college?" Jazzi asked her sister.

"There are a lot who are there to join fraternities and have frat parties. They don't seem as serious-minded as Foster is. Besides, when I've talked to them, I haven't felt 'it'."

"It?" Jazzi asked innocently.

"Yeah. That special something that makes you want to spend more time with a person."

"Mom went on a date," Jazzi informed Vi.

"She did? With who?"

"Cade Bankert," her sister answered.

"Girls, I'm right here," Daisy reminded them in a singsong voice.

"He's that real estate agent," Vi said, remembering their house hunt.

"And she went to school with him," Jazzi reminded her sister.

"That's right. You told us he took you to your prom," Vi said with a smile, then swiped her mouth with a napkin to clean off remnants of taco sauce.

"We had dinner out. That's all," Daisy murmured.

"I think she really likes Jonas Groft," Jazzi said. "The man who owns Woods. The one who's helping me find my birth parents."

"The tea garden and the two of you keep me busy enough. I don't need to date or to get serious about anyone," Daisy informed them all.

Now Iris included her two cents. "Don't you think it's time you date? Especially if the girls don't object. You need a life, Daisy. I thought I was finally going to find one with Harvey. Loving him put excitement in my days and gave me something to look forward to. You need that too."

All was quiet for a few moments until Violet said, "Aunt Iris, I forgot to tell you. Someone named Marshall Thompson came in and asked for you. He seemed disappointed when you weren't there."

Iris looked startled, and then she just waved her hand in front of her face. "Oh, he's a lawyer."

"Lawyer?" Violet asked.

"He's the lawyer we consulted when the police wanted to question us," Daisy explained. "Jonas advised us that would be a good idea and recommended Marshall."

"I see," said Violet. "But I don't think he was there to do anything lawyerly. He had a cup of tea and a scone, and then said to tell you he'd be in touch."

Daisy wondered if Marshall wanted to discuss the Harvey Fitz case or if he was interested in her aunt. Even if he was, Daisy knew it would take a long while for her aunt to get over Harvey.

Daisy worried about her aunt the next morning as she and Iris, Jazzi, and Vi went to church. Usually, Iris worked at the tea garden when Daisy didn't. But last night, she'd called Foster to take Iris's place, and he'd been able to work an all-day shift. Driving to church, Daisy made sure they weren't being followed, checking her rearview mirror often. Vi and Jazzi did too. They were determined to keep her aunt safe.

At church, though, Daisy found her mom and dad. They learned what had happened with Iris the evening before and said they'd take her to her house to gather up some clothes. She could stay with them for the afternoon. Soon they would be starting holiday hours and have little time to visit with her since the nursery would be open on Sundays. They would make sure no harm came to her. Daisy could pick her up later that evening, and they could all have dinner together. With Violet home, it would be a family time.

It seemed like a good plan, so Daisy agreed.

Back at home once again with Vi and Jazzi, Daisy suddenly knew how she wanted to spend the day with her daughters. "Why don't we pack a picnic lunch, take our backpacks, and go for a hike? It's been a long time since we've done that."

Vi teased, "Are you saying you don't get enough exercise?"

"I don't unless I walk around town."

"And visiting Woods isn't quite enough of a walk," Jazzi kidded.

"Hey, you two. Stop playing matchmakers. Let's get those sandwiches made."

While Jazzi and Vi worked on the sandwiches, Daisy put more kibble in Pepper and Marjoram's dishes. Marjoram playfully tapped Daisy's ankle with her paw in a thank-you, and Pepper meowed hers.

A half hour later, they'd taken a trail through a neighbor's farmland. The trees were turning now. Yellow, russet, orange, and shades of brown formed a canopy above them as they walked through maples, sycamores, elms, and birches. They didn't talk much, just enjoyed the beautiful Indian summer day. Rustling leaves as they walked, they stepped over fallen logs, tripped now and then over a protruding root or a rock, laughed, and caught each other's arms. Daisy realized how much she appreciated this day and having her girls with her.

They emerged from the woods near an old covered bridge where a stream burbled underneath. They were about a quarter mile from the Covered Bridge Inn, the ritziest place to stay and have dinner in the area. A gravel lane led to and from the covered bridge, and they heard the clump, clump, clump of a horse's hooves. Soon an Amish gray-topped buggy came along, clamored through the covered bridge, and continued down the lane to a farm over the hill. There was something about the horse-drawn carriages of the Amish that spoke of a slower pace of life and an earlier time where the things that mattered in life were always in the forefront.

Jazzi pulled a light blanket from her backpack while Vi plucked water bottles from hers. Daisy unpacked her insulated pack, which held the sandwiches, protein bars, and a chocolate and nut mix, along with carrots and celery in a Ziploc bag. They settled under a decades-old oak with the breeze rustling the leaves around their blanket.

After they ate, Violet leaned against the tree. "Do you really think Aunt Iris is in danger?"

"I don't know, honey. If she says someone was following her, I believe her," Daisy said.

"Maybe they don't mean her any harm," Jazzi suggested. "Maybe they just want to follow her and see where she goes, to see if they can find that coin."

That was possible. On the other hand, Daisy thought about Harvey Fitz's dead body and the unicorn statue that was missing.

The girls must have been thinking about the murder too because Violet shook her head. "Somebody must have had a really strong motive to kill Mr. Fitz. I can't believe it's all about a coin."

"Maybe it's not *just* about the coin," Daisy agreed. "Maybe that's only part of it."

"You know, we forgot to tell you that, besides Marshall, somebody else came in to the tea garden yesterday asking for you."

"Who?"

"A woman in her late twenties or early thirties. She said her name was Caroline. She had tea, but she wanted to see you and talk to you about a part-time job."

"She was let go from Men's Trends. Maybe her job interview with Gents wasn't successful."

"I can't see how men's clothing stores thrive," Violet said. "Just look at the discount department stores that have cropped up. And in this area, there are so many clothing outlets. Maybe Mr. Fitz had the right combination to make a success of his store, but that doesn't mean just anyone would. Taking on the store could be a financial risk that's too great."

"You might be right," Daisy agreed. "Did Caroline give you a number?"

Violet nodded. "She did."

Violet fished a slip of paper out of her pocket and handed it to Daisy. "I stuck it in my pocket, hoping I'd remember to give it to you. If you want to call her, go ahead. Jazzi and I want to explore that covered bridge, check out the initials inside, and see if there are more than the last time we looked."

Sweethearts who came this way carved their initials inside the covered bridge. It was a local ritual.

"Are you sure you don't mind?"

Violet answered for both of them, as she often did. "We don't mind." She and Jazzi rose to their feet and ambled off toward the bridge.

Daisy took her phone from her backpack and keyed in Caroline's number. She fully expected to leave a voice mail, but the young woman answered on the second ring.

"Caroline, it's Daisy Swanson. My daughter Violet said you stopped in at the tea garden yesterday."

"Yes, I did."

"What can I do for you?"

"I wondered if you're hiring. That other interview I went on didn't pan out."

"I have hired someone new, and he's working out. But my level of business has expanded in the past two weeks. If it continues, I'll definitely need more part-time help. Why don't you come in and fill out an application? I know you have sales experience. I'm sure we can teach you about tea, if you'd like to learn."

"That sounds good. I have another interview tomorrow morning at a women's clothing outlet. I might be able to get a benefits package there, and if I supplement it with working for you part-time, I can make my rent. You know, I'm not so sure this wouldn't have happened even if Harvey hadn't died."

"What makes you say that?"

"I don't know. Just a feeling that something had changed. The week before he was murdered, Harvey was out of the store a lot, which was unusual. He usually kept his eye on everything."

"Maybe he had meetings with his lawyer about his divorce and his will. I heard he changed it."

"I suppose that's possible. But only if his lawyer was in Philadelphia. That's where he drove to. When he returned from the meetings, he was always gruff and distracted. That wasn't like him either."

"You think maybe he was discussing selling the store?"

"Could be. Or it could be something entirely different. I certainly wasn't privy to what he was thinking. I'm not sure anyone was, unless maybe your aunt. He always seemed to be in a good mood when he was with her. And afterward. The employees kidded each other that the morning after a date with her, we should ask him for a raise. But I don't know if anybody actually did. You don't kid around with a man like Harvey."

After a bit more conversation, Daisy ended the call, assuring Caroline she'd talk to her when she stopped in. Violet and Jazzi were coming back from the tour of the inside of the covered bridge. They were smiling and talking like two sisters should.

Daisy thought about Caroline's words. *You don't kid around with a man like Harvey.* Maybe that was true. Maybe people knew that. Maybe someone had crossed Harvey and he'd found a way to get back at them. Or possibly his ruthlessness in business had been a two-edged sword. Possibly his desire to teach his children a lesson had backfired. What if Monica's resentment of him had turned nasty?

As soon as Daisy was alone with her aunt again, she'd ask Iris if she'd known why Harvey had been out of town the week before he was murdered. If she knew, that might give them a clue as to who had done the deed.

Chapter Twenty

On Monday morning, Daisy was surprised again at the number of customers who were present as soon as the doors to the tea garden opened. Helping to serve, she overheard several conversations. Many of the new tea garden customers were moms who carpooled and stopped in at Daisy's after they took their kids to school. She heard talk about soccer teams and parent-teacher conferences, trick or treat, and fast meals moms could serve on the run.

A busload of tourists pulled up at nine AM, filling both the green and yellow tea rooms. Vacationers were taking a bus trip through the area, viewing the leaves and the countryside in general. They'd started out in Chambersburg and were headed for King of Prussia Mall. Daisy had introduced a new orange pecan breakfast scone, and it was a hit. She was seriously considering hiring Caroline. They were getting a little backed up on the tea orders, and she didn't want that to happen.

She and Iris brushed elbows at one point at neighboring tables. Iris gave her a wink that said she understood business was good. Daisy thought about their conversation last evening after dinner with her parents. She'd inquired about those meetings that Harvey had had in Philadelphia. Iris had shrugged and said she'd known Harvey traveled to Philadelphia. But when he'd returned to Willow Creek, he'd merely told her the meetings were about business. She didn't know why she had assumed that they had something to do with his investments.

Now Daisy wondered if a Philadelphia investment firm took care of Harvey Fitz's accounts. If so, did that have anything to do with his murder?

Although Daisy felt sorry for her aunt, she was glad Iris had had her experiences with Harvey. Her feelings toward him had given her a new lease on life and the ability to dream again. The loss of Harvey would take a while to get over, but Daisy was hoping her aunt would see that she had the ability to fall in love again, no matter how old she was.

By ten o'clock, another tour bus had arrived. Along with those customers, Daisy's dad stopped in and waved her down. "Hi, honey. Got a scone for me?"

"Do you want to skip the line?" she teased.

"Actually, what I want is to unload fall planters for you that Mom sent over. She said you could use them in your garden, at least for a couple of weeks. We're bringing in holiday arrangements, and we have to make room. Do you want me to just set them out back?"

"That would be great. I'll arrange them when I have a chance."

"The marigolds might last longer than the mums. The snapdragons should last longest of all. They'll be good until we get a hard freeze."

Seeing that all the tables had been served and no customers were calling either her or Iris over to pour refills or to fetch another scone, she said to her dad, "Can I talk to you for a minute?"

"Sure. In your office?"

Before Daisy dashed into her office, she made a sojourn to the front cases, grabbed scones, and took them with her.

"Tea?" she asked him.

"You're busy. I'm fine without it. What did you need to know?"

Her dad studied her intently. Her mother said his bright blue eyes could convince her to do anything. But as far as Daisy knew, her dad only used that power for good. In jeans and a flannel shirt and wearing a ball cap that was Philadelphia Phillies all the way, he looked like many of the customers that came into her shop. But he was her dad, and she trusted anything he would tell her.

She knew he and her mom had investments. They'd had a college fund for Daisy and her sister, and now a retirement fund. She didn't know much beyond that.

"Do you have a financial adviser?" she asked him.

"We do. Our accountant recommended ours. Are you looking?"

She shook her head. "Not right now. I have the girls' college funds invested in no-load funds. I never felt the need for a financial adviser. After Ryan died, I just kept everything the way he'd set it up."

"So why are you asking now?" her dad inquired.

"Is your financial adviser around here?"

"He is. He's in Lancaster."

"So let me ask you something. If you had double or triple the money you and Mom have, would you still go to a financial adviser around here, or would you go to Philadelphia to find one?"

"I don't know if that depends on vicinity as much as contacts," her dad answered.

"I don't know what you mean," Daisy admitted.

"Word of mouth is important in that business," her father explained. "Friends recommend their financial advisers to other friends. A group of people who might work in the same business might go to the same financial adviser if they think he or she is doing a good job. It all depends on what a person is looking for, if he or she wants service, hand-holding, and many phone calls, in addition to investment strategies. The only way you know about those things before you settle on a financial adviser is to ask around and get valid recommendations."

"So if I wanted someone with a good track record, who kept me informed, and gave me good tips, I might go as far as Philadelphia if that person were recommended to me."

"Exactly."

"So it wouldn't seem unusual for a man like Harvey Fitz to go to Philadelphia to meet with people like that?"

"Philadelphia's really not that far. I don't think that would be unusual at all."

"The police would know who his financial adviser was, right?" Daisy asked.

"Most probably. They'd also have info about his accountant and his lawyer. They probably know his doctors too. Questioning all those people is tedious and takes time. I understand you don't like Detective Rappaport because he's been brusque with Iris, but that doesn't mean he's not doing his job."

"He won't tell us anything," Daisy grumbled.

"Daisy, you know he can't. The wrong word to the wrong person and the whole investigation could blow up in his face. They'll figure this out. You just have to give him time."

"I'm worried about Aunt Iris. She's under a lot of stress thinking she's in danger."

"Between you and the girls, and your mom and me, we'll make sure she's safe."

The bell above the front door dinged, and not just because customers were leaving; actually, more were coming in. Her dad ate the last few bites of the first scone. "I'll take the second one with me. You'd better get back to your service. Is Vi doing a good job today?"

"I think she's just waiting until she can see Foster again. He'll be in after lunch. But I'd better get top-notch work out of them both."

"Violet knows the tea garden is important, and its reputation is too. She won't let you down. I *am* worried about Jazzi, though. What happens if this friend of yours can't find her birth mother? Where does that leave her?"

"Still looking and still hoping. This is new territory for me, Dad. I just have to do what I think is right."

Suddenly, a man was standing at the door to her office. That man was Trevor Lundquist.

"Hi, Trevor," she said cheerily. "Did you come to try my new scones?"

"Did you read your e-mail this morning?"

"I haven't had a chance. Why?"

"Check your e-mail."

Since she was in her office, she decided to do it on her computer rather than on her phone. Sitting in the swivel chair at her desk, she brought up her e-mail program. In her in-box, she found an e-mail from David Ruiz. Quickly reading it, she saw he'd given the tea garden a four-star review in the travel guide.

"He liked us!" she said with a punch into the air.

"He calls us a charming place to spend a relaxing hour."

"What else does he say?" her dad asked.

She frowned. "He says he would have given us five stars if we'd had more staff."

Trevor's brow arched. "That's possible, isn't it?"

"I've hired someone, and I'm thinking about hiring someone else."

"If you do that, and if David comes in next year about the revised travel guide, you'll have that problem solved. Maybe you can go from four to five stars." Trevor was standing behind her, and she looked over her shoulder at him.

"Thank you for bringing David in."

Trevor negated that thought by saying, "The murder brought me in." At the door, he winked at her. "And you're going to tell me all about it when it's solved. I have a memory even better than an elephant's." Then he was gone.

"Are you beholden to him?" her father asked, sensing something in that interplay.

"We made a deal. He lived up to his end, now I have to live up to my end."

"I hope it's a legitimate deal."

"Oh, it is. I just told him I'd tell him everything I know about who the killer is as soon as I know."

"Daisy, the truth always comes to light. If the person who killed Harvey Fitz wanted something from him, or now wants something from Iris, believe me, we'll soon find out who he or she is."

Daisy thought that was the scariest thing her father had ever told her.

Maybe realizing that, Sean Gallagher gave her a big hug. "This will work out, Daisy Doo. The wheels are in motion. So just be careful who you talk to and what you say." Daisy Doo was an endearing name left over from childhood that always brought a catch to Daisy's throat.

After a kiss on the cheek, her dad said, "I'll tell your mom you loved the planters."

"I'll come with you and look them over. Then you can tell her the truth."

The truth. Did Daisy want to know the truth? What if the murderer was someone she knew? She put that thought out of her head as she followed her dad outside.

Daisy and Iris had finished with afternoon tea service and were wiping down the tables when Tessa motioned to Daisy from the main counter.

Daisy crossed to her and asked, "What's up?"

"Tornado warning," Tessa said in an undertone so none of their customers could hear. She pointed to the front door.

Monica Fitz sailed in, looking well put together in a red wool coat and a floppy red wool hat.

"A little overdressed for a Monday afternoon, don't you think?" Tessa muttered.

Daisy had to smile. "Maybe she came from someplace important."

"In Willow Creek? That would only be the country club," Tessa answered, returning to the kitchen.

Daisy wondered if she could snag Iris and go and hide. But that was a coward's way out. She didn't even have time to warn her aunt what was coming before Monica was at the counter.

"Hello, Monica," Daisy said amiably.

"I want to talk to your aunt," Monica demanded. "Where is she?"

Daisy couldn't very well say her Aunt Iris had gone home when she was in plain sight if Monica just looked through the doorway.

"She's in the yellow room," Daisy said, motioning that way.

Monica didn't hesitate a second but marched over there. Daisy followed, her cell phone handy in her apron pocket just in case she had to call in the police or 9-1-1. Who knew with this woman?

Iris was still wiping down tables, and Monica glared at her disdainfully. "What did Harvey give you?"

Aunt Iris's eyes widened. "Pardon me?"

"I'd like to, but your place was broken into. Somebody was looking for something. My guess is that Harvey gave you something valuable. He often did that with his paramours. Whatever he gave you should be part of his estate."

Daisy interfered, whether she should or shouldn't have. "I thought Harvey changed his will and his estate goes to charity."

"I'm going to be contesting that. My lawyer insists I have a good opportunity to succeed."

Monica was in Iris's face again. "Did he give you a diamond necklace or ruby bracelet? Or a sheaf of his ever-present coins? I know he was trying to hide assets from me so he didn't have to split them. That's illegal, and if you were any part of it, you were committing a crime."

Iris looked ready to cry, and Daisy stepped in again. "You're making unfounded accusations. If Harvey gave my aunt anything, and that's one very big *if*, it was a gift before he died and has nothing to do with you."

"So you're in on it too," Monica accused.

Now Daisy was close enough to smell alcohol on

the woman's breath. She wondered just how drunk this woman was. Would she act this way normally? Was this one of the reasons Harvey had divorced her?

"You've been drinking," Daisy said matter-of-factly.

"I was at lunch with friends. Of course, I've been drinking. Dirty martinis, if you must know." She pointed her finger at Iris, who was still holding a tablecloth over her arm. "You're nothing more than a glorified waitress. I can't believe Harvey got involved with you. Making me jealous was the only reason he did it."

"Mrs. Fitz, you've said enough. I think you should go," Daisy warned her.

"And I think you should stay out of this. It's between me and your aunt."

From the look on Iris's face, Daisy knew she had to get Monica out of here, or her aunt could possibly collapse. She'd had enough of all of it, and Daisy couldn't blame her. All she had done was fall in love.

For that reason, she decided to go for Monica's jugular. "Mrs. Fitz, maybe you should set a better example for your son so he can find a worthwhile life instead of attending happy hour."

Monica's mouth dropped open, and she just stared at Daisy. "You know nothing about my family."

"I know your daughter wants to change her life, and I know that Daniel needs to change his. But he can't do it with you as an example. He can't do it without your support. You need to pull yourself together and figure out how you can be a role model for him. Help him stop a downward spiral. You can't do that if you're spiraling downward yourself."

Monica's face turned red, and for a moment, Daisy thought the woman might slap her. Preparing herself, she took a few steps back.

In that instant, Daisy saw Monica's expression

change, and she wondered if the woman was having a sudden insight into what Daniel's problems were, as well as her own.

However, after that possibly insightful second, she pointed to Iris again, muttered, "I'll see you in court," and then spun around on her red high heels and left Daisy's Tea Garden.

Iris looked shell-shocked and lowered herself into one of the chairs.

Daisy asked, "Can I get you something—water, tea, something stronger?"

Her aunt gave her a wan smile. "You mean like hot chocolate?"

Daisy glanced into the other room and saw that Cora Sue and Foster were serving customers and had everything under control. She sat down next to her aunt. "She looked like the Wicked Witch of the West and acted like her. Goodness knows what Harvey had to put up with. And the drinking? Maybe that day she came into the twenty-fifth celebration she was drunk too, and that's what caused her behavior."

Iris put a shaky hand to her forehead and rubbed it, lowered her voice, and practically whispered, "Do you think she killed Harvey? She certainly seems capable of it."

It was quite possible that Monica, even if she'd been wearing a hat and high heels, could have scooped up the unicorn statue and walloped Harvey with it. Anyone who had just witnessed her in full witch mode would realize it.

"I think she's capable," Daisy agreed. "I'm wondering if we should tell Marshall about what just happened, or maybe even Detective Rappaport."

"The detective will just think we're trying to throw the blame on someone else," Iris said resignedly. "But maybe we should tell Marshall so he can document it. I'll call him. If he's busy, I'll leave a message."

"Are you sure you don't want me to do it for you?"

"No, I'll do it," Iris said. "Tessa should be starting batches of cookies so we can refrigerate the dough for the morning. Maybe you can help her."

Her aunt was right. She should help Tessa ready their baked goods for tomorrow.

She was on her way to the kitchen when she recognized the next customer who pushed open the door. It was Jonas. She realized how glad she was to see him and told herself she shouldn't be.

As he approached the counter, she realized he looked even more somber than usual. He might be here for more than a scone and a cup of tea.

When he reached the counter, he said, "I saw Monica Fitz fly by my window. She wasn't in here by any chance, was she?"

"Yes, she was. She had some things to say to Aunt Iris."

"Your aunt doesn't have to put up with her, you know. She can always get an order of protection."

"We'll keep that in mind," Daisy said. "What can I get you?"

"How about a chocolate scone to go. I came in because I have news about Jazzi's birth mother. How do you want to handle it?"

Two hours later, they were handling it the only way Daisy knew how. Honestly. She'd asked Jonas if he would come to the house so the two of them could talk to Jazzi there after Daisy had picked her up at choir practice. He agreed. So now here they were, and Daisy was probably as nervous as her daughter.

Sitting across the table from them, Jonas sent a gentle smile to Jazzi. "I had a break. I located the lawyer's secretary. She had moved several times, and that's why it's taken this long to find her. Since your birth mother's name, Portia, was unusual, she remembered the case. At first, she was reluctant to give me your birth mother's last name, but we had another break there. His secretary was adopted herself. So she absolutely understands your need to know. I told her you were registered on the adoption site, and she went to it to look. When she saw it, she knew I was legitimate and you were too. When she gave me your birth mother's last name, I wasn't so sure we had found another lead, because it was Smith! But Joan remembered that she was nineteen, though she didn't know any more about the case. She also doesn't know where Glenn Reeves's records are located. He's the lawyer who handled the adoption," Jonas reminded Jazzi. Then he continued, "Still, going on what she gave me, I think I've found your birth mother."

Jazzi's eyes widened, and she suddenly looked scared. Daisy put her hand on her daughter's shoulder.

Taking an index card from his pocket, Jonas pushed it across the table to Jazzi. "Her name is Portia Smith Harding now and she's living in Allentown. She married six years ago, and she has two children. That's her phone number and her address. What you want to do next is up to you." He looked toward Daisy.

But Daisy just shook her head. She couldn't make this decision for her daughter. She couldn't interfere. Jazzi could resent her for a lifetime if she did.

Daisy said gently, "It is up to you, honey. It's all up to you. You can put that number away in your jewelry box until you're ready to think about it again, or we can contact her. *You* can contact her."

Shifting on his chair, Jonas said, "There is another option. I can act as a go-between if you'd like *me* to contact her."

Studying Jonas's expression, Daisy was sure he hadn't made that suggestion lightly. She had the feeling that he didn't like to get involved, that he'd been too involved with sensitive matters as a cop or as a detective, and now he just wanted to live a quiet life without complications. But Daisy had brought him a complication, and now, it seemed, he was ready to help deal with it.

Jazzi looked confused and younger than her fifteen years. Pushing her chair back, she stood and just stared at the index card as if it were too hot to handle. But then she picked it up. "I have to think about this. Is it okay if I go to my room, Mom?"

"Of course, it is. I'll bring you something to eat in a little while. Warmed up mac and cheese okay with a sandwich?"

Jazzi nodded but had a distant look in her eyes as if she didn't really care what she ate or what Daisy brought her.

As Jazzi left the table, Jonas stood too. "I'd better go."

Daisy walked with him through the living room to the front door. There she looked up at him, noticed again the lines around his eyes, the few around his lips, the way his hair dipped over his brow. "Thank you for doing this."

"You might not thank me if she makes that call."

"I know. I'm as scared as she is, maybe even more. If she makes that call, our relationship could change forever. I could lose her."

Jonas shook his head vehemently. "No, that's not going to happen, and don't even think about it happening. She'll never forget what you've given her for fifteen years. Your love, your support, and your caring have been priceless. Do you think she'd trade that in for a hug from her birth mother?"

"I don't know. Maybe."

He shook his head again. "Trust her, Daisy. No matter how this goes, you have to trust your daughter."

That was true, and she knew it. Finally, she confided, "Ever since Ryan died, I don't trust as well. I worry more. I look for the other shoe to drop."

"Loss will do that," Jonas empathized, as if he knew. He reached out and squeezed her shoulder. "Somehow life works out, even if we don't think it will."

If it had come from anybody else, Daisy would have heard that line as a platitude. Coming from Jonas, it meant a great deal. His hand on her shoulder created a warmth inside of her that she hadn't felt in a very long time.

As if he felt some kind of heat too, he dropped his hand, turned, and opened the door. But over his shoulder he said, "Give her space, Daisy. She'll figure it out, and so will you."

Then he was gone.

As Daisy set the house alarm, she heard his SUV leave. There was something about Jonas Groft that made her want to spend more time with him. But she felt he was fighting the idea of spending time with her. Would she ever learn why?

Chapter Twenty-One

Daisy expected Jazzi at the tea garden the next afternoon. If they weren't busy, her daughter was going to seriously work on their cookbook. However, when Jazzi came in, she took Daisy aside.

"I know I'm supposed to work on the cookbook, Mom, but can we talk to Jonas?"

It was easy to see that whatever Jazzi wanted to tell Jonas was weighing heavily on her mind. Customers were arriving steadily, but Cora Sue and Iris were handling them easily. She said, "Let me call Jonas and see if he's busy." She did, and Jonas said no one was in the store right then. He could talk, if that's what Jazzi wanted.

Daisy didn't know if Jazzi had ever been in Jonas's store, but her daughter definitely wasn't interested in furniture. They spotted Jonas sitting on a stool behind the counter. With a slight hesitation and a sideways glance at Daisy, Jazzi approached him.

Jonas took one look at Jazzi and said, "You've made a decision."

Jazzi rested her hands on the counter and nodded. "Since my adoption was a closed one, that means my birth mother might not want anything to do with me. She might not be searching adoption sites like I am. I've registered on three. She might think I want something from her, like money, and I don't." Jazzi bit her lower lip, then went on. "I think it would be best if you make contact for me."

Jonas studied the teenager and then Daisy. "So that's what you want me to do?"

Daisy nodded too. "I think it's a wise decision."

"I found out more about Portia Smith," he said. "And I do think a visit might be better than a phone call."

"You'd drive to Allentown?" Daisy asked.

"For something as important as this I would. Portia's a graphic artist, and she works from home while she takes care of her children. My midweek is usually slow, so my clerks can handle the store. I'll drive to Allentown tomorrow."

"I have debate practice tomorrow," Jazzi told him. "That means Mom doesn't pick me up until around seven."

"No problem," Jonas said. "Your mom has my number. She can text me after you come home."

Relief stole over Jazzi's face now that a plan had been established. She said, "I'm going back to the tea garden and work on that cookbook. It will keep my mind off this." Then she looked at Jonas. "Thank you."

When Jazzi spun around, she seemed eager to leave Woods, eager to distract herself from what could happen the next day.

Daisy watched her daughter exit the shop, and her heart ached for her. She could only imagine how Jazzi was feeling, wondering if she would be rejected or accepted . . . wondering if her mother was a good person . . . or a not so good person . . . wondering if her life was about to change.

Jonas must have been watching her because he said, "I know you're worried, Daisy, but one way or another she'll have answers. You both will."

When Daisy turned around to face him, she could have gotten lost in his very green eyes. Her own eyes were a little misty, and she took a deep breath. "I don't know how to thank you for what you're doing. Not just anybody would do this for a stranger."

"You're not so strange," he responded with a crooked smile.

She gave a little laugh. "In the past few weeks, I've felt mighty strange, but now I guess we're not strangers anymore. Seriously, though, would you accept payment for your time?"

He shook his head. "No. Actually, I've forgotten how good it feels to help someone in this way. And as far as paying me back, sometime let's just make a time for tea for two."

Her heart sang at that suggestion, and she wasn't exactly sure why.

Although the following day was a busy one, Daisy was on edge all day. She knew where Jonas had gone and what he was doing. What had happened with Portia Smith Harding? Was he talking to her now or would he call on his drive home? Had Jazzi's birth mother been receptive, or had she shut the door in his face?

Daisy was sure those same questions had been running through Jazzi's mind all day. She was at debate practice now, and that should keep her well distracted for a little while.

The wind had picked up outside and blew leaves against the front of the Victorian as Daisy and Iris went through their closing checklist. Their staff had left. Daisy emptied the baked goods case and cleaned it while Iris inventoried the freezer and the walk-in refrigerator, making sure they were ready for morning. In a few more minutes, Daisy would switch the OPEN sign on the door to CLOSED.

After another look outside as dusk fell, Daisy said, "I think it's gotten chillier out there. How about a last cup of tea before we leave? I'm just going to work in my office until I have to pick up Jazzi."

"I have to sweep the front table area yet."

"Green tea?" Daisy asked.

"That sounds good."

A few minutes later, Daisy brought one of her favorite vintage teapots, painted with yellow roses and butterflies, to a table in the main serving room. She was about to snag two cups and saucers when she saw the shadow of someone at the front door. It was a man in a duster coat . . .

Bennett Topper opened the door and stepped inside the tea garden. He gave Daisy a smile. "Are you still open?"

As he paused at the door, Daisy glanced at the empty baked goods case in the front. She could always bring out the cookies she'd put in a bag to take home.

"We were just about to close, but we have time for you. Come on in. How are you doing?"

Iris stopped sweeping as Bennett came farther into the room. She still had her broom in hand and propped it beside her.

Bennett looked a bit unsure of himself as he said, "I'm still trying to absorb the fact that Harvey is gone."

"What can I get you?" Daisy asked, wondering if

Bennett had anyone to share his grief with. "Aunt Iris and I were just going to have a cup of green tea, and I have cookies in the back too."

But Bennett shook his head and admitted, "I'm just looking for some sympathy. Most people don't realize how close Harvey and I were. He was a father figure to me."

Iris said with a tinge of bitterness, "I imagine the family's getting all kinds of condolences, even his wife. But you and I . . . People don't consider how much we miss him."

Bennett responded, "Exactly." He glanced toward the side door and the serving area outside where Harvey was murdered. His eyes were troubled. "I just can't believe that someone would pick up a statue and kill Harvey in the garden."

It took Daisy a moment to realize what Bennett had just said. She tried not to react and prevented her expression from changing. She'd just realized who had committed the murder. Harvey Fitz's murderer was standing right before her!

No one had known Harvey was killed with the statue. The police had kept that quiet. Could she be wrong? Maybe Bennett had found out about the unicorn statue from Detective Rappaport somehow. Still, if she *wasn't* wrong—

She slipped her hand into the pocket of her apron for her phone.

Although she believed she'd managed a poker face, there must have been a change in her demeanor. Something had alerted Bennett that she was aware of him in a new way. In the next second, he pulled a gun out of his duster pocket and pointed it at Iris.

Iris gasped, and her hand went to her throat.

Shaking inside, Daisy tried to keep perfectly calm

and still. Her hand was on her phone. If she could just manage to dial 9-1-1. But she wasn't familiar enough with the changing screen and the keyboard on this phone, especially when she wasn't looking at it.

She had to keep her wits about her—her life and Iris's depended on it. Most important, she couldn't make Bennett nervous or freak him out. He didn't look like a man who was used to handling a gun. Was his hand shaking?

"Actually, there *is* something you can get me," Bennett said tersely. "Not tea, of course." He stared at Iris and pointed the gun directly at her heart. "You can fetch me the gold coin Harvey gave you for safe-keeping."

So Harvey's stash *wasn't* a secret. If Bennett was telling the truth and he and Harvey had been close, even confidants, he knew about that coin. Was there any point in either of them denying it?

Bennett shook his free finger at Daisy as if he'd read her mind. "And don't lie to me about it."

After he bit out his warning, he dug his hand into his coat pocket and pulled out a roll of duct tape. He addressed Iris again. "If the coin's not here, I'll just have to duct tape Daisy in her office and we'll go get it."

Bennett might panic if he learned the police were holding the coin. Daisy needed to stall Bennett and keep him talking. Maybe then she could dial the right number.

Her phone gripped tightly in her hand in her pocket, she asked, "Why are you doing this? Why would you kill Harvey, especially if he was your friend?"

"After fifteen years of working together, I *thought* he was my friend, my mentor, more like a father than a boss. But after fifteen years, fifteen long years that I gave him of complete service and loyalty, he was going to sell the store right out from under me."

"I'm so sorry about that, Bennett. That was a terrible thing to do to you, especially after all those years. Didn't he give you the option of staying on?"

"There was no option. If some chain corporation came in and bought his store, they wouldn't want me. They'd want someone they could pay a pittance to manage it. They wouldn't care about real fashion. They'd just truck in the latest menswear from the ready-to-wear line, baggy jeans, oversized shirts, and coats with no style. It would have been a nightmare."

"It would have been a nightmare since you had so much experience. But you could have found another job."

"How many men's stores are around here now, Daisy? I didn't feel like packing up and going back to New York, or even to Philadelphia. My life is here. But not if I lost my job."

"You said you and Harvey were close. Couldn't you tell him how you felt?"

"I did tell him. He didn't *care* how I felt. He was so wrapped up in divorcing Monica, so wrapped up in Iris, so wrapped up in the business of selling, he could hardly hear me when I talked. Even when I got him drunk, he didn't care about me."

"You got Harvey Fitz drunk?" Iris asked, sounding surprised.

When Bennett's attention shifted to her aunt, Daisy took a quick glance at her phone and changed the screen to her keypad.

He was still focusing on Iris as he answered her. "Yes, I did. You'd think he'd have better sense, wouldn't you? He'd had a particularly bitter meeting with Monica about the divorce settlement. I knew he stashed a bottle of one-hundred-year-old cognac in the bottom drawer of his desk. I motioned to it, and he got it out. One drink led to another. And that's when he told me."

Iris followed up with, "Told you what?"

Daisy managed to press 9-1-1.

"That's when he told me he wanted to start a new life—a new life with you," Bennett explained. Then he went on. "As if Harvey didn't have enough money even after he gave Monica a settlement, he felt he needed a hidden asset. He decided on a gold coin. And he told me what he'd done with it. He'd given it to you for safekeeping. I didn't think much about it at the time. I thought maybe it was a golden eagle or something like that because Harvey didn't tell me what it was worth. But I found out its real name and value when Guy Tremont came into the store one day. I overheard him arguing with Harvey. Guy had been all upset because he'd found a coin missing from Harvey's list of assets—a Coiled Hair Stella. I remembered the name. I researched a Coiled Hair Stella and was shocked at its value. But I wasn't shocked for long. And I knew why it was missing from Harvey's assets. He'd hidden it so he wouldn't have to declare it and include it in his net worth for his divorce settlement. I decided I deserved that coin or its equivalent after all those years of overtime and pandering to Harvey and his family. If Harvey wanted to sell the store from under me, fine. I'd have a million dollars, one way or another."

Daisy heard a voice coming from her phone—the dispatcher? Hopefully, Bennett was standing far enough away that he couldn't hear it. She asked, "So what happened the night you killed Harvey?"

"I didn't intend to kill him," Bennett answered

quickly. "I knew he was meeting Iris. I knew he often waited in your back garden until she came out. I followed him from the store that night. When he realized I had, I think he understood I wasn't here for a cup of tea. I didn't have murder on my mind. Who would? I was just thinking about blackmail. Knowledge is power, right? I had power because I knew about that gold coin. I knew what it would mean for Monica to know about it too. Harvey could make a deal with me in one of several ways. He could make me a partner in Men's Trends. I'd run it, and he could travel with Iris. Or . . . if Harvey gave me the coin, I wouldn't care if he sold the store. I'd researched a nice little village in Mexico where a million bucks could see me through my retirement."

"But I thought you didn't want to leave Willow Creek."

"That was before everything changed. That was before Harvey betrayed me by intending to sell Men's Trends. That was before I realized I could do whatever I had to do to make the rest of my life a happy one. You know, Daisy, no one ever thinks they're a murderer, that they're capable of violence. I never thought *I* was."

"Why did you kill Harvey?" The low voice had stopped coming from her phone. Was the dispatcher listening?

"Harvey laughed at me," Bennett answered bitterly. "Can you believe he laughed at me? Who does that to a friend? When I asked him for the Stella or a partnership in the store, he said I was crazy. He said I'd never have the guts to go through with blackmailing him. He said I might know about fashion, but I didn't know about real life and how ruthless men operated. If I tried to blackmail him, he'd destroy me. He had connections, he said. He had friends, he said. Did I know what blackballing was? He said I was going to find out if I tried to blackmail him. He said if I thought he'd make me a partner, I was delusional. He made me so angry that I just picked up that unicorn and swung it at his head."

With everything Bennett had revealed, Daisy believed he *was* delusional. Why did he think Harvey would have agreed to any of it? To elude fraud charges for hiding assets? To partner with Bennett so Harvey didn't have to concern himself with business issues? Because Harvey might feel some loyalty to Bennett based on their years of working together?

"But Harvey's gone now, and I want that gold coin," Bennett said. "Where is it, Iris?"

Daisy could see her aunt was trembling. "I don't have it," Iris assured him. "Honestly, I don't." She looked frantically at Daisy, trying to figure out what to say. If they told Bennett the police had the Stella, he could kill them both.

Daisy glanced at the teapot on the table, with its scalding tea. In the next instant, her gaze connected with her aunt's. Iris gave an almost imperceptible nod of understanding.

All of a sudden, there was a knock at the tea garden's front door. Why would someone knock when it was open?

But Jonas was looking through, bending down, trying to see the latch on the other side. Daisy realized the door *was* locked. Bennett had paused there when he'd slipped inside. He must have locked it.

Nevertheless, Jonas had given Daisy just the distraction she needed. She grabbed the handle of the teapot, rushed forward, and aimed the spout at Bennett's face. With a flick of her wrist, she jerked the pot upward. Hot tea splashed over Bennett.

When Bennett screamed, Iris took advantage of his injury and raised her broom. With a strong sideways hit, she swatted the gun from his hand. It skittered across the floor through the puddle of green tea and under another table. She ran to pick it up.

From the corner of her eye, Daisy saw Jonas take a metal plant stake that decorated one of the pots outside and slam it into the glass on the door. The glass shattered. Slipping his hand through the hole, he opened the lock.

Jonas rushed inside just as Bennett lunged at Daisy. "You burned my face. I'll be scarred for life!"

While Daisy tried to pull away from Bennett, Jonas crashed into him from behind. In a move she'd seen cops use on TV, Jonas spun Bennett around and pushed him to the floor on his stomach, his hands behind him.

In the next instant, Iris scooped up the duct tape that had fallen from Bennett's hand. She thrust it at Jonas. Swiftly, Jonas tore off a length of tape and wrapped it around Bennett's wrists. Then he took the gun from Iris.

As Daisy finally pulled her phone from her pocket, she put it to her ear. But before she spoke to the dispatcher, her gaze met Jonas's. She said, "Thank you," knowing those two words couldn't begin to convey the gratitude she felt.

Standing over Bennett, the man's gun in his hand, Jonas just smiled at her. "In thanks, you can have tea and scones with me once Rappaport cleans up this mess."

Daisy knew the night could be a long one, with questions to answer and statements to give. Tea and scones afterward with Jonas would be just what she needed. "It's a deal."

She suddenly remembered where Jonas had been today. "What about Portia Harding? What happened?"

A police car's siren screamed outside.

Any news about Portia Harding would have to wait.

Epilogue

It was an end-of-October day when the soft hum of two voices emanated from Daisy's kitchen into her living room. She looked up to Jonas for confirmation that they'd done the right thing by bringing Jazzi and her birth mother together.

Jonas had arrived with Portia Smith Harding about twenty minutes ago. He'd driven to Allentown to get her and was going to take her home again this evening. Daisy would be serving lunch in a little while. First, she'd wanted to give Jazzi and Portia time to talk.

Jonas suggested, "Why don't we go outside and give them some real privacy."

The sun was shining brightly on the Indian summer day. Daisy grabbed a sweater coat but still hesitated to go outside.

Jonas could see her hesitation. He reminded her, "We'll be right on the other side of the door."

Daisy took a last glance toward the kitchen and followed him out. On the porch, Daisy said to him,

"Tell me everything Portia said in the car. You had a long ride with her."

"Yes, I did, but we didn't talk much. I didn't learn much more than I already told you. She hasn't spoken to her husband about Jazzi yet. He knows nothing about her giving up a child for adoption fifteen years ago. She's not sure she wants to disrupt her life by bringing it all into the open."

"How did she explain you picking her up today?"

"Her husband's away on business, and her children are with her sister. I think she told her husband she was going shopping with friends for the day."

"Lies," Daisy said with a shake of her head. "One lie always begets another. I'm so afraid she's not going to want Jazzi as a constant in her life."

Gently, Jonas placed his hands on Daisy's shoulders. "That day I first met Portia, she was shocked when I told her about Jazzi and that her daughter wanted to meet her. We all understood she needed time to think about what she wanted to do next. She seems like a kind, if confused, woman to me. Anyone can see that Jazzi's a lovable young lady. After their conversations today, I predict Portia will accept Jazzi into her life. But she has to get used to the idea, and you have to give her time and space. Jazzi does too."

Daisy sighed, knowing Jonas was right, knowing she had to be patient with Portia as well as Jazzi for all their sakes.

Turning to another topic to distract herself from what was going on inside, she asked Jonas, "Have you learned anything more about Bennett?"

Jonas removed his hands from Daisy's shoulders and nodded. "From what I understand, Detective Rappaport found blood evidence in the trunk of Bennett's car, most likely from the unicorn statue.

He found the statue in Bennett's closet, wrapped in one of his expensive silk shirts. I thought Bennett would lawyer up. But he confessed and is awaiting sentencing."

"For a bright man . . ." Daisy let the sentence trail off.

"In my experience, I've found criminals are often stupid about their crimes. Maybe because they lose their heads in the moment. Maybe because their motivation outweighs logic. Is Iris still seeing a counselor?"

"She's had two sessions, and a third is planned for next week. I think it's helping. She says she wants nothing to do with the gold Stella coin even if a judge decides it's hers. She'd give most of it to charity. She's stayed at her house alone for the past two nights. That's the first since Bennett tried to kill us."

"And what about you?" Jonas's green eyes were steady on hers.

"*You've* been *my* counselor," she said with a small laugh. "You let me vent when I need to."

"All I do is listen."

Jonas had been doing a lot more than listening. He'd been supportive and helpful and kind ever since this whole thing had started. "I think the interview that Iris and I did with Trevor helped us deal with all of it too."

"I saw that the interview was picked up in area papers and on reporters' blogs. Trevor gave a fair perspective with his questions."

Daisy returned to the subject uppermost in her mind. "You said you predict that Portia will let Jazzi into her life. What makes you think that?"

"She has kids, and she did talk about them. From what little she said about her husband, he seems to be a good guy. Besides, when I make a prediction, it usually comes true."

When Daisy didn't respond, just gazed up at Jonas, lost in the caring she saw there, he said, "I have another prediction too."

"What?"

"I predict we're going to be more than friends."

Then he gave Daisy a hug, and she believed that his prediction could indeed come true.

...al Recipes

Daisy's Leek and Potato Soup

3 tablespoons high heat sunflower oil
1 cup onion
3 leeks, diced (about 2 cups)
1 cup celery, chopped
1 clove of garlic
3 tablespoons flour
1 quart chicken broth (I use Swanson
    100% Chicken Broth/99% fat free)
2½ to 3 cups peeled potatoes in small chunks
2 cups carrots, sliced
1 bay leaf
1 teaspoon salt
¼ teaspoon pepper
1 cup milk

Trim top and bottom of leeks. Cut lengthwise and soak in water 10 minutes.

In a 4½–quart pot, heat sunflower oil and sauté onion, leeks, and celery for about 3 minutes. After the mixture starts to sizzle, add garlic. Add flour and stir well. Add chicken broth and bring to a boil. Add potatoes, carrots, bay leaf, salt, and pepper. Bring to a boil again, then simmer until potatoes are tender (about 20 minutes). Add milk and simmer 5 more minutes.

Makes 6 servings.

Tessa's Carrot Salad

2½ cups shredded carrots
⅔ cup golden raisins
2½ tablespoons light mayonnaise
2½ tablespoons light sour cream
1½ tablespoons lime juice
1½ teaspoons honey
½ cup chopped pecans
2 cups seedless green grapes (washed and
    drained well)

Mix together carrots and raisins in a medium bowl.
Mix together mayonnaise, sour cream, lime juice,
and honey in a small bowl and pour over the carrot
mixture. Stir well. Add chopped pecans and grapes.
Stir and serve or refrigerate.

Serves 6.

Iris's Lemon Tea Cakes

Preheat oven to 375 degrees.

   1 cup butter, softened
   1½ cups granulated sugar (plus 2 tablespoons
      to garnish the baked cookies)
   3 eggs
   2 teaspoons lemon zest
   ½ teaspoon salt
   2½ teaspoons baking powder
   1 teaspoon lemon extract
   3 cups flour

Cream softened butter and granulated sugar until fluffy. Add eggs and beat until smooth. Add lemon zest and mix again. Add salt, baking powder, and lemon extract, and mix well with mixer. When you add the flour next, do it in ½-cup portions so batter is thoroughly mixed and smooth.

Drop rounded tablespoons of batter onto a well-greased cookie sheet. I don't use non-stick. Make sure there is space around each cookie because they grow.

Bake at 375 degrees for 11–12 minutes until golden brown around the edges. When you remove cookies from the oven, sprinkle with granulated sugar. Then quickly remove them from the pan and cool.

Makes about 34 cookies.

Please turn the page for an exciting sneak peek of
Karen Rose Smith's next
Daisy's Tea Garden mystery

MURDER WITH CINNAMON SCONES

coming soon wherever print and e-books are sold!

Chapter One

The Victorian house with its gray siding and white gingerbread trim loomed in front of Daisy Swanson as she and Tessa Miller approached it. The early January darkness had wrapped around the town of Willow Creek, Pennsylvania, early tonight with a cloudy pewter sky before sunset and the prediction of snow later. Daisy wasn't sure she should have let Tessa talk her into coming here to Revelations Art Gallery with her after hours. But Tessa was the chef and kitchen manager at Daisy's Tea Garden and Daisy's best friend. They'd been confidantes since high school. Still . . .

Daisy voiced her concern as a gust of wind blew her wavy shoulder-length blond hair across her cheek. She brushed it behind her ear, thinking she should have worn her hat. The temperature was below freezing. "I don't know if I should have come with you."

Walking along the side of the house to the back door of the art gallery, Tessa assured her, "I'm just going to pick up my sketchbook and leave your cinnamon scones on Reese's desk."

Tessa had been dating Reese Masemer, the owner of Revelations, since her show in October. She'd left her sketchbook there when she'd stopped in to have lunch with him.

Tessa went on, "You know you want to see the quilt display Reese set up. Quilt Lovers Weekend is coming up in a little over three weeks. I'm sure Reese won't mind you being in the gallery with me. He knows you and I are close friends."

Without hesitation, Tessa turned the key in the lock, stepped inside, and pressed in a security code. The long braid that kept her caramel-colored hair relatively confined swished across the back of her purple down jacket as she switched on a light. "He trusts me with the key and the code now."

And Daisy knew why. Often Tessa spent the night with Reese in his apartment upstairs.

Even in the dim light, Daisy could see Tessa blush a little. Her friend's relationship with Reese was fairly new, and Daisy wasn't sure what to think about it yet.

She stepped inside with Tessa and looked around at the office. It was business—messy, with a few paintings positioned on easels and art books spread across a large maple desk. Papers—invoices and such—were scattered over the surface of the desk too. A computer station sat at the far wall, and the computer was off. At least it looked as if it was off, but it could have just been sleeping, Daisy supposed. Tessa's sketchbook rested on the corner.

"I'm surprised you and Reese aren't out on a date tonight," Daisy said. Reese and Tessa had been spending most evenings together.

Approaching the desk, Tessa set down the foil-wrapped package of cinnamon scones and picked up her sketchbook. "He has a meeting with a client tonight in York, and he said he won't be back until late."

Willow Creek, in the heart of Lancaster County, was

close to Lancaster as well as York, making it an ideal small town with other accessible services close by.

"I *am* interested in the quilts display." Daisy unzipped the first few inches of her fleece jacket, which was patterned with cats. "Especially if Reese has any album quilts. But then I want to get home."

"Vi only has a few more days at home before returning to college, doesn't she?" Tessa asked.

Her friend knew how much Daisy had missed her oldest daughter. "Yes, and I want to spend as much time with her as I can. And Jazzi—"

Her fifteen-year-old had had a lot on her plate the past six months. Not only had she missed her sister, Violet, who had gone off to college, but Jazzi was adopted, and she had decided to search for her birth parents. After weeks of silent and secretive behavior in the fall, Jazzi had finally confided in Daisy. She knew her girls missed their father, who had died three years ago, and Jazzi had been especially close to Ryan. Putting her own feelings about the search aside, Daisy had supported Jazzi's efforts to find her birth mother. Now she wanted to be available to her younger daughter because Jazzi had an upcoming visit planned for this Sunday with Portia Smith Harding. Jazzi might want to talk about it. Although her daughter had spoken with Portia, she hadn't seen her face-to-face since their first meeting in October.

"Come on," Tessa said, disrupting Daisy's thoughts. Crossing to the doorway that led into the other rooms of the gallery, Tessa paused.

When Reese had bought the old Victorian to use for his art gallery, he'd kept its charm and only done renovations that would help show off work in the gallery. Now Tessa guided Daisy through a dark room into a larger one where ambient light glowed from a track along the ceiling.

"I have to find the light switch," Tessa said.

Daisy stayed perfectly still so she didn't inadvertently knock an elbow into an art piece. Most of the work Reese carried was from new artists, but some of it was still valuable.

There was an eerie quality about the Victorian that manifested in several ways. A light mustiness always floated in the air. Did that come from the house being over a hundred and fifty years old? Possibly. Or perhaps it was from the antiques that Reese used for display tables. The floorboards, although they had been refinished to their original character, creaked. It was hard to find one that didn't.

She and Tessa stood in one of the rooms toward the back of the house. As she peered through the duskiness toward the front room, shadows appeared to be waving in the streetlights. Those were tree branches swaying in front of the huge bay window.

When there was a bump and swish, as if a branch had brushed against the side of the house, Daisy jumped. She wasn't a nervous person, anxious only when she had concerns for her daughters. But this gallery, devoid of patrons, was giving her the creeps.

Finally, Tessa found the light switch. An overhead light glowed mildly over the room. Daisy knew Reese didn't want glaring illumination to disturb the atmosphere of his displays or damage any of the works.

"Over there." Tessa pointed to a corner where Daisy could see quilt stands and several quilts folded over chairs. Another was spread across a table. The array drew her to it as she forgot all about the eeriness of the Victorian house. She went straight for one of the quilt stands, where she recognized an album quilt.

It *was* beautiful. The tag on the quilt read BALTIMORE ALBUM QUILT.

"Isn't this gorgeous?" she whispered.

Tessa came up beside her. "Reese said that one's worth about fourteen thousand dollars."

"Just look at this fine needlework."

"It's hard to believe it's from the nineteenth century. I can't imagine anyone sewing so evenly with those tiny stitches."

"It's appliqué and reverse appliqué, embroidery, and more padded appliqué that make up the three-dimensional blocks. I really should learn to quilt. Rachel Fisher teaches it." Rachel and Levi Fisher, friends of Daisy's, owned Quilts and Notions. They not only sold quilts but cloth and sewing supplies too.

"Reese believes the Quilt Lovers Weekend will bring in a lot of business for Rachel and Levi."

Daisy knew the Amish family well. Although she'd moved away from Willow Creek after college, she remembered her childhood as if it was yesterday. Rachel's parents had grown shrubs and trees for Daisy's mom and dad to sell at their nursery, Gallagher's Garden Corner, and Daisy had spent time on their farm. She admired the family and their Amish way of life.

Reluctantly, she moved away from the Baltimore Album Quilt to study another.

Suddenly, she heard a noise coming from another room. It didn't emanate from the office or the front gallery. If she remembered the downstairs layout correctly, it was coming from the stairs that led to the second floor.

"Someone else can't be here," Tessa murmured, stepping toward a sculpture of an old man sitting by a tree stump. She picked it up as if she intended to hit someone with it.

Daisy held her breath, unsure what Tessa would do next.

Tessa hadn't yet taken a step when Reese appeared in the doorway.

They were as surprised as he was.

Reese Masemer wasn't quite six feet tall, but he was fit and lean. At forty-something, his hair was sandy brown, thick, and long. It shaggily splayed over his denim shirt collar. His dark brown eyes landed on Daisy and Tessa. His face, which had seemed too pale, showed a little more color.

Tessa spoke first. "What are you doing here? I thought you had dinner and a meeting with a client."

Appearing a bit shaken, Reese shrugged. Then he smiled. "I thought I had intruders. I'm glad to see it's the two of you. I was worried I might have to invest in a new alarm system."

Crossing to Tessa, he wrapped his arm around her waist. "My client canceled, so I was spending the evening working on my laptop upstairs. I have a lot to catch up on—invoices to input from the sales over the holidays." He wiggled his brows at Tessa. "Including two of your paintings that sold. I'm ready for you to bring more to the gallery."

Daisy's woman's intuition told her that Reese was trying to distract Tessa from the fact that he was still here and hadn't told her.

Her friend, a bit besotted by her relationship with him, let him do it. "I came over to bring some of those cinnamon scones you like so much and pick up my sketchbook. The scones are on your desk in the office. I asked Daisy along because I knew she'd like to see the quilts before we had to scramble through people to view them. They're going to be a big draw."

"I suspect they will be," he agreed. "Those album

quilts are a real find. But that's another reason I'm concerned about security."

He did seem troubled, Daisy thought. But did his concern really have to do with the album quilts?

Reese gave Tessa another squeeze. "Remember, we're going to have a candlelit dinner in York on Saturday evening. Is that still good for you?"

"It is. But I hope we can spend some time together before that. "Are we still on for dinner tomorrow evening?"

"We are."

With Reese and Tessa gazing into each other's eyes, Daisy felt like the proverbial fifth wheel. This was Wednesday. She imagined Tessa would be staying overnight again before Saturday. "I'll let you and Tessa say a proper good night." Crossing the room, she headed for the office and the outside back door.

It wasn't long before Tessa joined her, rosy-cheeked and looking just kissed. However, she was quiet as they left the gallery and closed the door. Once outside, she glanced up at the apartment on the second floor, where all the blinds were drawn. No light escaped. Had Reese really been working up there?

A cold wind buffeted them, and Daisy pulled the zipper on her jacket up to her neck and turned toward the tea garden, where her car was parked.

Tessa took a few quick steps to keep up and asked, "Do you think Reese rushed us out?"

In spite of the wind, Daisy stopped. "What's on your mind?"

"Reese's assistant, Chloie Laird, flirts with him constantly. What if she's been doing more than flirting? What if she was upstairs with him?"

Daisy watched as Tessa took another look up at the second floor. "Are you saying you don't trust Reese?"

"You know it's hard for me to trust anyone."

Daisy *did* know that. But before they could delve into that subject, Tessa changed it. "We're going to be passing Woods. We could stop in and say hi to Jonas."

Tessa was aware that Daisy and Jonas Groft had spent time together. Daisy enjoyed his company—if she had to admit it, more than enjoyed it. However, Jonas had closed his shop from Christmas to New Year's and gone to Philadelphia to spend the holidays with good friends. They'd spent New Year's Eve together, though, with her girls. That was a few days ago. Since then, she hadn't heard from him. She wasn't sure she should visit Woods because she didn't want to push.

Because of his background as a former detective in Philadelphia, Jonas had gotten pulled into her life to help Jazzi search for her birth mother. It was quite possible he didn't want a serious relationship. To be honest, she wasn't sure *she* did.

Still, Tessa caught her arm and pulled her along, saying, "Come on. You've got to take risks in your life. You don't very often."

"Opening the tea garden with my aunt was a risk." After her husband had died, she'd returned to her hometown to start over. She and her Aunt Iris had bought a house to establish Daisy's Tea Garden, and Daisy had also renovated an old barn, where she and the girls now lived.

"Your aunt knows more about tea than Wikipedia. And the two of you created a place where everybody comes to chat and relax, eat good food, and drink the best tea. How could it have missed?"

"It still could. You know the track record with small businesses."

"I do. But we're growing. We hired more help."

"When you become a rich and famous artist, you won't want to be my kitchen manager."

With a frown, Tessa studied Daisy. "If I ever do become rich and famous, I'll still be your best friend. And if I have to quit my job, I would find you the best kitchen manager on the face of the earth."

"Now that reassures me," Daisy said wryly as they stood in front of Woods.

"Come on," Tessa urged again, opening the door and pulling Daisy inside. "At least we'll get warm for a few minutes."

Daisy just shook her head and gave in to the inevitable enthusiasm Tessa usually exhibited. To her relief, Jonas was nowhere in sight within the store. However, Elijah Beiler was. He was an Amish woodworker who sold furniture through Jonas's shop. In his forties, Elijah wore black pants with suspenders and a dark blue shirt. His beard signified he was married.

"Good evening, ladies," Elijah said with a broad, welcoming smile.

"Evening, Elijah. Is Jonas around?" Daisy asked.

"No. He went searching for reclaimed wood. He's thinking about adding a line of furniture created from it."

"I've seen furniture crafted from reclaimed wood on those building shows on the Home and Garden Channel," Daisy recalled. "It's beautiful."

Elijah went to the counter in the back of the store and reached underneath. After he brought out a few sketches, he carried them to Daisy and Tessa. "Would you like to look at these? They're what Jonas has in mind."

When Daisy had renovated the old barn that she now called home, she'd included an island in her kitchen. She'd examined many in her search for the best one for her use and was familiar with the styles. She admired the plans for islands that Jonas had designed, as well as those for a sideboard table and a practical desk.

"You and Jonas are both very talented," Daisy said, meaning it.

A humble man, like most Amish, Elijah reddened at her praise. "Like me, Jonas takes pleasure in bringing the real nature of wood to life."

"I'm looking forward to seeing what the two of you come up with," Daisy assured him. She glanced at Tessa. "We'd better go. I want to get home to the girls."

"I'll tell Jonas you stopped in," Elijah assured them.

Daisy wasn't certain she wanted him to do that, but she kept silent. After a round of good-byes, she and Tessa left Woods.

They walked briskly up the street. In front of Daisy's Tea Garden, they paused and glanced at *their* Victorian. The tea garden took up the first floor. Tessa lived in the second-floor apartment and used the attic for painting.

A light that came on at dusk and went off at dawn glowed on the front porch. It illuminated the pale green exterior with its white and yellow trim. On the first floor, Daisy and her aunt had furnished the be-served or buy-it-to-go room with oak, glass-top tables. She'd painted the walls the palest green. A second tea room on the first floor was a spillover area. It was also the room they used when they took reservations and served afternoon tea by appointment. That room had walls that were the palest yellow.

Daisy's office was located to the rear of the tea room, and the kitchen spread behind the walk-in room. They also had a side patio where they served customers outside, weather permitting. A private parking area for Daisy, her aunt, and Tessa's vehicles ran in back of the Victorian.

"Business is still good," Tessa reminded her, "even

though it's early January and the tourist season has slowed down. That means the community is embracing Daisy's, and the tea garden is an integral part of the area."

"I hope that's what it means. The uptick in business could still be from the notoriety of the murder that happened here."

Daisy's Tea Garden had been the scene of a murder in the fall, and there had been publicity from that, with local TV coverage as well as discussions on online blogs.

"Foster has really helped to spread the word about Daisy's Tea Garden on social media too," Tessa added. "You have to give him credit for that."

Foster Cranshaw was a college student Daisy had taken on when they'd gotten busier. He and Violet dated when she was home, and Daisy had mixed feelings about that. Yes, she wanted Violet involved in relationships so eventually she could find a permanent life partner. Daisy was sure marriage and vows would mean as much to her daughters as they had to her and Ryan. On the other hand, Violet was still young, and she hoped her oldest and Foster weren't too serious.

"Foster has been a huge help," Daisy agreed. "I don't know what we'd do without him. He has a way with customers, and his tech skills are a godsend."

They were walking along the lane that lead to the private parking lot when a shrieking alarm pierced the silence of the night.

Tessa spun around toward the direction from which they'd come. "That sounds like it's coming from Revelations."

The alarm was so loud and piercing that Daisy supposed it could have come from any of the businesses along their street. But she followed Tessa as she raced down the sidewalk. Daisy wasn't going to abandon her friend now.

As Tessa streaked past a candle shop, an insurance office, and a store that sold hand-sewn purses and travel bags, as well as Woods, Daisy kept up with her pace. Elijah had come out of Woods and was staring down the street too.

Tessa ran by him, and so did Daisy, realizing now that Tessa had been right. It was the alarm from Revelations that had sounded. Running along the side of the building to the back entrance, Tessa didn't hesitate to go inside when she saw the door was opened.

Daisy called after her. "Tessa, wait! We don't know what's happened. It could be a fire . . . or *anything*."

But Tessa didn't wait. And when Daisy ran inside and caught up with her, she saw Tessa holding up Reese, who leaned heavily on her. There was blood on his forehead and down the side of his face.

Daisy pulled out her phone to call 9-1-1.

Reese saw her do it and held up his hand. "You don't need to call anyone. The alarm alerted the PD. They'll be here."

Tessa led Reese to a wooden captain's chair, and he flopped into it.

"What happened?" Daisy asked. Certainly, Reese didn't do that to himself. Could someone still be in the gallery?

"An intruder got in before I reset the alarm. He hit me and escaped. I managed to smack one of the panic buttons."

Reese had definitely been hurt by someone. Papers from the desk were strewn across the floor. But something about his story didn't seem to ring true. How could anyone have known the alarm was off? Why hadn't Reese reset the alarm after she and Tessa had left? Had a break-in really occurred?

Or had something else happened that Reese didn't want anyone to know about?